Once and For All

Once and For All

AN AMERICAN VALOR NOVEL

CHERYL ETCHISON

An Imprint of HarperCollins*Publishers*

This is a work of fiction. Names, characters, places, and incidents are products of the author's imagination or are used fictitiously and are not to be construed as real. Any resemblance to actual events, locales, organizations, or persons, living or dead, is entirely coincidental.

Excerpt from *You're Still the One* copyright © 2016 by Darcy Burke.
Excerpt from *The Debutante Is Mine* copyright © 2016 by Vivienne Lorret.
Excerpt from *One Dangerous Desire* copyright © 2016 by Christy Carlyle.

EPub Edition MAY 2016 ISBN: 9780062471055
Print Edition ISBN: 9780062471048

Avon, Avon Impulse, and the Avon Impulse logo are trademarks of HarperCollins Publishers.

10 9 8 7 6 5 4 3 2

For V.

Chapter One

February 2012

DANNY MACGREGOR STARED at the black screen, knowing he was good and screwed. The dead cell phone meant he had no way to call for an exfil, no GPS. Aside from the fact that he was standing on the deck of a million-dollar beach house, he had no fucking clue as to his whereabouts. Only one thing was for certain—no way was he going back inside to wake last night's distraction and ask for directions. Or worse yet, ask her to drive him to his daddy's house.

Not just no, but hell no.

"God. I'm getting too old for this shit."

Danny shoved the useless piece of tech in his back pocket and buttoned the fly of his jeans. So what if he was in a bit of a jam. Not a big deal. He'd made it out of far worse situations before. And this time he had the luxury of not being shot at in the process.

The sun was breaking over the Atlantic, painting the

cloudless sky shades of pink and orange as the tide eased its way farther and farther onto shore. He'd seen plenty of sunrises all over the world, but for him none were more beautiful than those in Myrtle Beach. He breathed the cool, salt-tinged air deep into his lungs, soaking in the moment, imprinting it to memory. As much as he loved home, he couldn't stay. There were other places in the world where his talents were put to much better use. But it would be a moment like this he would recall in the future, when the world around him went to shit and he would briefly close his eyes in desperate need of peace.

After pulling on the rest of his clothes and tying his boots, he made his way across the expansive deck and down the stairs, following the boardwalk over the dunes. Then, using both hands, he shielded his eyes from the sunlight reflecting off the ocean waves. He looked first to the south, then back to the north as he tried to get his bearings. A half mile down the beach, a long wooden pier jutted out into the water, giving him a good idea of his whereabouts. He turned back to the south and began the solid six-mile run back home.

The temperature was cool with a light breeze out of the north, making running conditions damn near ideal. Even so, within the first hundred meters his head began pounding in time with his heart. Jack Daniel's pulsed through his veins and soured his stomach, causing it to burn and churn with every step. The nausea finally got the better of him, forcing him to stop and puke in a nearby sand dune. But with a swift kick of his boot, he covered the mess and resumed his steady, albeit slower than normal pace.

He felt like hell and probably looked far worse considering the stares he was getting from a few of the early-morning beachcombers. Or maybe they just weren't used to seeing anyone running on the beach wearing the same clothes they wore out to the bar the night before. Even with a raging hangover, it was still one of the more pleasant runs he'd taken since enlisting in the army.

For almost a decade the 75th Regiment had conditioned and trained his body to run under far worse circumstances, for far longer distances. Time and time again he pushed his body beyond normal limits, depriving himself of food, of sleep. But more important, ignoring twinges of pain or fatigue until it became second nature. He'd run in rainstorms, in sandstorms. In one-hundred-degree heat and bone-chilling cold. He'd run during the day, carrying a sixty-pound rucksack on his back and a gas mask on his face. He'd run through fields and forests in the dead of night with only night-vision goggles to help him see the way, all part of his continued physical training so he could run down a target the government wanted captured, or run for his life when all hell broke loose and the only way to safety was on his own two feet.

After hitting the halfway mark home, Danny glanced at his watch. Twenty-five minutes. It wasn't close to his best time. Hell, it wasn't even the Ranger minimum. If the guys in his squad ever found out he'd certainly catch hell for it. But if he could maintain this pace, he'd be back at his father's house in another thirty. Which meant within the next hour, after a shower and maybe some breakfast, he could fall into bed and sleep off what remained of his hangover.

Then he'd spend the rest of the day doing absolutely nothing. And hating every minute of it.

Goddamn mandatory block leave.

For Danny, two weeks forced vacation from the job he loved was the worst kind of torture. He handled life far better when things were balls to the wall. Functioning on less than three hours of sleep. Blowing shit up. Training guys up. Jumping out of perfectly good aircraft. Anything, *anything* to keep him busy and out of trouble.

Before he completed another mile, the familiar roar of a big block engine approached from behind, forcing him onto the shoulder. The faded red and rusted truck from his youth gunned past and pulled to the side of the road only yards in front of him. Danny came to a standstill, taking a moment to brace his hands on his knees and catch his breath.

The driver-side window eased down. "Morning, sunshine. Nice day for a run?"

From where he stood at the side of the road, Danny could see his brother's shit-eating grin reflected in the side mirror. Being the ever respectful enlisted man, he snapped to attention and bestowed upon his officer brother a well-earned middle-finger salute.

Mike laughed. "Get in, dipshit."

As he walked to the passenger side, Danny wiped the sweat from his brow with the tail of his button-down.

"Where the hell is your truck?" his brother asked.

"Sitting in the parking lot of Eve's." At least he hoped his truck was still sitting there. All too often, nice truck plus dive-bar parking lot equaled stolen.

Danny yanked open the door, the old steel frame groaning beneath the added weight as he climbed in. After slamming the door shut, he studied his perfectly coiffed brother. They were polar opposites when out of uniform. Danny always dressed for comfort while his brother appeared to have stepped from the pages of a fashion magazine. In his high-dollar golf shirts and perfectly pressed pants, most would assume Michael MacGregor was part of the country club set. Which is exactly where Danny thought he belonged. Or at the very least, working at Walter Reed or Brooks or some other VA hospital. Someplace stateside. Someplace nice and safe and far away from trouble. He sure as hell shouldn't have joined regiment just so he could babysit his little brother.

But that age-old argument could wait for another time.

Danny cranked the window down halfway and leaned his head back against the cracked vinyl headrest. He closed his eyes, letting the cool morning breeze wash over him as the truck rumbled down the street. If he was lucky, his brother would save the inquisition for another time.

"Good time last night?"

So much for luck.

"Oh, come on. Why the silent treatment?"

Danny kept his eyes closed, silently praying to the hangover gods for a quick and merciful death.

"Say something, dammit!" His brother's words were punctuated by a dull thump, most likely the palm of his hand meeting the padded steering wheel.

His eyes snapped open and he turned to face his brother as best he could, squinting against the glare of sunlight. "What the hell do you want me to say?" Between the liquor, the vomiting, and the impromptu run, his voice sounded like someone had scoured his vocal cords with sixty-grit sandpaper. "Yes, I drank too much. Yes, I went home with some random woman from the bar. No, I don't remember her name. Yes, I feel like shit. Good enough? Anything else?" Danny glared at his brother, daring him to ask one more idiotic question.

Mike glanced at him warily. "I guess that about covers it."

Finally, that was over and Danny relaxed back into the seat. The silence, however, was short-lived.

His brother turned on the radio, the volume a low hum as it scanned from station to station. But once it landed on the heavy metal station, Mike cranked it to the highest level the factory-installed system would allow. Danny felt the pound of the bass in his chest, hands, and feet. Not to mention his head. He took slow, measured breaths but refused to complain. No way would he give his brother the satisfaction. After all, it was something he would have done.

Halfway into the second song, the truck came to an abrupt stop and the engine shut off. Danny opened his eyes, expecting to be parked in the driveway of their childhood home. Only they sat in a grocery-store parking lot.

"I thought we were going home."

"Should've asked," Mike answered with a laugh. "I needed to make a grocery-store run and decided to drive around town a bit to see if I could find your dumb ass. Lo and behold, I did." Mike pulled a folded sheet of paper from his pocket, tore it in two and handed one half to him. "Look at it this way, we'll get the shopping done in half the time."

"I'll just stay here," Danny said, avoiding the piece of paper held out in front of him.

Mike took hold of his brother's hand and forced the list into his palm. "Not unless you want to walk home from here."

Danny stared at the grocery list, contemplating the lesser of two evils. The unexpected detour had added at least two more miles. He could easily run the rest of the way, but he felt like hell. And this was supposed to be his vacation.

Reluctantly, he snatched the paper from Mike's hand and followed him inside.

BREE DUNBAR TUGGED on her pageboy cap in hopes of hiding the obvious. Having beaten cancer for the second time, she'd woken up feeling stronger, more confident than she had in months. A little rebellious, even. Which is why she'd said goodbye to the wig and hello to her stylish new cap. Only now that she was out in public it didn't seem like the smartest of moves.

People weren't just noticing her, but staring. Stopping

dead in their tracks with mouths gaping open in an "I'm not even trying to hide the fact that I'm staring at you" kind of way. With her earlier confidence now wavering, she felt more than a little . . . exposed.

She closed her eyes and took a steadying breath. "Screw it. Doesn't matter," she told herself. After all, they didn't know what she'd been through. What she'd given up. So in her mind, feeling this good was still a milestone worth celebrating. Worthy of cheesecake, even. Who cared it wasn't even noon.

Bree shoved her cart in the direction of the bakery, where she perused the refrigerated display case. Turtle. Strawberry swirl. Double chocolate.

She sensed someone hovering and her earlier irritation reared its ugly head.

"When a woman is stalking the cheesecake case first thing in the morning it can only mean one thing," a man whispered in her ear.

Bree spun around, prepared to kick this guy in the nuts and tell him exactly what he could do with his one thing, but her plan of action died the moment she laid eyes on him.

"Oh. My. God."

It had been years since she'd seen Michael MacGregor, but he looked just the same as he always did with his preppy clothes and dark blond hair cut in a traditional military style.

"Definitely not God," he said with a hint of Southern twang. "God complex? Maybe."

With a wink and a smile, Michael extended his arms

wide and Bree practically leaped into his waiting embrace, wrapping her arms around his neck. Then, just as he'd done when they were younger, he lifted her feet several inches from the ground and spun her in a tight circle. She laughed as they narrowly avoided a bread rack and towering cupcake display. Then with her feet firmly planted on the ground, he kissed her forehead and released her.

"How you doing, kiddo?"

"I'm good. Really good," she said with a smile. And for the first time in a very long time, she wasn't lying. "What on earth are you doing in town?"

"I'm on leave. Came home to visit Dad. Play some golf."

"In February?"

"Got to play when I can."

Some things never changed. "You're still in the army, then?"

Mike scrubbed the palm of his hand over his crew cut. "Still have twenty months left on my contract."

For as long as she could remember, he was the big brother she'd never had. After Lily MacGregor died, it was Mike's job to look after his younger brother, Danny, while their father worked. And since she and Danny were inseparable for most of their youth, Mike played mother hen to her, as well.

His smile slipped a bit. Bree braced herself, knowing what was coming.

"You look good. Considering."

And if that wasn't a wet blanket on her morning.

So much for going an entire day without talking about cancer. Bree did her best to shake off the irritation. If anyone deserved a pass, it was Michael. After all, he was a doctor. And one of her oldest friends. So for him, she'd let it slide. This time.

"Considering?" Bree held on to her smile as best she could and took a playful swipe at his chest. "Thanks so much for qualifying your statement."

His cheeks and ears tinged pink in response. At least he had the good graces to blush.

"You know what I mean," he said. "All done with treatments?"

"Last one was nine weeks ago. Just trying to get on with life now."

"Good girl. That's the right attitude." He smiled and patted her shoulder, probably with the same bedside manner he was taught in medical school. Then his gaze drifted from right to left across the back of the store. "Have you seen Danny? He's around here somewhere."

Of course he was.

At the mention of his name, her heart stuttered in her chest. Daniel Patrick MacGregor. The boy she'd loved her entire life. The man she'd hated for a decade. Or at the very least, tried to.

To know he was in such close proximity made her want to jump for joy as much as run screaming for the door.

"There you are," came a voice from behind her. "I've been looking all over for you."

Bree closed her eyes, knowing exactly who that voice

belonged to. And she wasn't so naive as to think he was talking to her. But now simply turning and walking away was an impossibility.

For ten years she'd prepared herself for this moment, rehearsed what she would say if ever given the chance to confront Danny face-to-face. Only now the time had arrived and she couldn't remember a damn word of any of it. Out of options, she pasted on a smile and turned to face her demons.

Or more like one devil in particular.

"Hello, Danny."

If she had any lingering delusions his words were meant for her and not his brother, they quickly disappeared. His gaze shifted to her, then to Michael, and back to her. Confusion gave way to realization then surprise.

"Long time, no see, huh?" She smiled so hard it was a wonder her face didn't crack. And before she realized what she was doing, she leaned in to give him a quick hug. Although she couldn't remember the plan, Bree was pretty damn sure this wasn't part of it. But she recovered quickly and pulled away, giving him a little finishing pat on the arm. The kind of gesture typically reserved for old schoolteachers or distant cousins you haven't spoken with in a million years. To be honest, he didn't deserve that much affection, but she was trying to be the bigger person. Let bygones be bygones and all that crap.

Nope, no hard feelings here. No deep-seated resentment that had been festering in her heart for years.

Bree took a deep breath and turned her attention back to Michael. Even heard herself ask a million questions about who knows what and not really hearing the answers. Occasionally, she'd glance in Danny's direction so as not to appear rude, but she purposely avoided looking at him too long; otherwise he'd realize the effect he still had on her.

She jammed her shaking hands into her pockets. Kept her words clipped and short to hide the tremor in her voice. Although she focused on Michael, her skin prickled under the weight of Danny's stare. She could practically feel all the questions waiting on the tip of his tongue. Things she didn't want to talk about with anyone, but especially not with him.

Bree glanced at her wrist only to realize she didn't wear a watch. Hopefully neither noticed. "I'd love to stay and chat but I've got to go. It was nice seeing both of you."

She smiled and grabbed her cart, ready to make a hasty exit.

"What about your cheesecake?" Mike asked.

"I shouldn't be eating that anyway." She waved goodbye as she rushed toward the closest aisle.

As her luck would have it, the bakery was located in the far back corner of the store. She raced toward the front door, blazing her way through the maze of shelves and freezer cases. In the detergent aisle she abandoned her half-full cart due to a temperamental front wheel that only slowed her down. Her eyes burned from unshed tears, and Bree could only hope to make it outside before the inevitable meltdown began. With the front entrance in sight, a sense of relief washed over her.

Right until a hand captured her elbow.

DANNY GRABBED HOLD of one arm and when she spun around, he took advantage and grabbed hold of her other arm, as well. "I need to talk to you," he said, tugging her by both elbows from the main aisle into one stocked with charcoal and citronella candles. He had only a matter of minutes, seconds maybe, before someone walked by and alerted security.

He quickly assessed the woman in front of him. Brown stubble peeked out from beneath an awful-looking hat. Her clothes hung off her slight frame. She'd always been thin, genetics giving her a dancer's body, but this wasn't quite right. And there had always been a brightness in her eyes, a glow about her. That was missing, too.

"Is everything okay with you?"

"I'm fine. Now, if you don't mind—" She attempted to free herself from his grip, but he held firm.

"You're hardly fine. You look like hell."

His words definitely lacked finesse but would have to do for now. She didn't look like she'd just had a bad night or even a bad week. She looked sick. Frail. He probably hurt her just by wrapping his fingers around her elbow. Hell, he'd likely bruised her already. His stomach rolled at the thought of physically hurting her.

Danny relaxed his grip, hoping she wouldn't run away. Not just yet, at least.

"I've got to give you credit, Danny, that's one hell of a pickup line." She took advantage of his eased grasp and pulled her arm free. "Do you use that on all the girls?"

"I just want to know what's going on. Is it . . . ?"

He couldn't bring himself to say the word *cancer*

aloud, although the lack of hair indicated she was likely a chemo patient. It was his best guess. But one thing was certain—he'd definitely pissed her off.

Bree stepped closer now, anger flashing in her eyes as she stared up at him. "You have some nerve demanding answers from me."

"I get that you're still angry, but this is different."

"Really?" She must have said it far more forcefully than intended, judging by the way she looked around to see if any onlookers had gathered. She composed herself and began again, poking him in the chest with her index finger. "Who do you think you are?" Another poke. "I haven't heard from you in ten years. Ten. Years." She punctuated each word with a jab. "But it shouldn't surprise me in the least. You always did have far bigger balls than brains."

Like a prizefighter surprised by a swinging left hook, Danny rocked back on his heels, stunned she would say something so cruel. By the time the initial shock wore off, she'd escaped through the automatic front doors. He started after her, determined to chase her down a second time. Only this time it was Mike who stopped him with a hand on his shoulder.

"Let her go, Danny."

He tried to pull free from his grasp, but his brother's vise-like grip only tightened. "This doesn't concern you."

"Quit being so goddamn stubborn and listen to me a minute," Mike said, his voice low and threatening. "In the middle of the grocery store is not the place to have that kind of conversation."

Danny stilled and turned to look his brother in the eyes.

"You know what's wrong with her."

Mike nodded. "Like I said, this is not the place. Besides, we have shit to do." He shoved the cart at his brother and with a look that could kill, silently commanded him to head in the opposite direction.

Reluctantly, Danny obeyed, pushing the cart with one hand as he rubbed at the place where she'd jabbed him repeatedly. It hurt like hell. Like she'd stabbed him with a dagger instead of a bony little finger. And he'd acquired more than one Purple Heart during his time in the army, so he knew pain.

Or maybe that pain in his chest had less to do with her finger poking and more to do with ten years of guilt.

Chapter Two

HER HANDS SHOOK with such force it took three tries just to get her car key into the ignition. Bree swiped away the hot tears streaming down her cheeks, angry that after all this time Danny still had the power to make her so damn . . . angry.

How many times had she rehearsed that scenario over and over again in her mind?

She'd decided long ago to not let the eighteen-year-old whose heart was shattered into a million pieces come to the surface. To keep that girl stuffed deep down inside to prove she'd moved on. To show that he couldn't hurt her anymore. To show him her life was fabulous and he no longer had an effect on her.

But her life wasn't fabulous. It was pure crap. No amount of rainbows and unicorns could fix it at this point.

She slammed on the brakes for a red light and

screamed at her own stupidity. Even gave the steering wheel a few well-deserved smacks with the palm of her hand.

Ten years. Ten years since she returned from an afternoon lab only to find out from his roommate Danny had packed up his things and left school. No note. No text message. No email. Nothing.

And he didn't just leave college and return home to Myrtle Beach. No, he went all extreme, joining some gung-ho division of the army. Jumping out of airplanes, toting a machine gun. Going as far as halfway around the world and into a goddamn war zone to get away from her.

Obviously, the universe was having fun at her expense, dumping pounds of salt into that ancient wound, because Danny had definitely improved with age. Oh hell, this morning he looked like something the cat dragged in and smelled even worse, but the fates had been very kind to him. Little creases at the corners of his eyes. The dark beard covering his jaw. A small scar slashing his brow added to his manly ruggedness.

Even his voice was deeper, more mature. Although her memory might be playing tricks on her, he seemed bigger, taller even. And from the breadth of his shoulders and the look of his hands, he was stronger, too, with a chest as solid as a brick wall. She had an aching finger as proof. The teenage boy she once knew had disappeared and been replaced by something new and improved.

And what did he see when he looked at her for the first time in ten years? Obviously nothing good. His reaction had been one of shock then pity.

And that made her blood boil. How dare he pity her.

She pulled into the garage of her parents' home and stared in the rearview mirror at the house across the street where Danny used to live. The same one where he was now staying. She had no idea how much longer he'd be in town, but odds weren't in her favor he would just leave her be. She'd thrown down the gauntlet and Daniel Patrick MacGregor had never been one to back down from a challenge.

Hitting the garage remote, the house slowly disappeared from view as the door lowered to the ground. Bree headed inside, her mother greeting her at the back door as she opened it.

"Can I help you carry some things in?" she asked while drying her hands on a dish towel.

"Nothing to bring in."

Bree scooted past her mother, not yet ready to rehash the morning's events.

"I thought you were going to the store?"

"I'll go back later."

She grabbed the ibuprofen from the cabinet by the sink, the dull ache behind her eyes now reaching epic proportions. After swallowing two small tablets with a single drink of water, she headed for her bedroom.

"Is everything okay, sweetheart? You look flushed."

"Fine," she said, ducking out of her mother's reach. Twenty-eight years old and her mother still wanted to check her temperature with the back of her hand.

"Are you sure? You're not running a fever, are you?

Your immune system still isn't where it needs to be. You need to be careful—"

"I'm fine, Mom. I swear. Just going to lie down for a bit."

Bree darted upstairs, escaping to the relative peace and quiet of her bedroom. She closed the door behind her, sighing in relief to see her mother wasn't hot on her heels.

She loved her dearly and wouldn't have survived chemo treatments without her, but sometimes her mother's care and concern was too much. Suffocating. And despite her best intentions, she was always reminding Bree that she'd been very sick, when all Bree wanted to do was put it behind her.

For now, she'd settle for crawling into bed and trying to forget the morning ever happened. As she closed the blinds, a familiar old truck pulled into the driveway across the street. The door flung open and booted feet hit the concrete. Instinctively she jumped back from the window, not wanting Danny to think she'd been standing there, watching, waiting all this time for him to return home.

Bree held her breath and with the tips of her fingers lifted a single wooden slat so she could peek out. The old truck's passenger door sat open wide, but there was no sign of either brother. The screen door swung open and Danny bounded down the porch steps, reaching the truck in four long strides. He grabbed the last few grocery bags from the floorboard and shoved the door closed with his elbow. On his way back into the house he suddenly stopped and turned to look across the street. At her house. At her bedroom window.

Despite peering through a tiny gap no wider than an inch, she knew he could somehow see her. She could feel his gaze locked on hers. But he didn't drop the grocery bags on the front porch or storm across the street toward her. Instead, he just stood there. His expression completely unreadable.

Surely he wouldn't march across the street and start things up again right now? He wouldn't dare.

Oh, but he would.

Maybe he expected her to do something. Wave. Stick out her tongue. Flip him the bird. Instead, like a deer caught in a hunter's sight, she stood frozen, unable to will herself away from the window. Then he did the very last thing she expected him to do.

He smiled.

A smile so wide, so bright, she hadn't seen the likes of one in over a decade. Although she didn't want to admit it, she'd missed that smile desperately and her heart squeezed painfully in her chest. Finally, Danny looked away, breaking eye contact, releasing her from his spell. As he turned to go inside, he shook his head, apparently unable to believe it himself.

For a long time after he went inside, Bree stood there looking out the window. And the more she replayed it in her mind, the more she began to wonder if she'd imagined the entire thing.

Only one thing was for certain—things between them were far from over.

DANNY SHOWERED, ATE and tried to rest, but each time he closed his eyes her face was there in front of him, haunting him. Finally, he gave up on the idea of sleep and wandered into the living room where his dad and brother had just returned from their round of golf. If he had hit the links with them, maybe he could've cleared his head for a few hours. But it wouldn't have been that easy. After all, ten years had passed and he still hadn't been able to completely shake her from his thoughts.

His first year in the army, he hardly had time to eat and sleep, much less think about Bree. Fourteen weeks in Infantry OSUT. Another three weeks in Airborne, followed by a month of hell known as the Ranger Indoctrination Program. From there he was assigned to 75th Ranger Regiment's 1st Battalion in Savannah, Georgia.

But he wasn't there long enough to settle in. Instead, by the end of the week, he was a newbie on patrol in Iraq. Kicking in doors. Blowing shit up. His training an extreme version of sink or swim. Suddenly he was a scared shitless nineteen-year-old doing his damnedest to follow orders and stay alive.

Twenty-seven weeks later 1st Batt returned stateside and Danny had his first mandatory block leave. Then with the freedom to go where he wanted and do what he wanted, he felt lost. His only guidance came from his squad leader. *"Stay out of jail and, for the love of all things holy, wrap it up no matter what she says."*

Good, solid advice, for sure, but not very helpful for a kid needing direction. So he packed his duffel and borrowed a car, intending to drive home to Myrtle Beach.

Instead, he found himself on campus at the University of South Carolina.

He had no plan. No idea what he was going to say when he found her. *If* he found her. He had since lost her cell number and didn't know where she lived. Hoping she still majored in finance, he figured the business building was his best bet. Finding a comfortable place to sit, he prepared himself to wait hours, days, if necessary. Only it didn't take anywhere near that long. Within thirty minutes she came out the main entrance, smiling and laughing with a group of friends. Danny rose to his feet, picked up his backpack from off the ground. In that brief moment he looked away, some guy he didn't recognize appeared from nowhere, draping an arm over her shoulder and kissing her cheek.

And that was that.

He was too late. Waited too damn long to try and make things right and she'd moved on without him. And he had no one but himself to blame.

"What the hell is wrong with you?" Footsteps pounded across the living room's wooden floors. "What's with him? Just standing there staring out into space."

Danny turned to see his father, Mac, settle into his favorite chair, careful to not upturn the plate of food he held in one hand or the beer in the other. Since he now directed his attention to the television, Danny assumed the question to be rhetorical. He turned back to look out the large picture window and stare at the house across the street.

"We ran into Aubrey at the grocery store," he heard his brother say.

Only then did Danny turn back again to look at the two of them. His father nodded in understanding and took a bite from his sandwich. He chewed thoughtfully as if in deep contemplation then washed it down with a pull from his longneck.

"Goddamn cancer. Although she's doing much better now. Pete said she's out of the woods for now, mostly because they caught it sooner than last time."

Last time?

The words hit him like a round to the chest, knocking the air from his lungs and his weight off his feet. Danny moved to the end of the couch and sat down, waiting for the shock to wear off. But soon the shock was replaced by rage.

"Bree's had cancer twice? Which I assume means she's gone through chemo and whatever the hell else twice. And no one thought to tell me?"

Mac shrugged his shoulders. "I wanted to tell you, but—"

Danny held his hand up, silencing his father. He didn't want to hear excuses. He wanted answers.

"Is that why she's back in Myrtle Beach? What about her job in Columbia? I remember you talking about this great job she got after graduation." Danny waited as his father and brother exchanged a knowing glance, the kind that only meant more bad news. "What about her job in Columbia?"

Mike folded his arms across his chest, refusing to succumb to Danny's questioning. So again his father answered. "She was laid off a few years ago."

"Because of the cancer? They can't do that. She should sue their asses for wrongful termination or something."

"The second diagnosis came after. But your brother understands these things far better than I do. All I do know for certain is things have come a long way since your mother—"

Now his father fell silent.

Lily MacGregor had been dead twenty-three years and his father still couldn't bring himself to say the words.

Danny looked to his brother. "I understand Dad knowing and not saying anything, but how long have you known?"

"From the get-go," his brother answered nonchalantly. "Bev sends care packages on occasion and she always includes a letter filling me in on all the goings-on. Kind of like those Christmas letters Aunt Grace used to send each year."

Danny held up a hand to stop him. His head was spinning as he tried to process all this information at once. "Bree's mom sends you care packages?"

His brother shrugged as if this was no big deal. "Has from the time I was in medical school. Last one came around Thanksgiving while we were in Afghanistan. Had these really good oatmeal cookies with cranberries and nuts and stuff."

What. The. Hell?

"Does she always send you cookies?"

"Not always. Sometimes it's brownies. Sometimes cupcakes. Depends on where I am at the time. If she's sending it overseas it has to be vacuum-sealed. And that would really mess up the icing on cupcakes."

Danny's jaw went slack from the shock of it. He looked to his father, who shook his head. No point in looking for answers from him. He glared at his brother. "You mean to tell me Bev's been sending you cookies for what . . . eleven . . . twelve years? I never got any cookies! Why the fuck didn't I get cookies?"

Mike grinned then took another drink from his beer, making him wait for an answer. "Might be a wild guess on my part, but could it be you broke her only daughter's heart?"

Danny clenched his fists. It took every ounce of self-restraint to not wipe the smug look from his brother's face. Even so, that wouldn't do any good. This conversation needed to be with someone else. He turned on his heel and headed for the front door.

"Where are you going?" his brother called after him.

"Where do you think?" Danny yelled back as he crossed the threshold. "I'm going to get answers."

Chapter Three

BREE SETTLED UPON the old wooden swing hanging from the large oak in her backyard, hoping the fresh air and sunshine would settle her mind. But she couldn't escape her thoughts of Danny.

At every turn, the memory of him haunted her like a ghost. It's why she found her life in Columbia so much easier. Yes, he'd lived there for a while. But memories of him didn't permeate every nook and cranny. Here in Myrtle Beach, no matter where she went, no matter how hard she tried, she couldn't escape memories of him.

Even worse were the times she didn't want to.

"How you doin', pumpkin?" Her father's low, slow Southern drawl pulled her from the past and brought her back into the present. "Everything okay?"

If it had been her mother, she would have said whatever it took to make her mother feel better. No matter how big the lie. But Pete Dunbar had always been a straight shooter and asked everyone he knew to be the same in kind. Anyway, lying to him served no purpose. The man had a nose for bullshit.

"I've been better."

From the nearby storage shed Pete grabbed an empty five-gallon paint bucket, overturning it on the grass. He took a seat on the makeshift stool, waiting for her to fill the silence.

"Ran into Mike MacGregor at the store."

"Oh yeah? Mac told me a couple of weeks ago the boys would be home for a visit."

It took a great amount of restraint, but Bree chose to bite her tongue for the most part. "Would have been nice to know."

"I thought I told you they were going to be in town. Huh." Pete shrugged his shoulders. "Guess I didn't."

Sometimes her highly intelligent father could be so dumb. What she wouldn't have given for a little forewarning. If she'd known there was a possibility of running into Danny she could have prepared herself mentally, emotionally.

Or taken up temporary residence in a convent. Somewhere far, far away.

"So, how is Mike?"

"Good, it would seem."

"He's always been a good kid. Good man, I should say." Her father crossed his thick arms over his round belly. "So seeing Mike got you all upset?"

The aluminum screen door slammed against the frame, immediately followed by heavy footsteps across the wooden deck. No need to turn around to know who it was. To be honest, she was surprised he'd waited this long for a second confrontation.

"Should've known," her father grumbled. "Do I need to kick his ass?"

Despite being annoyed with her dad, that made her smile. Having had both knees replaced, there were some mornings her father had difficulty getting down the driveway to pick up the morning paper. No way in hell would he ever be able to kick anyone's ass, much less the ass of a man in prime physical shape almost thirty-five years his junior.

But it was the thought that counted.

"I can handle this."

He studied her for a long moment, then, satisfied she could deal with Danny on her own, braced his hands on his knees and stood. After a quick pat to her shoulder, he crossed the yard to the back deck. Stopping only inches in front of Danny, he stared him in the eye. No words were exchanged, but plenty was said between them. Danny held his ground, unflinching, then with a slight nod, respectfully stepped aside, giving way to her father.

After the back door closed, Danny strolled across the yard to where she sat. A shining example of calm, cool and collected, although history taught her he was likely anything but on the inside. If there was one thing this man learned early in life, when it came to those of the female persuasion, he could catch more flies with honey.

"Mind if I sit down?" he asked, gesturing toward the makeshift chair her father had vacated.

There was no point in answering him. If she said yes, he'd count it as a victory. No, he'd sit down anyway just to prove she couldn't get rid of him that easily.

A breeze kicked up as he passed by, carrying his clean, fresh scent with it. Clearly, he'd showered, although he hadn't shaved. He now wore a gray henley, the first few buttons undone, exposing the hollow of his throat, the sleeves shoved up to his elbows, revealing muscular forearms and a large black watch. The heavy-duty kind. One that was more utilitarian than fashion statement. His jeans were faded and worn in all the right places, the soft fabric cupping his ass.

Bree gave herself a mental shake. The last thing she needed was for Danny MacGregor to catch her checking out his butt.

Danny smiled at her as he made himself at home on the overturned paint bucket and rested his elbows on his knees.

"Stop it."

"Stop what?" he asked, feigning wide-eyed innocence.

"You know. Waltzing in here all charm and swagger with that dimple on display." Of course he only cranked up the wattage of his smile. Bree leveled a finger at him. "I'm immune to your charms, Danny MacGregor. So why are you here? What do you want?"

"So that's how it's gonna be? Cut right to the chase?"

Bree folded her arms across her chest. "The way I see

it, the sooner you say what you want to say, the sooner you'll leave. Again."

A decade of rehearsed conversations finally paid off when her jab hit the mark.

Danny hopped to his feet and marched halfway across the backyard before he stopped. With his back turned to her, he looked to the sky. His broad back expanded as he took a deep breath then another, and another. Finally, he turned to face her, the epitome of restrained fury with his clenched jaw and flexed muscles. Even his fingertips were white where they dug into his hips.

"I'm sorry," he said, throwing his hands in the air. "I'm sorry I left Columbia without telling you. I'm sorry about this morning in the grocery store."

"That sounds sincere."

He scrubbed both hands over his face and head in frustration before letting them fall to his sides. "I *am* sorry. But dammit, Bree, what do you expect? It's a little shocking to see you this way. I get that you didn't want to tell me personally, but swearing my dad and brother to secrecy? That's not excessive?" His voice grew louder with each question. "How long were they supposed to keep your little secret? What if you'd died? Would they have been allowed to tell me then?"

Her chest hurt where he landed a verbal blow of his own and now she felt . . . guilty. Because when he put it that way, what she'd done was childish. And petulant. And selfish. And a whole other list of adjectives that should never be used to describe a twenty-eight-year-old woman.

"You're right." Her body sagged beneath the weight of her admission. "And I'm sorry."

Thankfully, he didn't feel the need to rub it in. Instead, he closed the distance between them and crouched down to bring his face level with hers. "I know I screwed things up royally ten years ago, but that doesn't mean I stopped caring about what happens with you. Got it?"

Bree nodded, and Danny retook his earlier seat.

"So Dad's filled me in for the most part. But what's next for you? Where do you go from here?"

And that was the million dollar question. With companies still trying to recover from the economic downturn, jobs were few and far between. And financial analyst positions numbered even fewer. The longer she was out of work, the harder it would be to get back into the job market.

"It will be a while before I can really start looking for a job." She lowered her gaze to her feet, watching as she pushed the ground just enough to rock the swing back and forth.

"Does that have anything to do with your treatment?"

She shook her head. "I can't interview right now because companies take one look at me and see their insurance rates skyrocketing."

"They can't do that."

"Oh, but they do. So until I'm back to looking like my old self, I'm stuck here living with my parents."

"It can't be that bad."

Bree put her feet flat to the ground, bringing the swing to a halt, and lifted her face to look at him. Danny waited for her to speak, all the while watching her carefully with his deep, dark blue eyes.

"You know I love my parents dearly. They mean well, but I can't breathe here." She glanced toward the house to make sure no one was listening. Then when she realized her parents had given her this privacy, she felt like an ungrateful traitor of sorts. But she needed to talk to someone and despite all his faults, she knew Danny was someone she could trust to keep her secrets. "Every time I go out I run into someone who wants a full medical history because they want to compare my treatment to their cousin's next door neighbor's sister's treatment. Even worse is when someone's read some crap on the internet and becomes a self-proclaimed expert and starts telling me I should be eating this or doing that. I swear it won't be cancer that kills me. It'll be everything else. I'm ready to move on with my life and here people want to treat me like I'm sick."

"So leave."

"It's not that easy, Danny. I have little savings left and what I do have goes toward keeping my insurance current. I have no choice but to be patient."

He stared at the ground in front of him, rubbed his bristled jaw with his knuckles, his brows drawn together in concentration. She remembered that look from when they were younger and knew one thing was for certain—he was plotting some sort of cockamamie scheme.

"Okay then," he said, slapping his palms to his thighs. "Let's get married."

That was not the scheme she was expecting. Surely he was joking.

She searched for a mischievous twinkle in his eyes or slight quirk of his lips, something that signified this was all a joke. But there was no sign of amusement in his eyes, which left only one other possibility.

"Are you insane?"

Chapter Four

THE WORDS POPPED out of his mouth before he'd completely thought it through, but Danny knew this idea had real possibilities.

"Just hear me out a second." He rose to his feet, ready to make his argument before she had time to shoot it down. "You want a fresh start, right? You can have that in Savannah. And I think you'd like it there. It's muggy as hell a lot of the year, but it's nice."

Bree watched him closely from beneath the brim of her cap, a hint of wariness in her eyes, but intrigue, as well.

"If we get married, your insurance will be covered by the army. You won't have to pay for coverage out of pocket in addition to your medical bills." She reluctantly nodded in agreement and he knew the first little battle had been won. So he pushed forward. "It gets you out of your parents' house," he said, ticking off each reason on his fingertips. "You can find a new job or go back to school, whatever you want to do. And since I'm gone a lot you'll have my place to yourself most of the time. You get freedom, space. You get your life back. And when you're back on your feet and ready to move on we'll get a divorce."

Bree shook her head in disbelief. "This is your great idea? You want me to marry you? I don't know if I even like you anymore."

He flashed his best smile. "Well then, you'll fit right in with a bunch of the other wives and girlfriends since they don't like me, either."

Not one giggle or smirk. Not one single reaction from her. Maybe she really was immune to his charms now. Instead, she just sat there, studying him carefully while absentmindedly chewing on her thumbnail. A bad habit of hers for as long as he could remember and a sure sign of her indecision.

"You're really serious about this?"

"Now's not the time to cut off your nose to spite your face, Bree," he said. "When faced with a problem, I find a solution. You know this is one hell of an offer I'm making." He paused a moment for the punchline. "Besides, I happen to like your nose."

At least this time she narrowed her eyes at him and he couldn't help but chuckle.

He waited patiently, somewhat surprised she hadn't grabbed this lifeline with both hands by now. But Bree had always been independent and self-sufficient. Relying on others for help never had been her style. They were alike that way. So when she described how trapped she felt, he could only imagine how crazy he'd be if he were stuck in her shoes.

"You're acting like this is no big deal. Couldn't you get in trouble for this?"

"Obviously, you don't know about life in the military." He knew of guys who advertised on Craigslist for a contract wife. All for a bump in pay and the right to move out of the barracks. Luckily for him, he ranked high enough to live off post and had been doing so for some time. No one would accuse Bree of being a want-ad wife. "Trust me when I say this will not be a problem. As a matter of fact, I bet no one even notices."

"No one will notice?" This time her laugh lacked amusement. "What about my parents? They'll flip. And not in a good way. Then there's your dad. What do you think he'll have to say about all of this?"

"It'll be fine. And if not, they'll get over it."

Bree shook her head in disbelief, but at least now she was smiling. "You haven't changed a bit. That used to be your answer for everything."

"True." Danny rose to his feet and made his way toward the side gate. "Think about it, but not for too long. Mike and I are heading back to Savannah at the end of the week."

"I'd always assumed there'd be music and flowers and a ring," Bree called out to him. "Maybe the guy would get down on one knee. Hell, buy me dinner at least."

He laughed at that. "Guess I'll have to leave that to the next guy." He tapped the face of his watch. "But for now you have a decision to make. Time's ticking."

Danny strode back across the street feeling better about things. A lot better, as a matter of fact. Helping Bree was the least he could do, considering her situation. He'd been a spineless little prick when he left Columbia. He'd known she'd be heartbroken and yet he'd left without saying a word anyway.

Although what happened then had nothing to do with the predicament she found herself in now, he'd never forgive himself if he just went on with life as usual. What kind of man would that make him, knowing he could help her but doing nothing instead?

He might be an asshole, but he wasn't *that* big of an asshole.

"It appears there was no bloodshed." His brother stood on the front porch, obviously waiting for him to return. More likely contemplating whether or not he needed to cross the street and intervene.

"None at all. As a matter of fact, we ended up having a nice conversation." Danny made his way up the steps and continued past him to the front door.

"Is that right? I find that hard to believe."

"Believe what you want, big brother, but the truth is things are just fine between me and Bree."

INSANITY HAD TO be contagious because she was suddenly straight up certifiable to even consider marrying a man she hadn't seen in over ten years.

Ridiculous. And unrealistic.

Although it pained her to admit it, Danny's proposal

had ignited a flicker of hope within her. The possibility of starting over someplace new, of escaping this deep, dark rut in which she was stuck excited her. A quickie wedding. A move south. A little paperwork with the army and just like that, so many of her problems would disappear. He'd made it sound so very easy.

And it'd been a very long time since her life had been easy.

Then there was the fact he had zero problem raising his voice and calling her out on her crap. He was the only person in what seemed like forever who treated her like a normal human being instead of handling her with kid gloves, fearful she might shatter into a million pieces if someone dared to upset her.

Bree headed inside, opening the back door just in time to see her mother disappear around the corner into the kitchen. She'd likely been keeping a watchful eye on matters, at the ready in the event she needed to run a little interference for Bree. Undoubtedly her mother would be heartbroken if she'd up and left. But just maybe, by her leaving, her mother would find some freedom, as well.

"Need help with anything?" Bree watched as her mother gave a quick stir to a pot on the stove and covered it.

"All under control." Bev gave a quick smile then returned to her chair at the island and a partially filled-in crossword. "Are you okay? Danny didn't upset you, did he?"

"We got off on the wrong foot this morning. But we sorted things out. He apologized. I apologized."

"That should make any future run-ins go a little smoother." Her mother watched her from over the rim of her coffee cup as she took a careful sip.

"Yep. Especially since those run-ins could become a daily occurrence." Her mother quirked an eyebrow but waited for more. "I told him everything. About the cancer. All of it. He thinks if we got married it would make life a little easier for me."

The cup hit the counter with a dull thud, coffee sloshing over the side and spilling onto the counter. "He asked you to marry him?"

"No. He *offered* to marry me. Not the same thing." Danny had proposed out of a sense of duty. Not love. And Bree knew she'd be better off to not forget that.

Grabbing up a dish towel from near the stove, her mother wiped down the counter then slumped onto her bar stool. She closed her eyes in exhaustion as if the conversation had physically drained her. For the first time in a long time, Bree saw her. Really saw her. Her mother, who was still young and vibrant, looked so very tired. The dark shadows under her eyes. Her hair in need of a good color. Nails in need of a good manicure. Clothes that were a little worn and out of style.

It wasn't just Bree who'd suffered financially and emotionally all these years. Her parents had taken a hit, as well. She couldn't remember the last time they took a vacation, something her parents had done regularly until her first diagnosis.

What Danny didn't realize when he proposed marriage was that he'd be helping them as much as her.

Bree reached across the counter and grasped her mother's hand. "I think this could be really good. For all of us."

Her mother's eyes widened in horror. "Don't do this for our benefit."

"Okay. I won't. I'll just live here. For-ev-er."

The corner of Bev's mouth quirked upward on one side. "Sheesh. No need to go to extremes."

They sat there smiling at each other, enjoying the moment. Until Bree picked up the cordless phone. "Guess there's no time like the present," she said, dialing the only other phone number she knew from memory as she made her way back upstairs.

THE HOUSE PHONE rang and Danny walked into the kitchen where the thirty-year-old Slimline was still mounted on the wall. Fairly certain it was Bree on the other end, he waited until his brother wandered out the back door then lifted the phone from its cradle. She was off and running before he could even say hello.

"I feel there needs to be some ground rules," she began.

"And those would be?"

Danny made use of the overstretched spiral phone cord and sat down at the kitchen table. Might as well get comfortable. This was probably going to take a while. Bree had always been more of a planner than a fly-by-the-seat-of-her-pants kind of gal.

"Just because I'm going to be your wife on paper and

we're living together doesn't mean I'm your indentured servant. Or anything else, for that matter."

"Wouldn't dream of it."

"But I am willing to help out since it's the least I can do. Like grocery shopping. Of course, I'd need to borrow your car."

"You don't have a car?" No wonder she felt held captive here.

"I turned it back in when the lease expired. Is that a problem?"

"No, not really." He could always hitch a ride with Mike or one of the guys. "Next item." Undoubtedly, she'd made a list of demands or house rules, whatever she was calling it. If he could hazard a guess, living with Bree would likely have more restrictions than he'd ever had while living in the barracks. At least she was prettier. And smelled better.

"I don't mind washing your stuff if I'm doing laundry, but I don't iron and I'm not folding your boxers or briefs or whatever the hell you wear."

"Not a problem since I don't wear any."

"I swear," she huffed in exasperation, "you're still such a pain in the butt. I can't believe I'm even considering this."

"You love it and you know it."

Only when he was met with silence did he consider his words. He said them more out of old habits than really believing it to be true. Amazing how things like that come back so quickly. Danny cleared his throat then tried to restart the conversation. "What else is on that list of yours?" He heard the shuffle of papers in the background and chuckled to himself. She really did have a damn list.

"I'm not going to pick up after you or clean up your messes. And as far as the toilet goes, I'm just a glorified guest. So you clean it."

No sweat off his brow. Like he'd never cleaned a toilet while in the army. During basic training, the US government taught him to scrub a latrine to a sparkling shine using only a toothbrush. "Fine. I'll clean the toilet. But I get to leave the seat up."

"On second thought—"

"Nope. No take backs. I get to leave the seat up." She swore and he chuckled. Who knew negotiations with Bree could be so much fun? He waited for the next demand.

She cleared her throat. "What will the sleeping arrangements be?"

Now this was getting good. "What do you mean? Like right side, left side or top and bottom? Because to tell the truth, sweetheart, any which way works for me."

"Oh, God. Maybe this isn't such a good idea, after all."

He always did love to poke the crazy with her. "I'm just teasing you, Bree. Of course you can have the bed. I'll sleep on the couch."

Even as the words escaped his mouth, he regretted them. If he had one prized possession, it was his bed. His big, fluffy "girlie" bed as his brother called it. With a super-thick pillow top and feather down pillows, it was like sleeping on a cloud. And he didn't give a shit if it wasn't considered manly.

"That's very generous of you. Thank you."

"You're welcome. Any other questions? Concerns?"

Who knew what else was on that list of hers. Whether or not she was gutsy enough to demand it remained to be seen.

"None that I can think of at the moment," she answered. "But I reserve the right to revisit this discussion."

"Got it. Do I get to set some ground rules?"

"Go for it."

"I just want to make it clear the army is my life now and this marriage is just a temporary solution. Anything related to my work is my decision alone. You don't get a say."

"Fine. Whatever. So we're really doing this?"

"Yep. I'll call the courthouse to find out what the procedures are and get back with you."

She hung up the phone, leaving him with their conversation replaying in his head. Just like she'd said, it sounded so very cold, businesslike. No hearts and flowers. No romantic declarations. Probably not what his mother had wished for him—for the two of them—but it was what it was. Still, he couldn't shake the idea of his mother looking down from heaven and enjoying the hell out of the show.

Danny headed out back to the screened porch where his father and brother were trading stories. Leaning a shoulder against the doorjamb he listened to their conversation as they rehashed their day on the golf course. His brother glanced once in his direction then did a double-take, stopping in midsentence.

"What the hell are you smiling about?"

He hadn't realized he was, but there was no denying it. He'd probably been standing there the entire time with a grin on his face. Danny dropped into an empty deck chair and pulled a beer from the cooler. He twisted the cap off then tapped the longneck against the one Mike held in his hand.

"Congratulate me, big brother," he said, raising his bottle for a toast. "I'm getting married."

Chapter Five

DANNY STOOD IN front of the bathroom mirror, fumbling with the silk tie he'd bought the day before. First he tied it too short, then too long. Then the knot somehow ended up being the size of his fist. He took a steadying breath, let it all out as he shook his hands, the blood rushing back to his fingertips.

Why the hell was he so anxious? It wasn't as if this was a real wedding.

Well, it was real. Papers signed, sealed and delivered by the power vested in a county judge. But beyond that, the entire arrangement was a total sham. And yet he found himself deeply afraid of disappointing Bree. Again.

Hence, the new tie. And suit and dress shirt. Not to mention shoes. He dropped a small fortune to buy an outfit he'd likely wear only once and for a couple of hours at best.

Danny continued with his tie. Over. Over. Around.

What if she wears jeans and a T-shirt?

He paused. Surely not.

He completed the half-Windsor and again it looked like shit, which was ridiculous considering all the practice he'd had tying knots. During trainings and missions, his belongings were tethered to his person using 550 para cord, especially when bailing out the side door of a C–17. He could tie knots in the pitch-black, practically in his sleep. And yet, today of all days, he couldn't make a presentable looking half Windsor with a silk tie.

"To hell with this."

He unknotted it and in one swift motion pulled the fabric from beneath his collar then unfastened the top two buttons of his shirt. All the better. A tie had a way of making everything a little more formal. The last thing he wanted was to give the impression this marriage was anything more than a short-term solution.

"Daniel." His father stood in the doorway. "Come with me," he motioned before heading in the opposite direction.

He obediently followed his father through the house, down the darkened hallway to his parents' room. Mac flicked the switch by the door, instantly bathing the room in a dull, yellow light. Without so much as looking at Danny, he pointed to the foot end of the bed, silently ordering him to have a seat before he disappeared into the closet.

Danny sat on the threadbare comforter, the same one that had covered the bed since he was a child. Although his father had added a few things to the house over the years, most everything remained unchanged from the time of his mother's death. Walls had been repainted but always in the same color. Every picture, every painting, returned to its original hanging place. His parents' wedding photo sat atop the bureau. His mother's photo sat on the bedside table. A husband's way of honoring the wife he loved so dearly and lost far too soon.

"Hold out your hand."

He did as instructed and his father grasped Daniel's hand between both of his. It took a moment to register the press of metal against his palm. His already nervous stomach turned.

"Dad." Danny shook his head. Even attempted to pull his hand free from his father's grip. "No. Absolutely not. I cannot take Mom's wedding ring."

"Hear me out first." His father sat beside him on the bed, still clutching Danny's hand between his. "I know you say you're only doing this to help Aubrey out from between a rock and a hard place. That's commendable. Everyone should have as good a friend as you. But whether this marriage is for the short term or the long haul, one thing is for certain—you love this girl."

"Dad . . ." His throat tightened, making breathing difficult and words impossible. How did he know that he still loved Bree? That he always had? Was it so obvious? Despite all the mistakes and bad decisions and straight-up idiotic behavior, the countless one-night stands and weekend flings.

"As a matter of fact, we all love her. Even your mother loved her." Tears shimmered in his father's eyes. "I'd like to think I knew your mom pretty well and I'm absolutely certain she would want Aubrey to have it."

He knew his dad was right, but his mother's ring represented so many memories, promises. So many expectations for the future. Suddenly, Danny feared failing not only Bree, but his mother, as well.

"We're getting married at the county courthouse. In front of a judge. That's not the kind of place—"

Mac held up a hand, silencing him. "Where you get married doesn't matter. It's what's in your heart that matters. I might not have told you this enough but you're a good man, Daniel. I'm proud of you. And your mother would be, as well. All I ask is that you treat Aubrey right. Be the man we all know you are deep down inside. You never know what the fates have planned. Maybe this marriage was meant to be all along."

He had to smile at that. Never in his entire life had he heard his father speak in such a way. He was damn near waxing poetic.

"Mac MacGregor. The romantic."

"My boy," he said, slapping Danny's back, "I've always been a romantic. Sadly, you were too young to remember. I wooed your mother even long after we were married. That woman had me wrapped around her slender finger," he said, holding up his pinky to demonstrate. "And I loved every minute of it."

The earlier sadness had passed, replaced by a twinkle in his father's eyes.

"I can't believe what I'm hearing."

Mac laughed. "Oh, you better believe it. Raising you boys

didn't leave much time for me to go on and on about my love for your mother, but that doesn't make it any less true. Besides, for the last decade when I've seen you two, the conversation has been about blowing stuff up, shooting stuff, or who had the worst case of trench foot. Doesn't really lend itself to hearts and flowers, if you know what I mean."

He smiled at his father, but only for a moment. "Does Mike know about the ring? Can't imagine he'd be too thrilled about this."

From the moment Danny shared the news he and Bree were getting married, Mike had made it quite clear he was completely against the idea, although he never gave specific reasons as to why.

"Worry about Bree, not your brother. You two will be just fine."

They rose from the bed simultaneously and Danny held the ring up between them. "Thank you for this. It means a lot."

His father pulled him into an embrace, arms wrapped around his shoulders, holding him tight for one moment longer. A kiss on the cheek and two slaps to the back later, he released him. "Get on out of here. Your girl is waiting."

Holding the gold band between forefinger and thumb, Danny gave his father a little salute and headed for the door.

THE DOORBELL RANG just before nine and immediately the butterflies took flight in her stomach. Only thirty-six hours had passed since she'd agreed to this crazy, hatched-up scheme of his, which could only mean she was as insane as he was. Quite the pairing they made.

A few moments later her mother appeared in her doorway. "Danny's here."

"I'll be down in a second," she said while slipping on her heels.

Bree took one last look in the mirror and hoped she'd made the right decision. Living with Danny, being his wife, what would that mean, really? After all, she hadn't liked him very much for the past decade. Definitely never had happy thoughts about him. Tried her damnedest to hate him. But even after all this time apart, he could still make her smile, make her laugh. Make her crazy in a good way, it seemed. To suddenly be in each other's personal space on an almost daily basis . . . could she handle it?

More important, would her heart survive it when all was said and done?

Then there was not only the uncertainty about the marriage, but also about what to wear for her nuptials. Unfortunately, every wedding website she found lacked advice on "what to wear for a marriage of convenience." Surprising, since the internet seemed to have an opinion on almost everything. After spending way too long surfing, she came to the conclusion that for this particular occasion she was on her own.

So she made up her own rules. Which meant anything white, anything remotely bridal, was out of the question. As was black. She and Danny might be marrying for the wrong reasons but there was no need to be morbid about it. Strewn across her bed was everything else in her wardrobe that didn't fall into either of those two categories. She finally settled on a blush pink sheath dress with lace overlay. One she'd always loved but never had much occasion to wear.

"Are you sure you don't want to get married in the church? I'm sure Father Bryant would be willing to perform the ceremony even on such short notice."

"Mom," she said sharply. "No church."

It wasn't that she was against religion or being married in a church. It had more to do with the memory of waking up from surgery to see Father Bryant, eyes closed, Bible in hand, rosary beads dangling from his fingers while praying over her bed. There are those who would find comfort from the gesture. Unfortunately for her, she couldn't shake the feeling of last rites. Going into surgery that morning she understood the long battle in front of her, but she was far from dying. Then Bree woke up to a prayer vigil and for one brief moment wondered if they were already digging her grave.

"What about the beach? The backyard?" Bree cut her eyes at her mother, but the woman refused to take the hint. "Anywhere but a courthouse," her mother continued. "It might be . . ."

Although she didn't say them aloud, her unspoken words whispered through the room—*it might be the only wedding you ever have.*

Bree looked at her mother, saw the heartbreak in her eyes. No grand wedding. No large celebration with friends and family. Her dreams of a day to remember replaced with a quickie set of "I dos" at the county courthouse.

Since witnesses weren't required, she and Danny had decided to forgo an audience.

"I'm sorry, Mom." She hugged her mother close. "I know this isn't what you wanted."

"I just want what's best for you. If you think Danny will be the one to give it to you—"

She raised a hand to stop any wrong ideas before they steamrolled into something bigger.

"You know what this is. Marrying Danny, moving to Savannah, is a short-term fix, not a plan for the long run. It's not a question of *if* we will divorce, but *when*. It's not the ending you might prefer, but it most definitely is the kickstart I need."

Her mother nodded in agreement although tears welled in her eyes. Bree didn't like causing her mother this pain, but she wasn't about to back out now. This needed to be done. For all of them. Whether that change was for better or worse didn't really matter to Bree, just as long as her life moved in some direction instead of remaining in idle.

After grabbing her coat from the closet, she headed downstairs to find Danny waiting in the front entryway along with her father. He stood tall, shoulders back, hands clasped behind him with his feet placed shoulder-width apart. The charcoal-gray suit and crisp white shirt did nothing to hide his military background. His posture simply screamed soldier. His hair had been trimmed, the top still damp from the shower. He'd also shaved, his jaw clean and smooth, revealing the faint creases in his cheeks and shallow cleft in his chin. The definition of handsome. Then he caught sight of her, his eyebrows drawing together for just an instant before schooling his expression.

She'd never considered herself a vain person. Even as a teenager she never spent a great deal of time in front of the mirror. But the look on his face told her something was wrong, and panic set in as she ran down a self-evaluating checklist as she eased on her coat.

Matching shoes? Check. Hem tucked in underwear? No. A lipstick situation, perhaps? She ran her tongue across her teeth and swiped at the corners of her mouth. That left one thing. She flicked the ends out from under her collar and smoothed her palms over the long brown strands, discreetly adjusting her wig, although it didn't feel lopsided to begin with.

Had he expected her to wear something more formal? More wedding-like?

"Is this okay or should I change into something else?"

Danny shook his head. "No. It's fine. You look . . . nice."

His smile was an afterthought. Forced. Something knotted in the pit of her stomach and for the first time she considered that this was a terrible, *terrible* idea.

Her father must have sensed her discomfort. "Beautiful as always, pumpkin," he said with a wink.

Bree pressed a kiss to his stubbled cheek. "Thank you, Daddy."

Danny stepped forward and offered his hand to her. She looked into his eyes, needing some kind of reassurance and he gave it to her with a confident smile. Bree placed her palm in his and watched as his strong hand folded around her own, providing that little bit of security she needed to push forward.

"I'm not sure how long we'll be," he said to her parents. "Depends on how many others they have scheduled in front of us. But if we won't be back until this afternoon, I'll let you know."

Hesitantly, Bev stepped forward and embraced him, pressing a kiss to his cheek. Pete nodded in understanding and offered his hand to Bree's future husband. "Good luck." Danny reached out to accept it only to be pulled in unexpectedly, her father whispering something in Danny's ear then slapping his shoulder to punctuate the point.

"Yes, sir." Danny smiled, seemingly amused by what transpired.

After one last hug and kiss from both her parents, he pressed his palm to the curve of her lower back. Even through the layers of her dress and jacket, she could feel the strength of his hand as he escorted her out the door and to where the car was parked along the curb.

"What did my dad say to you that was so funny?"

"He told me if I hurt you that he had a gun and a shovel and that no one would miss me."

Bree rolled her eyes. "That man really needs some new material."

"Tell me about it," Danny laughed. "I'm pretty sure he said the exact same thing before I took you to senior prom."

Mac stood on the sidewalk to see them off, happy

and smiling and kissing his daughter-in-law-to-be on the cheek before she climbed in. Michael kept his distance, remaining on the front porch, arms crossed over his chest. Even if Danny hadn't mentioned Michael was against their marrying, she would have caught a clue. Only when she waved did he give a half smile and wave in return. The smile, however, quickly disappeared and he turned to go inside.

Whether he was upset with her or Danny or both remained to be seen, but it looked like their four-hour car ride south was going to be an interesting one.

Chapter Six

ASIDE FROM THE low hum of the radio, they drove to the county seat in silence. Which meant she had far too much time alone with her thoughts. Just the occasional glance from him had Bree going crazy inside. What the hell was running through his mind? Was he regretting his offer of marriage? There'd been that momentary look of surprise in his eyes that disappeared just as quickly. Something was up and once again he was keeping his true thoughts from her.

"Are you sure you want to do this?" She watched his face carefully, his eyes briefly making contact with hers before returning to the road. "This idea of yours, it was pretty impulsive. Even for you. So if you don't really want to go through with this I'll understand."

"And do what instead?" he replied without looking in her direction.

Here she was one giant bundle of nerves spiraling out

of control and he was calm. So damn calm. Which was just so like him. Danny loved this kind of crap. Spontaneity. Living moment to moment. Whereas she was a planner. She liked neatness and structure, and this was far from orderly.

"I don't know. Don't you have a girlfriend?" Or two? Maybe three? God, she hoped there weren't three. "What would she have to say about this?"

"You're asking whether or not I have a girlfriend? Now?" he asked, not hiding the amusement in his voice. "We're on the way to the courthouse, Bree. And no, there's no girlfriend. I don't do girlfriends."

"You used to."

"Not in a very long time."

She couldn't help but wonder how long it had been. Two years? Five years? Surely he'd been in some kind of long-term relationship since they were together in college.

"So what happens after?"

She didn't dare look at him now; instead she took great interest at the passing scenery as the heat of embarrassment burned through her.

"After?"

"After we get married since we won't be . . . you know." She idly waved one hand between them without looking in his vicinity.

"Since we won't what? Be having wild hot monkey sex 24/7?"

Jesus. He loved tormenting her and she couldn't not look at him now.

Having hit a red light just blocks from the courthouse, Danny focused his attention solely upon her. His blue eyes twinkled with mischievousness, his lips quirked. He was having way too much fun with this.

"Well, yeah. I'm just—"

A car horn alerted them to the stoplight changing to green, and Danny returned his attention to the road. Which meant she could now ogle to her heart's content. Her gaze landed on his hands, how they alternately gripped then smoothed over the leather-wrapped steering wheel as he made a turn. She still remembered the feel of those hands. Smoothing across her skin, over her breasts, down her stomach. How they could lift her from the ground and gently pin her to the bed.

"What are your plans?" She placed a hand at her throat. Her pulse raced beneath her fingertips, her skin hot to the touch. If she were wearing a string of pearls around her neck she'd certainly be clutching them right about now. Which was pathetic, considering she was a grown damn woman having a conversation about sex with her husband-to-be. Instead, she was on the verge of dying of embarrassment.

"My plans?"

"Because I sincerely doubt—" Bree cleared her throat in an attempt to free the words. "I doubt you'll go without you-know-what for however long we're married."

He found a spot in the courthouse parking lot, pulled in and shut off the engine. Danny repeated her sanitized phrasing in amusement just before his eyes widened with surprise.

"You're expecting me to be unfaithful?"

The temperature in his vehicle had skyrocketed twenty degrees in the last sixty seconds and she desperately needed fresh air. Bree made a play for the door handle, but he hit the child locks, effectively holding her hostage.

"LET ME OUT, Danny."

"Not until we talk this out, Bree."

At first it was amusing listening to her spurt and sputter as she fought the embarrassment to get to the heart of the question. But in the end she'd successfully gotten under his skin. He realized it'd been ten years since they were close, but even as a horny college freshman he'd been faithful. So to question his loyalty, his ability to keep his libido in check, well, in short, it pissed him off.

"It's not really cheating since it's not a real marriage."

Danny took a deep breath, counted to ten and reminded himself to not lose his shit. Resting one arm atop the steering wheel he turned to face her.

"You think I'm going to marry you, have you move in with me then go off and screw around with someone else?" he said so calmly he impressed the hell out of himself.

"You aren't?"

"No!" Bree flinched when his answer slipped out with a little too much force. He needed to regain his composure. Not to mention change the subject, if possible. Time for a little designed distraction. "I mean no," he repeated, the calm having returned. "Not unless you're into that kind of thing." She blinked once, twice, her eyes going wider each time. He was definitely on the right track. "Are you into that kind of thing?"

Her jaw dropped open. With his index finger Danny lifted her chin and closed it for her.

"You don't seriously think—" Her blush now reached epic proportions.

He leaned across the console well into her personal space. "It's been ten years, Bree." His voice dropped to an even lower register. "Who knows what you're into now. What kind of naughty little things are packed away in those boxes in your bedroom?"

Bree covered her face with both hands, the only way to hide from his gaze as he had a good laugh at her expense. "You're so mean," she whined.

Danny pulled one hand from her face and waited until those big brown eyes focused on him.

"To be honest, I'm a little bit insulted. As you should be. You'd let me humiliate you that way and just sit back and take it? That's not the girl I knew." He released her hand and pressed the button on the driver-side to unlock the doors. Hopefully he'd convinced her unless . . . "Was that what you were planning to do?"

"Me? I have no plans," she said, the picture of innocence. "I'm just along for the ride on this one."

"Yeah. Right. Why are we even having this conversation if you haven't been thinking about it? Maybe I should have asked if you were planning on screwing someone else while we're married. Have *you* been seeing anyone?"

"I'm twenty-eight years old, unemployed, and living with my parents. And I've yet to mention the cancer part. That's *so* sexy. For years I've practically been beating men back with a stick," Bree deadpanned.

Danny shook his head. "You're terrible."

"What?" she shouted as he climbed out of the truck and made his way around the front. "It's the truth."

He opened her door, offering his hand to her. "Listen up, Dunbar. There won't be any other women. I promise."

"But that's the point. You don't have to."

God dammit. He could just tell she was on the verge of saying something stupid, like suggesting he take a lover. So when she didn't take his hand, he placed it over her mouth instead. Her brown eyes widened to the size of saucers.

"No, I do. *Got it?*" He'd definitely shocked her. About as much as he shocked himself. But she didn't fight him, didn't squirm to get away. "Nod your head once to show you understand."

Almost immediately he felt her smile against his palm as she nodded in agreement.

"Good," he said, smiling back at her.

His knuckles brushed across her soft cheek, his attention dropping to her now uncovered mouth, temporarily mesmerized by his thumb skimming across her full lower lip of its own volition. Her pink lips parted beneath his touch, her soft exhales fanning over his calloused skin in an erratic rhythm. In an instant their past came rushing back. How he'd tasted those lips, that tongue. How there once was a time he'd spent hours lost in the feel of her mouth on his.

But reliving the past wasn't part of their agreement and he'd be far better off to remember that.

JUST BEFORE DUSK they reached the outskirts of Savannah due to a longer than expected wait at the courthouse. After which they'd returned to her parents' home for a late lunch, and Danny loaded up her things. Somewhere south of Charleston, the whirlwind of the past few days caught up with Bree. She curled up on the second-row bench seat with a pillow and blanket and slept peacefully despite all the boxes and luggage piled around her.

In the rearview mirror he could see the long strands of her brown wig draped over her cheek, the contrast between light and dark only making her skin appear paler. More sickly. He knew why she wore it, but secretly wished she wouldn't. Something about it dulled her natural vibrancy. And the woman that wore it was far from dull.

At least she didn't used to be. As much as he hated to admit it, Danny didn't really know much about the woman she was now.

"What do you think the guys are going to say when they find out the great Daniel MacGregor has fallen into the clutches of marriage?"

Of course Michael's first attempt at conversation in the past three hours would be a doozy. Why pussyfoot around the subject? Just go for the damn jugular right out of the gate.

"I'm going to catch a ration of shit, that much is cer-

_Checkout Receipt

_ Henderson Library
_ 30 Aug 2017 12:02

****

_ Once and for All /

_CALL #: FICTION ROM ETCHISON
_ 33097080422493
Due Date 20 Sep 2017

_TOTAL: 1
****

Manage Your Account Online or By Ph[illegible]
Renewals * Notices * Online Payments
Call TeleMessaging at 204-986-4657 or
1-866-826-4454 (Canada/US toll free)
Go online winnipeg.ca/library
****

Overdue Fines:
Adult Items 40 cents/day per item
Children's items 20 cents/day per item
Express, Bk Club kits $2.05/day per item

tain." If Danny never thought it possible he would return from block leave with a wife, then the guys in his platoon certainly didn't.

"Think your past is gonna come back to haunt you?"

Danny shrugged his shoulders and focused his attention on the road. "Can't do anything about that now."

Mike chuckled. "Maybe you shouldn't have talked so much crap for the past several years to every guy who got married. Which reminds me, are you going to change your cell phone number? How many women have that number anyway?"

"Quit—" Danny checked himself, quickly lowering his voice before he woke the woman sleeping in the backseat. "Quit blowing shit out of proportion. You make it sound like I fucked anything in a skirt."

Danny continued to check the mirror, hoping Bree was truly asleep and not listening in on the conversation.

"Let's be honest here. You've definitely plowed through a lot of terrain."

"And who are you? The Pope? I don't think you've been the greatest of Boy Scouts, either."

"Have you given her any idea of your past? What are you going to do when you two run into one of the many notches on your bedpost? Because at some point in time, it will happen."

"It won't be a problem. Things aren't like that between us. There are no expectations."

Thankfully, the conversation ended before Bree woke and they arrived at the apartment complex where both he and Michael lived. Taking the first of several boxes from the truck, Danny led Bree upstairs to his second-floor apartment.

Michael dropped his load and headed out the door for more. Danny followed to do the same, until Bree called out to him.

"Are things okay with you two?"

Danny shrugged. "No different than always."

A worry line formed between her brows. "I hate that I'm the cause of tension between the two of you."

"He's not angry with you. He's angry with me." Danny skimmed his palm across her shoulder. "And you of all people should know that's nothing new."

"Maybe we should all go out to dinner? Smooth things over before it gets worse?"

With the way their conversation went in the car, the last thing Danny wanted to do was break bread with his brother. But he'd suck it up and do it. For Bree. Not for his brother or himself, just so she'd stop worrying about it.

By the time he reached the parking lot, Michael had already removed several boxes from the back of his truck.

"Bree wanted me to ask if you wanted to go out to eat with us."

"I've got plans."

"With who?"

"Hatton."

First Lieutenant Raymond Hatton was an asshole of the highest order. A guy who knew more about writing military history than actually conducting it. After more than a few close calls during their last rotation in the 'Stan, he finally let go of his micromanaging bullshit style and let the guys who'd been fighting the fight all these years do their job. Even if there weren't rules against fraternization, Danny wouldn't hang with Hatton unless it was a direct order. But it made sense Hatton would try to hang with Mike. After all, they were both officers. Both single, since Hatton's wife filed divorce papers and moved back to wherever they came from during the last deployment.

"Since when do you hang out with that dickhead?" Mike gave him a look. "Sorry. I meant Lt. Dickhead."

"Consider it a pity outing. I'll take him out, let him blow off some steam, maybe then he won't be such an asshole. Besides, I'm sure as hell not going to hang out with the two of you on your wedding night."

"I told you it's not like that between me and Bree."

"That may be the case—"

"That is the case."

"Either way, if the three of us go out and run into any of the guys, they're going to get suspicious. So I'll help carry up the rest of her stuff, but then you two are on your own." Mike stacked one box on top of another and picked them up off the ground. "You're not afraid to be alone with her?"

Yes. No. "Why would you think that?"

"There's a lot of history there, Danny. This arrangement you've come up with might not be so easy to disentangle yourself from."

Making a big deal out of nothing. Again. There was absolutely nothing to worry about. Both he and Bree were adults. They'd made a deal. He'd help her for as long as she needed. A year, maybe two at the most. After that she'd probably move back to South Carolina or maybe to Atlanta and he'd go back to doing the same thing he was doing before he slipped that ring on her finger. Back to a life filled with random hookups, short-term arrangements and recreational flings.

Oddly enough, the prospect of rushing back to his old life didn't seem all that appealing.

BREE TOOK UP residence in the kitchen where she'd be out of the way as the brothers brought in box after box of her things. Danny's apartment was sparsely decorated, with not much more than a loveseat, recliner, and television. A small table with two chairs was shoved against the wall to allow for a path through the tiny breakfast nook.

The boxes continued to stack up, many of them filled with stuff she didn't really need. But Danny insisted she'd feel more at home if she brought more than just the essentials. Since he had plenty of room for her things and her move was indefinite, she might as well bring everything they could haul.

"Okay you two, I'm outta here," Mike said, making his way to the front door.

"Want to run in the morning, or do you think you'll be out too late?"

"If it's anything like the last time I went out with Hatton, I'll be in bed before eleven. Give me a call at six. If I don't answer, go on without me. 'Night, Bree."

Mike waved goodbye and pulled the door closed behind him.

"How is he going to get home?"

"Walk. He lives on the other side of the complex." Danny pointed in the general direction before disappearing down the hallway.

Bree made her way to the front window that looked out over the courtyard. Sure enough, there was Mike, duffel thrown over one shoulder, golf clubs over the opposite, walking across the grass to an identical building just beyond the pool. At least he was nearby if she ever needed someone to talk to other than Danny.

For now, it would be just the two of them.

The two of them.

The full impact of what that meant hit her like a Mack truck and she couldn't help but wonder if she'd just traded the frying pan for the fire.

Chapter Seven

BREE FELT LIKE a fool, arms wrapped around her middle, her insides a giant ball of nerves. Standing in the center of the living room, unsure what to do or what to say, it reminded her of once when she was a teenager and left alone for the first time with a boy who wasn't a MacGregor brother.

Oddly enough, never in their past had she felt this kind of nervousness. When they were teens, they somehow skipped right over all the awkwardness that comes with a new relationship. Probably because they were too stupid to feel any differently.

"Bree, can you come here a sec?"

She followed the sound of his voice down the single hallway. The first door she came to was a small bedroom, now filled with boxes of her things, along with a mountain bike, golf clubs, and a few boxes of his own. Across the hall, louvered doors hid what she assumed was storage or laundry. Then came the only bathroom. Through the last door on her right was where she found him.

She watched Danny stretch across the king-size mattress to pull free the last bedsheet corner. "That's a pretty big bed," she said once he noticed her standing in the doorway.

"I'm a big boy," he said, adding a wink.

Instantly, her stomach knotted. Knowing Danny like she did, he'd put it to more than good use. As teens they'd put backseats, sofas, twin beds, sleeping bags, all through their paces. He was probably one hell of a showman with that much floor space.

And why was he stripping the bed? To rid the evidence of his last encounter?

"The answer is no."

She tore her focus away from the bed to find him standing directly in front of her, sheets and pillowcases bundled in his arms.

"You were saying?"

"I'm not washing the sheets because I just slept with some chick before going back to Myrtle Beach."

"I wasn't thinking about—"

"Yes, you were," he said with a devilish smile. "You forget who you're dealing with." He stroked the furrow between her brows. "This always appears when you're considering the worst. And this—" he lowered his hand to touch the hollow of her throat with his fingertip "—this place right here always turns beet-red when you're thinking about sex."

"That's not true." Instinctively she lifted her hand to

bat away his touch and hide her neck from view. For the second time in a day she could feel the heat coming off her skin.

"Whatever you say." He pushed past her into the hallway, pulled open the louvered doors to reveal the washer and dryer. "The ugly truth is I didn't wash them when I got home after the last rotation so they have roughly six months' worth of dust on them. It didn't bother me to sleep on them a couple of nights once I came back since I spend the majority of my life in the sand and dirt and mud. But what's good enough for me shouldn't be good enough for you."

She cleared her throat, needing to change the subject. "So is that why you called me? I thought I made it clear I wasn't going to be your maid."

Danny chuckled. "Hardly. I made some space for you in the dresser if you want to unpack some of your things."

He disappeared down the hall and soon returned with her suitcase in tow, hefting it onto the mattress. "I've got nothing in the fridge. We can either go out to eat or have something delivered. Any preference?"

Since Mike begged off, they'd be alone together either way. At least if they stayed put she could always find an excuse to distance herself from him. But trapped in a restaurant or in the car, there would be no escape. "Do you mind if we eat in?"

"After the long day we've had, I'd actually prefer it."

"Chinese?"

"Can do. I tell you what, there's a place just down the street that's great when you go inside for carryout, but shit if you have it delivered. Doesn't make any sense, but there you have it. So I'll run out and grab it. Anything else? Beer? Wine?"

"Just water. Or whatever you're having is fine."

"Okay. Make yourself at home. I'll be back in a bit." He pushed away from the door frame and headed down the hall. Over the hum of the washing machine, she heard the jangle of keys followed by the turn of the dead bolt.

The empty drawers he'd designated for her use were left pulled open. Bree unzipped the largest suitcase and placed T-shirts and yoga pants in the bottom drawers, her lingerie and smaller items in the top. Out of curiosity, she pulled open the drawer next to hers and found rolls and rolls of—were those shirts or boxer briefs?

Bree picked up one soft cotton roll and studied it a moment before placing it back in its spot. Every bit of his clothing had been rolled and tucked and shaped to the size of a toilet paper roll. Bree looked back at her drawer, how a few items were neatly folded but for the most part things were just tossed in there. She quickly closed both drawers, embarrassed by her lack of organization.

In the closet she found an extra hanger for her winter coat. His things didn't fill half of the walk-in, but what he did have was neatly arranged. She ran her hand over half a dozen button-down shirts, a dozen or so golf shirts. Only one other time in her life had she gone through this process, sharing a space with a man. A month after graduating from college, she met Brandon when he moved into the apartment next door. Tall, blond, and lanky, he was Danny's opposite in almost every way, from his CPA to his plaid button-down shirts. They began dating a few months later and when his lease came up for renewal, he moved in with her since it only made good financial sense. For a long time she convinced herself she could love him enough to make it last and that he could be a good enough man for her.

Until he proved himself not.

But this would not end like that. Danny was loyal to a fault. When this marriage ended, it would be on her terms and not because of something he did. That she knew for certain. Because he said so. She could trust in that. And that idea of control, of being able to call all the shots, should have left her with a feeling of empowerment. Instead, thinking of a day when all of this would come to an end a second time, left her feeling a little sad.

She sat on the end of the bed and stared at the ring he'd placed on her finger earlier in the day. Not until the judge said "until death do you part" had the idea of not making it to a divorce ever crossed her mind. And whether or not Danny realized it, the odds were stacked against them. She'd battled cancer twice. Came out the other side a little bruised and battered each time, but she'd made it. The next time, if there was one, she'd probably not be so fortunate.

And then there was Danny. She didn't know exactly what his job in the army entailed, but her father had hinted it was a dangerous one. They were both like cats who used up one life after another. The only question that remained was which one of them would use all nine the quickest.

But worrying about tomorrow didn't do any good. All she needed to do was get through today. And the next day. Then the next one. Sooner or later she'd find out where they ended up. Until then, she was just going to keep on living.

Deciding a hot shower was in order, she gathered a change of clothes and toiletries and headed into the bathroom. A clean towel and washcloth were stacked on the counter as if Danny knew even before she did that a shower would be on the agenda. The lights were bright, the mirror large, spanning the length of the counter. There would be no hiding here.

She studied her reflection, the cut of the wig, the color of it. No matter how many people said to her they thought her wig looked real and natural, all she ever saw was something completely fake. But it got the job done, hiding her away from the outside world.

With one hand she pushed it off her head and laid it upon the counter. Today had been the longest she'd worn her wig in months. Her hair was coming back, slower than it had the previous time, which was nothing out of the ordinary. Short, baby-fine strands of brown hair covered her head. In some places, the strands were dense enough her scalp barely showed, whereas in others, it was as bare as a baby's bottom.

If there was one perk to chemo, it was that it made showering quick work. No need to shave legs, arms or bikinis. No need to lather, repeat then condition. Just a quick wash and done.

However, after the shower, that was when the real dilemma came. Put the wig back on or just go as-is? She'd never been one of those women who rose early to put on a full face of makeup before facing the man she lived with. So how was this any different? Despite her trying to convince herself it wasn't, she knew the two reasons were worlds apart. After all, it was when she lost all her hair the first time that she lost Mr. Good Enough, as well.

DANNY PATIENTLY WAITED in the living room, having heard the shower turn off ten minutes before. In the meantime, he'd tossed the sheets into the dryer and set the table. He'd give her another five before asking if she was okay since the last thing he wanted was for her to think he was hovering. One reason they married was to help her escape that.

He clicked on the television to distract himself. Two more minutes and he'd check on her. Surely that would be okay. Just then the bathroom door opened and she darted across the hall, registering as a little more than a blur in his peripheral vision. But one thing was for certain; the wig she wore all day was in her hand and not on her head.

"Dinner's getting cold," he called. That should work. Just a way to let her know he was back in case in her rush across the hall she hadn't noticed him sitting there. He rose from the chair and headed into the kitchen where she appeared before him all soft and warm-looking.

"I hope you don't mind that I changed into my pajamas already." Her fingers fiddled with the mousy brown strands, twirling the ends between her fingers just as she used to do as a girl then as a teenager.

"Don't mind at all." While he placed the containers of food on the table, he noticed the thick, fuzzy socks on her feet. "Is it warm enough in here for you? I can turn the heat up."

"I'm fine. Just my feet are cold, really. And my hands."

He chuckled. "Not much has changed there. Your feet were always like a block of ice, even in the middle of summer."

The dinner conversation remained in the safe zone as they stuck with topics like their parents, old friends from high school, and places they'd each like to visit. In silent agreement they avoided speaking of Michael, the war and her remission status.

" '*Doing what you like is freedom. Liking what you do is happiness.*' Seems fitting," she said, handing him back the small slip of paper from his fortune cookie. "You should keep this one. Play the lottery numbers on the back. It's probably good luck."

"What does yours say?" he asked around a mouthful of cookie.

"Nothing really. It's stupid. '*A new job opportunity awaits you.*' "

"You should save that. Could prove lucky."

Bree rolled her eyes. "I was diagnosed with cancer, lost

my job, and was forced to move back in with my parents all in the same year. If it weren't for bad luck, I wouldn't have any luck at all."

"Yeah, but you're married to me now. Maybe your luck is changing?" He waggled his brows and flashed her his signature heartbreaker smile.

Bree mumbled under her breath, something suspiciously sounding like "arrogant asshole" before she wadded up her small fortune and bounced it off his forehead.

God, she was fun to mess with.

"Do you have room for dessert?" he asked while shoving his chair back from the table. "There's a bakery next door to the Chinese place so I bought a little something."

He went to the refrigerator and pulled out a pale pink pastry box. From a drawer he grabbed two clean forks and a knife before returning to the table and placing the box in front of her. "For you."

She raised a brow. "If it's for me then why did you bring two forks?"

"Touché, smart-ass." He laughed. "If you don't want to share, fine. But I really doubt you can eat the entire thing. Especially not in one sitting."

"I'm kidding," she said as she lifted the lid. Instantly, her face softened, her eyes welling with tears. Her sarcasm gave way to a soft gasp.

"Don't cry, please?" he begged. "I didn't buy it to make you cry. I just thought you deserved a little something nice. You know, since I didn't get down on one knee and all that."

She lifted the small cake from the box, holding it at eye level. He didn't know squat about wedding cakes but was glad she liked it. Initially, he'd been unsure about all the fake little pink flowers on top, even if they were edible. And the sides looked like a puffy quilt with little polka dots where the lines crossed. The baker assured him Bree would love it and damn if it didn't look like she was right.

"Where did you get this?"

"Like I said, there's a bakery next to the Chinese place. I told them my wife and I eloped today and I wanted a nice cake that would go with dinner. They gave me that."

"It looks like a real wedding cake," she whispered.

"I think it is. Or the top of one, at least. There were several women working on these big cakes in the back and when I told this little white-haired woman working the counter what I was looking for, she disappeared into the back room and brought this out. She patted me on the cheek and told me to take it home to my bride."

She smiled at that. "The good ol' Danny MacGregor charm. Still have women young and old eating out of the palm of your hand, huh?"

All of them but one.

He sliced them each a piece and Bree squealed when she realized it was Italian Crème cake. Her favorite. Which was purely by accident, but damn if he didn't need to go back and give that baker a huge tip.

After they were done eating, Bree stifled a yawn. "I'm sorry. It's not the company, I swear."

"It's been a long day. Why don't you head off to bed?" As soon as the words escaped his mouth, he worried she'd consider that hovering. "That's if you want to," he quickly added.

"I want." Bree rose from the table and pushed in her chair. "Are you sure you're okay to sleep on the loveseat?"

"Positive."

"Okay then." Bree nodded. "Good night."

He boxed the cake and returned it to the refrigerator. Then cleared the empty Chinese containers and trash from the table. Under the edge of his plate was the fortune she'd wadded up and thrown at him. Danny unwrinkled the piece of paper and turned it over.

It's easier to resist at the beginning than at the end.

Wouldn't he love to know what ran through her mind after reading that? And why would she make up something completely different? Likely a smart move on her part since it would have been difficult to resist teasing her about it. Watching that rosy-pink blush rise from her chest and up to her cheeks used to be a favorite pastime of his.

He intended to drop it into the trash can but stopped himself. Unable to let that be the end of such a great fortune, he tucked it into a junk drawer for safekeeping.

After hauling the trash out to the dumpster, Danny returned to find the hallway now dark, a pillow and blanket left neatly stacked upon the couch. He bolted the door, turned out the lights, and powered on the TV, quickly muting it. He stared blindly at the sports ticker on the bottom of the screen, rolling score after score. But nothing registered in his brain. Instead, his thoughts were focused on the woman down the hall. A woman, who until a few days ago, he hadn't seen in forever. A woman who was now his wife and sleeping in his bed. While he slept on the couch.

The irony was not lost on him. How they spent so much of their high school years stealing moments here and there. Always worried that someone would return home and catch them in a compromising position. And now they were married, living under the same roof but sleeping in separate rooms.

By the end of their sophomore year in high school, they'd been "together" for well over two years. And while many of their classmates had already lost their virginity and assumed the same of them, they'd both been too nervous to do the deed. Until one day, just weeks after her sixteenth birthday, they were caught in a summer rainstorm as they walked home from the beach. Not that the rain was a problem, but everything they wore was soaked through. And somewhere along the way, Bree lost the key to her house. With her locked out and her parents at work, she had no choice but to come inside with him. Although they kept a spare to the Dunbars' front door in a kitchen drawer, Danny pretended to not know where it was kept.

It was the first time he ever outright lied to her. And she knew it. Her smile told him so.

Her Myrtle Beach High T-shirt clung to her skin. The bright pink triangles of her bikini shone through the white cotton fabric. Bree grasped the hem and pulled it over her head, letting it fall with a wet slap to the floor. Her short denim cutoffs soon joined her bag and flip-flops in a pile.

He remembered his body drawing tight, his mouth going dry at the sight of her. Which was odd because he'd seen her wear that same bikini a million times before. But this time was so very different. They were all alone. No friends around. No fear of interruption. No chance of being caught. Just four little tugs and all that pink would join all of that already on the floor, and everything would change between them.

She smiled then shivered as the air-conditioning kicked on, her flesh erupting into a sea of little bumps.

He stepped closer, using his palms to stroke her arms and warm her chilled skin.

"How is it your hands are so hot?" she whispered.

What he said in response, he couldn't recall, only that it made her smile. And he knew in that moment, with her staring up at him with big brown eyes and heart-stopping smile just for him, Bree Dunbar was without a doubt the most beautiful girl in the entire world. Brave, too. Far braver than him. Of course she always had been. After all, she was the first to ride a bicycle without training wheels. The first to jump off the end of the Second Avenue Pier into the deep and murky waters below.

The first to slowly pull one skinny pink string securing her bikini top.

With that little bit of encouragement, he pulled the remaining strings while guiding her down the hall and into his bedroom. The pink fabric fell away, revealing all of her beauty. Until this moment, everything between them had remained so very innocent. Stolen kisses. Soft caresses. Brief touches of skin still hidden from view beneath clothing. But this time she bared herself completely to him, and breathing became impossible. He tumbled her onto the bed, his hands touching, his mouth tasting every inch of skin within reach. Her fingertips threaded through his hair, her blunt nails scored his back. Her long, willowy legs first twined with his then wrapped around his body. She encouraged every motion with a soft sigh or whisper of his name.

Silently he prayed to God that the condom wouldn't break as he rolled it on and asked her one last time if she was certain. Bree answered by pulling him closer, kissing him deeply, encouraging him to rest his weight upon her waif-like body. He remembered the hint of uncertainty in her eyes in contrast to the smile on her face since they both knew there likely would be pain on her part.

They fumbled their way through that first time, as short-lived as it was. When all was said and done, what amazed him most, she invited him to return to her body again and again and again.

Chapter Eight

THE LOVESEAT WAS too short, too narrow, and lumpy as all get-out. To say he'd slept like shit would be an understatement. Of course the late-night stroll down memory lane hadn't helped things, giving him the mother of all hard-ons. Then, as he slipped his boxer briefs from his hips, preparing to take matters into his own hand, one hell of a fucked-up thought popped into his head. Which segued into the next sleepless hour as he debated whether or not he was some kind of sick perverted freak for getting hard at the memory of a sixteen-year-old girl.

So he spent most of the night moving from the loveseat to the recliner and back again, never getting comfortable. Around 0300 he seriously considered reneging on his agreement with Bree and relocating to his bed. Lord knew she didn't need all that space. Danny made it as far as the bedroom door, took one look at the situation, and stormed back to his recliner in disgust.

The damn woman didn't even know how to make the most of a bed like that. His big, comfy bed was going completely to waste. Bree was curled up on her side, sleeping on the far edge of the bed with the covers still neatly tucked in place. At the very least he wanted to drag her to the center of it, spread her arms and legs out like a starfish, and draw all the blankets into the middle and twist them around her body.

When did she become such a polite sleeper? Did she no longer know how to hog blankets?

At 0530, Danny rolled off the couch and tried to straighten the kink in his spine. After quietly changing clothes and lacing up his running shoes, he scribbled a note for Bree then headed out the door and into the darkness.

Still fuming about Bree's poor sleeping habits, his irritation powered him through the first five miles. Then as the sky began to lighten and the world began to wake, his thoughts transitioned to work. All the paperwork he'd have to file, the changes in benefits and such.

While Mike couldn't wait to see how things went down with his Ranger buddies, Danny was more concerned about how the hell he was going to explain his sudden marriage to his superiors. One thing was certain—there would be questions. Lots of questions.

They all knew him well enough to know he'd never planned to marry. Especially since he was *that guy* in his company. The one with the reputation. The one they'd all tell stories about for years to come. The one who rarely spent more than one night with the same woman, let alone a full week. He was that guy mothers warned their daughters about. That same guy commanding officers threatened with finishing out his military career in the fucking Antarctic if he so much as looked in the direction of their virginal daughters.

And if by some miracle his superiors had been zapped by that memory-erasing light Tommy Lee Jones used in *Men in Black* and had forgotten all about his reputation, his asshole friends would be oh so happy to remind them.

Then there was the fact he actually married a woman whom he didn't intend to have sex with and, in an attempt to be a better man, his dumb ass agreed to not have sex with anyone. Fucking brilliant on his part. If the guys ever learned the whole story of their arrangement, he'd be better off cutting his own parachute cord during the next practice jump.

Either way, it was time to pay the piper.

Not that he regretted marrying Bree one bit. If given the option to do it all again, he still would. No way did she deserve the hand life had dealt her. Not to mention he felt like he put all that bad mojo into motion by his leaving her, even though it had been the right decision for his life.

As the sun rose and the temperature warmed, his newest accessory made its presence known as he continued to run. The metal band constricted the blood flow, making his finger pulse. Danny turned the ring with his thumb on the same hand, unable to stop himself from smiling at the memory of their courthouse wedding.

Danny slid his mother's ring onto Bree's finger then

pulled from his pocket the ring she bought for him on their way to the courthouse and handed it to her. At first she stood there frozen, staring at the plain gold band she held with both hands. He held his breath, fully expecting her to turn tail and run. Only when the judge prompted her a second time did she look up at Danny. Her hands shook with nervousness and she dropped the ring, the two of them watching it fall in slow motion to the floor only to see it bounce once, then twice, and roll across the hard marble floor, coming to rest under a large wooden desk on the far side of the room. Dutifully, he went after it, ending up on hands and knees to fish it out from where it rested against the baseboard. As he rose to his feet and dusted off the knees of his pants, Bree covered her mouth. While she stifled the giggle, the smile showed in her eyes. The spark of it. And he knew from that moment on, life for Bree would only get better.

THOSE FIRST FEW moments after she woke, Bree was confused by her surroundings. Then it all came back to her. The exchange of rings. The vows. The apartment in Savannah. Although she was now a married woman, she'd spent her wedding night sleeping all alone in a king-size bed.

Still in her pajamas and stocking feet, Bree pulled on her wig and padded out to the kitchen. On the counter she found a note scribbled on a restaurant napkin. *Out for a run.*

Most mornings she arrived downstairs to find her

mother had made a huge breakfast. And more often than not, if she wasn't feeling nauseated from the chemo, ate whatever was made so as not to offend her mother. But there were plenty of mornings when she looked at the fresh-baked muffins and eggs and bacon and thought she'd love nothing more than a slice of cold pizza. It was the little freedoms like that she missed. Not that her mother would have stopped her from eating what she wanted, but in the end the guilt she would've endured wasn't worth the price of admission.

Bree shuffled across the cold ceramic tile floor to the refrigerator only to learn Danny wasn't kidding when he said there wasn't anything in the place to eat. She would've sworn there was some Kung Pao left over, but no containers were to be found now. That left her with Red Bull, Tabasco, a bottle of yellow mustard, and jar of bread-and-butter pickles. Sliced.

Her gaze drifted to the pink pastry box.

There's always cake.

Bree closed the refrigerator door and opened the freezer. Even less in there. In the cabinets she found coffee, boxes of protein bars, steel-cut oats, and an open bag of sunflower seeds. Um, no.

Her stomach grumbled. It knew there was cake in the immediate vicinity and would not be denied.

Bree took the pink box from the refrigerator and a plastic fork from the drawer. The first bite was heaven, just as she remembered. The second, even better. The third bite to reaffirm her earlier evaluation was correct. The fourth because, "Damn, that's good." And the pink fondant rose met its fate for simply being in the way of bite five.

Oh, hell.

She'd made a mess of the pretty cake. If Danny got a look at it he'd know in an instant she'd been in it. Time for a new strategy. Just a few more bites to even it out.

Without warning the front door opened wide and in walked Danny, hot and sweaty and absolutely breathtaking. The gray T-shirt he wore stretched tautly across his shoulders and chest, the fabric darkened with sweat and clinging to his form like a second skin.

He sure didn't look like this ten years ago.

She shoved the largest chunk of Italian Créme yet past her lips, if only to keep herself from drooling.

"Good morning," he said with a smile, wide and bright. "And here I was worried about there not being anything to eat and hurried back to take you out for breakfast. We can do that if you're still hungry."

She narrowed her eyes at him, carefully licking the crumbs from her lips after she finished off her mouthful of cake. "That was just a snack," she muttered, closing the pastry box.

"Okay, then." Danny chuckled. "Just give me a few minutes to hop in the shower and we'll go."

AFTER A LEISURELY breakfast, Danny gave Bree the nickel tour of Savannah, beginning with Hunter Army Airfield where he and Michael were stationed. From there they headed downtown, past the historic squares and brick-paved streets until they reached the river. As the tourists began to emerge from their hotels and the traffic picked up, he changed gears and headed for the shopping center near home.

They weren't in any rush and the store was empty for the most part, so he and Bree took their time shopping, going up and down each aisle. Until they turned into one aisle where it appeared two rowdy boys were arguing over boxes of cereal.

Oh, shit. He recognized those two kids.

"Anything you want down this aisle?" he asked.

Bree wrinkled up her nose. "Not a big fan of cereal."

Worked for him. He made a U-turn with the cart to go back the way they came when suddenly another cart was blocking their exit. And his best friend was pushing it.

Fuck.

So much for telling people in his own time.

"And here I was wondering if you were back from your dad's yet." The smug look on Ben's face was as if he'd just caught Danny with his hand in the cookie jar.

"Got back just last night."

"Have a good trip?"

Asshole. He was looking at Bree like she was a late-night hookup that ran over until morning. No point in beating around the bush; he only hoped Bree was ready for this. Feeling more than a little protective, he took a step closer toward her, taking her left hand in his. Ben noticed and raised a brow in interest.

"Bree, this ugly guy here," punctuating it with a slap

to Ben's chest, "is Ben Wojciechowski. Everyone calls him Soup. He and I've been in regiment together from the get-go. Ben, this is Bree Dunbar. MacGregor. My wife."

The smirk disappeared as Ben's face turned serious. "I'm sorry. Did I hear that right? Did you say *wife*?"

"I did. We got married yesterday morning."

"Wow." Ben took a moment to compose himself then extended a hand to Bree. "It's very nice to meet you," he said with complete sincerity. Then quickly added, "And only the a-holes in regiment call me Soup. Please, call me Ben." Then he turned to face Danny, clapping his shoulder. "Congratulations, man! Clearly, your vacation was far more interesting than mine. All I've been doing for the past two weeks is peeling off a hundred years' worth of wallpaper and working on the boys' jump shots."

"Basketball?" Danny asked. "I thought they were doing wrestling."

"Ah, yes. The nice thing about basketball is it requires a ball and a hoop. Which makes that an outside sport in our house. Unlike wrestling, which can be done anywhere. Speaking of which—" Ben's attention shifted to behind them. Danny and Bree turned to see those two little hell-raisers scrabbling on the ground, a twist of skinny arms and legs as boxes of cereal lay in carnage on the floor surrounding them.

"Jesus Christ, guys! Come on! Just pick one so we can get the hell out of here."

Bree stifled a giggle. "They're yours?" she asked.

"Afraid so," Ben said with a laugh. "Which reminds me, I'm supposed to buy a bottle of wine for the wife."

"Better make it two," Danny added.

"It was nice meeting you," Ben said, pushing his shopping cart past them. "Hope to see you again soon."

Bree smiled. "Same here."

Ben gathered the boys, threw two kinds of cereal in the cart then gave a quick wave before disappearing around the corner at the opposite end.

Her eyes met Danny's and she shook her head in amazement. "Wow. I'm worn out from just watching them."

"I know, right?" He chuckled. "And that was good behavior for them. You should see those little terrors when they're really going at it."

"No, thanks."

They headed back the way they came, Danny pushing the cart past refrigerated cases as Bree walked alongside him.

"Why do they call him Soup?"

He stopped and looked at her, a bit taken by surprise. Calling Ben by his nickname had become such a habit he'd never thought it might be considered odd by others. "When we were in RIP together . . ." Bree crinkled her brow in confusion and he suddenly remembered she didn't know army lingo. "The Ranger Indoctrination Program," he explained. "Basically, it was a month of hell to get into regiment. Anyhow, one of the instructors looked at his name and said 'Your name has more fucking letters than my bowl of alphabet soup.' " Danny shrugged. "It stuck."

Instead of a slight chuckle or polite giggle, she laughed right out loud, the sound music to his ears.

"You guys are weird."

He smiled back at her, unable to argue the point. Truth be told, she didn't know the half of it. And if the day did come she found out about all the crazy shit they'd done over the past decade, she might very well want that divorce sooner rather than later.

WHILE DANNY RETRIEVED the last few grocery bags from the car, Bree began putting things away. When his phone chimed the first time, she realized he'd left it sitting on the breakfast bar. Before she turned back around to finish what she was doing, it chimed a second time. Then a third. Clearly, someone was trying to get his attention. For the briefest of moments she considered taking a peek at his screen, but quickly reminded herself that would be an invasion of his privacy.

"Your phone is going crazy," she blurted out the moment he walked in the door.

Danny placed the last few bags on the kitchen counter. "Who is it?"

Was that a test? To see how jealous a wife she'd be? "I don't know. I didn't look." Although she was telling the truth, she couldn't help but sound guilty to her own ears.

"I've got nothing to hide, Bree. Mi casa es tu casa." He grabbed the phone and smiled to himself as he scrolled through the messages on his phone. "Well, that didn't take long. Looks like Marie knows."

"Marie?" Just as she'd feared. Her stomach twisted at the thought of an ex-girlfriend, ex-lover, whatever she might be, text messaging him the moment she found out he married.

"Ben's wife," he answered and the knot in her stomach loosened a bit. "And it would seem she's angry she found out about our marriage after the fact." He looked up from the small screen to meet her eyes. "Which is really just code for 'she's pissed Ben found out before her.' " He typed a quick reply. "I wonder how long it will take for everyone else to find out."

"Really?"

"News, good or bad, travels like wildfire on a military post. Sadly, sometimes the guy it directly involves is the last one to find out."

"That's terrible."

"Tell me about it. I probably should have forewarned you that people will be all up in your business if you let them. Just be sure to establish clear boundaries right from the start. If you share too much too soon, they'll come to expect it." His phone chimed once again. "She wants us to come over for dinner tonight."

To be honest, she hadn't considered this aspect of their marriage. That Danny would have longtime friends here who cared for him. Which meant this dinner would be an interrogation of sorts. To see if she was worthy of him.

"You've got that look on your face."

"What look? I don't have a look."

"The hell you do. You look like a deer in headlights. There's nothing to worry about. And to be completely honest, I'd feel a lot better if there was someone else in town you could call if I'm away for training or you can't get ahold of me."

"Then I'll just call Michael."

"For the most part, when we're not in rotation, we stay close by. But there are times even when we aren't in Afghanistan that we're off training somewhere far away for a couple of weeks. Like when we go to Thailand next fall. And Michael will be there, too, so you won't be able to call him. That's just how things work."

His argument made complete sense and it's not as if he was being unreasonable. She couldn't avoid them forever. Add the fact this was what she wanted. A fresh start. New beginning. New people.

"So, are you up for it?"

Bree put on her best brave face. "No time like the present."

Chapter Nine

"ARE YOU SURE we shouldn't stop to get something else? A dessert or something?"

"Trust me," Danny said, glancing at her briefly before looking back at the road. "We'll be read the riot act for bringing wine."

Bree clutched the bottle of Merlot in her hands a little tighter. How could he be so calm at a time like this? Here her insides felt like one massive knot and he was the epitome of cool. As if introducing his new from-out-of-the-blue wife to longtime friends was an everyday occurrence. No big deal. At least no bigger deal than strolling into the Horry County courthouse and marrying a woman he hadn't seen in almost ten years.

"Do they live on base?" she asked, not really wanting to be left alone in her thoughts.

"On post." With traffic stopped at a red light, he turned to face her, although his eyes were hidden behind the dark lenses of his sunglasses. "Army is a military post. Marines and Air Force are a military base. Some of the lingo is different between the branches. Not a big deal, but every once in a while you'll come across someone who gets their panties in a twist if you use the wrong terminology." He returned his attention to the light, lowering the visor to block the sun glaring through the window. "Anyhow, Ben and Marie don't live in military housing. There's a pretty long waiting list here so they got used to living off post. Then, several years ago, she inherited some money and talked him into a fixer-upper in Ardsley Park."

The red light went on forever. Danny tapped his index finger impatiently atop the steering wheel. That tapping was a tic of his. A tell when he was nervous. He wasn't as calm as he'd like her to believe.

"Finally," he mumbled as the light changed from red to green. Within minutes they turned down a tree-lined street with historic homes as far as the eye could see. At a white picket fence, he turned into the driveway of a large, two-story home with glossy black shutters and a bright red door. An American flag proudly waved from the small front porch. Just like an image from a magazine.

"Their house is beautiful."

"Definitely not military issue." Danny waited as she walked around the front of his truck then placed his hand at the small of her back. "Marie's an interior designer and works out of the house so their place is kind of a portfolio for her. But believe me when I say it used to be a real dump."

They made their way past bicycles and scooters abandoned along the front walk. After Danny rang the bell, almost immediately several dogs went on high alert, their collective barks nearing the front door as they made their way through the house. As loud as they were, a woman's voice could be heard over the top of their commotion, yelling for someone to answer the door.

"That would be Marie," he said with a chuckle. "She runs the place."

Bree smiled, although the twist in her stomach tightened a bit more. Thankfully, they appeared to be as informal as Danny said they were, but the nervousness remained. Her heart pounded in her chest and out of nervous habit, she smoothed the strands of her wig. But before she finished, her fingers were captured in his, pulling her hand from her hair.

"There's absolutely nothing to worry about," he whispered. "I promise."

She focused on their hands, his grasp strong, confident. He gave a reassuring squeeze.

Footsteps echoed from the opposite side of the door just before it flung open to reveal Ben with a baby girl in his arms. Just as he opened his mouth to speak, two dogs of considerable size but unidentifiable breeding rushed out the front door. Squeezing between him and the door frame, they rushed past Bree, nearly knocking her over as they made their great escape. Danny's hands came to her waist, steadying her.

"Sorry about Cosmo and Wanda. Are you okay?"

"I'm fine," she answered. "But will they come back on their own?"

Ben shook his head in disgust. "Probably not. They're stupid, *stupid* dogs. Both failed remedial obedience school. I don't think the dog whisperer himself could fix those two yahoos." He then turned his attention to the baby he held in one arm. "Look who's here, baby girl. It's your Uncle Danny," he said, handing her off to the man in front of him.

With large, dark eyes and dark, glossy pigtails tied with bright red ribbons, she resembled a doll off the shelf. She smiled brightly at Danny, revealing three little teeth across her lower gums. With one slobbery hand, she reached for him.

Danny obliged, taking hold of her, but keeping her at arm's length from his body. "Her diaper better not be full of—"

"Uh, uh, uh," Ben said, waving a finger at him. "You know the rules, MacGregor. Besides, I just changed her. You're good to go."

"I've heard that before."

Ben laughed then slapped Danny's shoulder as he jogged down the steps. "You guys head inside. I have some dogs to chase down."

After a hesitant sniff, Danny finally caved and pulled her to his chest. A buzz to her cheek, a little kiss to her ear and she squirmed and squealed in delight. Just another female to have fallen for the irresistible charms of Daniel MacGregor.

"This is Hannah Banana," he said, manipulating one of her chubby little arms like a puppeteer.

Bree grasped the waving, albeit very wet little hand. Dark eyes studied her for a moment, then Hannah abruptly pulled her fingers free. She turned her attention back to her admirer, slapping both hands on his face and babbling undoubtedly words of adoration.

"In the kitchen, Danny!" yelled the same voice from before. Only now her accent was more prominent and Bree couldn't help but be reminded of the *Real Housewives of New Jersey*. She expected big hair, big boobs, big everything, to go along with the booming voice. Instead, the woman they found in the kitchen was tiny, with shiny black curls and dark eyes. A grown-up version of the little girl Danny held in his arms. Minus the ribbons.

After closing the oven door, she turned to them. "Danny," she cried, arms outstretched until she grabbed hold of his face, pulling his down to hers so she could place a kiss upon both cheeks. Cheeks now pink from embarrassment.

"So you went and got married. I can hardly believe it."

"Couldn't wait around for you anymore," he said, punctuating his words with a wink.

Bree watched as the smile on his face reached his eyes, his affection for this woman obvious.

"Always the charmer." She took the baby from his arms and settled her on one hip. "You know, if you'd been an officer or a doctor, things might have been different between us."

"Never worked for Mikey."

She waved off the idea. "Michael is Michael. Besides, you've always been my favorite MacGregor brother."

Danny laughed. "I'll be sure to tell him."

"Oh, he already knows," she said with a laugh of her own as she buckled the little girl into her high chair. "I told him myself after you spent two weeks' leave helping Ben renovate the upstairs bathroom and he was off golfing somewhere. But enough of that," Marie said, now turning her attention to Bree.

Almost immediately, her palms went damp to the point the wine bottle she held nearly slipped from her grasp. Thankfully, Danny saved her, taking the bottle from her hands.

Refocusing his attention, Ben's wife smacked him across the arm with the back of her hand. "Are you going to just stand there looking pretty, Daniel? Or are you going to introduce us?"

Bree bit her lip to keep from laughing out loud. This woman was petite and Italian and bossy as hell. Despite her nerves and sweaty palms, she liked her already.

For the next half hour, Bree sat at the kitchen island, letting the conversation between old friends swirl around her as she enjoyed a glass of wine for the first time in years. With each sip, her muscles relaxed and her earlier anxiety gave way to warm fuzzies. Her fingers tingled. Her toes tingled. Even the tip of her nose felt a little ticklish.

And if the wine wasn't enough, there was Danny. Who

smelled so good and felt so warm, standing right beside her, lulling her into an extreme state of relaxation. His hand skimmed up her spine, across her shoulder, down her arm only to retrace its path and do it all over again. Always moving, never stopping. Spreading his warmth all across her body.

With her anxiety levels no longer at DEFCON 4 status, Bree felt good about how things were going. All that worry for nothing. At least until that bossy little woman handed her saint of a husband a platter of steaks and forced both men outside to the grill.

Her fight or flight instincts kicked in and Bree turned to escape. Within inches of the back door, Marie called her back to the kitchen under the guise of wanting to "get to know her better."

"Have a seat," Marie said, gesturing with the tip of her knife to the seat she vacated only moments before. A seat positioned directly beneath the white-hot bulbs of low-hanging pendant lights.

How convenient. Obviously, the time had come for the interrogation portion of the evening.

"So . . ." Marie began. The blade of her Santoku knife pounded into the butcher block as she julienned a carrot with the skill and speed of a professional chef. "How did you and Danny meet?"

Bree kept her eyes on the knife, the bright light glinting off the blade with each rhythmic chop. "I don't remember how we met, really."

"Could it have been in a bar, by chance?"

She detected a hint of a snort at the end of Marie's

question as she dropped the knife and cutting board in the sink and went about warming a bottle.

"We've known each other for as long as I can remember. He and Michael grew up across the street from my family. His father still lives there, as a matter of fact."

Marie's expression softened immediately, surprised. "Really?"

"Mmm-hmm," Bree answered as she took a fortifying sip. "Our mothers were best friends. And everywhere they went, we went. Together."

Bored with Cheerios, Hannah began to fuss in her high chair. Armed with dinner for one, Marie sat down for the first time since she and Danny arrived. As Marie fed the baby, the conversation naturally shifted to the topic of children, and Bree learned they not only had two boys, but two girls, as well. The oldest, Leah, whom her mother described as eleven going on twenty-five, was currently at a friend's house. Their identical twin boys were eight, while the baby was ten months. At one point, Ben returned to grab two longnecks from the refrigerator, pausing on his way out to kiss his wife and ruffle his daughter's hair while she chewed and sucked on her bottle.

Bree took a long drink from her glass, wanting to drown the burn of jealousy in her gut. There once was a time she'd thought her and Danny's future would be just like this. With a family that was loving and happy and loud. Instead, they were glorified roommates, counting down the days until their divorce.

She wanted to cry. She could actually feel the burn

behind her eyes. It would be so easy to go there, but Bree refused to let it happen. She reminded herself to be thankful for what she had. She was alive, for one. She wasn't alone in this world and knew the love of family and friends. Even had one friend who cared enough to give her that new beginning she'd long believed to be only a pipe dream. No, she was far better off than so many others. It would be best to never forget that.

Proud of saving herself from drowning in a sea of self-pity, Bree rose from her seat, needing to be productive. Bree asked Marie to direct her to where the tableware and things were kept. Armed with a stack of dishes and silverware, she went about setting the table. But even as she moved from place to place, she felt Marie watching her.

Bree carefully smoothed the long brown strands and turned to face her hostess. "It's a wig."

Marie's eyes widened in surprise. "Excuse me?"

"My hair, it's a wig. Just in case you're wondering." She smiled, hoping to put her at ease. "I finished chemo a while ago but my hair hasn't grown back yet."

"Oh," Marie whispered as she patted Hannah's back, now drowsy and draped over her shoulder. "I'm sorry if I appeared to be staring. I mean, I was staring, but not for the reason you were thinking. I promise I hadn't even noticed your hair." She then politely excused herself to take the baby upstairs.

Shit.

She let her own insecurities get the best of her and ended up making Marie uncomfortable. What a way to make friends. Clearly, years of self-imposed confinement had damaged her social skills.

Marie returned several minutes later with a baby monitor in hand. She turned it on, the soft static filling the room.

"I'm really sorry—"

Marie cut her off with the wave of a hand. "If anyone should apologize, it should be me. After all, I was staring. But I'm still just trying to figure this whole situation out." She gathered the tiny bowls and spoons, along with the high chair tray and tossed them all into the sink. "I've known Danny a very long time. Love him like a brother. My kids think of him as an uncle. And not once in all these years has he ever been serious enough about a single woman to bring her to a company function let alone around here."

"Really?"

"Can I tell you something?" she said, shutting off the faucet and lowering her voice to a conspiratorial whisper. "For the longest time I thought he was gay." Bree laughed out loud in response and Marie joined in. "I mean, sure there were stories of him with a flavor of the week, but I thought maybe it was all just an act."

"No," Bree giggled. "Definitely not gay."

Marie raised an eyebrow. "Oh, really now?" Instantly, Bree felt her entire body heat, especially from the hollow of her throat to her blazing cheeks. Damn him. "You can try to blame that blush on the wine, but I know better."

"Is there a statute of limitations on firsthand knowledge? Because up until last week, we hadn't seen or spoken to each other since before he enlisted. I'd be willing to bet my knowledge is out-of-date."

Their laughter was interrupted by the ringing telephone. "Sorry. I need to get this. It's likely my eldest."

Within seconds it was clear her daughter didn't want to come home yet, and Marie entered into negotiations with her child. Bree turned her attention to outside only to find Danny watching her from where he stood on the back porch. Unsure what to do, she gave a simple wave. He smiled and gave a little salute back. Even though he was no longer standing right beside her, that earlier warmth returned, knowing he was still looking out for her.

And having ended her phone call, Marie appeared to have caught the entire exchange.

"So he sees you for the first time in almost ten years and proposes? That's very romantic."

"More practical than romantic. He married me so I wouldn't have to pay for my own health insurance."

"So you're not—"

"Having sex?" Bree shook her head then took another drink of wine.

"Interesting." Marie settled onto a bar stool next to her. "This has the makings of a Lifetime movie of the week."

"He married me out of pity. Because I lost my job. Because of the cancer."

"I take that back," she said, her glossy curls bouncing as she shook her head. "This sounds more Nicholas Sparks than Lifetime. Of course, that would mean one of you would die at the end and we don't want that. So on second thought, scratch Nicholas Sparks. Stick with Lifetime. I wonder who they would get to play me."

"Wait. What?" The woman talked a mile a minute and Bree's wine-soaked brain was slow to catch up. "You're making too much of it. This is his way of helping me out."

"For how long, then? A month? A year?"

"I don't know. The goal is for me to find a job, save some money so I can stand on my own two feet, and then we'll get divorced."

"Or maybe not," she said with a wink.

"No, really. That's the plan."

"Oh, honey." This time Marie placed her hand on Bree's forearm. "I don't doubt that's the plan. But if there's one thing I learned years ago, not all things in life go according to plan."

Chapter Ten

DANNY TOOK ANOTHER long pull from his beer and tried not to worry about leaving Bree alone with Marie. Not that Bree couldn't handle herself. But Marie could be a real pit bull if and when the mood struck. In his mind, this evening could only end one of two ways: either they'd be at each other's throats or they'd become thick as thieves. Both of which were equally frightening prospects.

Ben manned the grill, taking account of hot spots and rearranging his steaks accordingly. His perfectionist side showed when he placed them at a forty-five degree angle to get that crosshatch pattern. If it wasn't for the fact the man knew his steak, Danny would give him hell for watching too much Food Network.

"Pretty quiet over there." Ben lowered the lid and dropped into a nearby deck chair.

"Just wondering if those steaks are kosher."

"Highly doubtful. It's not as if all those MREs I've eaten over the years were kosher, either."

"Isn't that against your religion, being Jewish and all?"

"Emphasis on the *ish* part." Ben chuckled and took another drink from his beer. "Isn't it Lent? You Catholics aren't supposed to be eating meat, either."

"Fridays, man. We don't eat meat on Fridays."

"Right. Next time I'll be sure to invite you for dinner on a Friday. Spaghetti is easier on my wallet."

Danny couldn't help himself from checking to see how things were going inside. So far, so good, it would seem. He returned his attention to his beer, picking at the label until the entire thing pulled free.

"So." After a prolonged silence, Danny looked up and realized that was exactly what Ben had been waiting for. "Are we going to talk about the elephant in the room?"

Danny shook his head. "Bree's hardly an elephant."

"That's true."

And then Ben went silent like a goddamn therapist. Just sat there, patiently waiting for him to start talking. He never did this shit in their early years, but as he and Marie had more kids and those kids grew older, it became his go-to tactic. One he'd perfected. Now he liked to sit in front of them, arms crossed, not saying a word. Just making those kids squirm until the guilt got to them and they spilled their guts.

"I know what you're doing. You can knock it off with the PSYOP mindfuck bullshit any day now." Ben smiled in response, but still said nothing. Asshole. So Danny caved. "Go ahead. Let's hear it. I'm sure you have a million questions."

Ben laughed at that. "Marie is the one with a million questions. I, on the other hand, only have one."

"And that would be?"

Without any hint of sarcasm he asked, "Do you love her?"

A nervous laugh escaped him. "That certainly isn't the question I expected you to ask."

"You thought I was going to ask if she's pregnant."

"Pretty much, yeah."

"You know how I feel about that." Ben shifted forward in his chair, his elbows resting on his knees. "That's a terrible reason to get married. And just because Marie was pregnant when we married, doesn't mean that's why I proposed. We might have married sooner than we planned, but from the day I met her I knew she was the one I wanted to spend the rest of my life with."

Danny had heard him say the same thing before. A story he shared through the years with plenty of guys who knocked up gate bunnies. Never once in all those times had Ben's advice been directed at him.

Although he and Michael were close, the bond Danny had with Ben was far different. They suffered through RIP then Ranger school together. Had been deployed three times to Iraq and another six to Afghanistan together. They'd mourned friends killed in war and celebrated life together. But never once, in all the years they'd been friends, closer than brothers, really, had they ever spoken of love.

"It's pretty simple, Danny. Either you love her or you don't."

"It's not as simple as you're making it out to be. She was in a bit of a jam. I'm helping her out."

"So you don't love her?"

There wasn't an easy answer to that. Of course he loved her. He'd always loved her. Probably would always love her. But the woman he was married to? He didn't know her. And she didn't know him. Neither of them was remotely close to being the same person they once were.

"Just because I care about her and want to help her—"

"And marry her," Ben added.

"And marry her, doesn't mean I'm *in* love with her now."

From where he stood on the back porch, he could see Bree and Marie just as he'd left them. Then Marie huddled close and a roar of laughter came from the two of them so loud it startled both him and Ben. Bree turned to look outside, her eyes meeting his. She lifted a hand in a slight wave and smiled. He felt himself smiling back at her, saluting her with the beer in his hand.

And of course when he looked back at Ben he had that same know-it-all smirk on his face as before.

Danny gestured toward the house. "Sounds like the two of them are hitting it off."

"Yep." Ben nodded. "You do realize absolutely nothing good can come from that?"

Danny laughed. "Tell me something I don't already know."

THE FOUR OF them talked well into the evening, long after the kids had been tucked into their beds. All the times before when he'd been invited over as a single guy, prolonged exposure to such domestic bliss would have made him itch. Would have chased him out the door not long after dinner was over so he could meet up with some of the guys or rendezvous with the flavor of the week. Not this time.

The stories Ben and Marie told Bree were ones he knew by heart, but he didn't mind hearing them all again. Instead, he liked watching Bree, how she reacted to their stories, the punchlines. He liked seeing her in their home, smiling and laughing, a world away from what her life was only a few days ago. He stretched his arm across the back of the couch, his palm resting on her shoulder. He expected her to knock his hand away when she turned to face him. Instead, she smiled and shifted a little closer before returning her attention to the conversation.

Sitting this close he caught the scent of her perfume or bodywash or whatever it was she used. He'd never smelled anything like it. Only two days they'd been married and already his brain associated the scent with her. He liked how it greeted him whenever he walked in the front door of his apartment, a pleasant reminder he no longer lived alone.

After checking on the baby for a second time, Marie

returned downstairs, this time dropping into Ben's lap, her legs casually draped over the arm of his leather chair as she reclined against her husband's chest.

"So give me an idea of when we can expect news of another kid on the way? I want to get in on the early betting." Danny leaned closer to loudly whisper in Bree's ear. "Hannah is a welcome-home baby."

"That was all Marie's fault," Ben quickly added.

"My fault?" She shoved her husband's chest. "Oh, I think not. It's not as if you weren't there when it happened. But there's no point in betting since there most certainly won't be any more. What is it you guys always say, Danny? We got our stuff in order and locked it down tight." She patted Ben's crotch. "Isn't that right, honey?"

Ben winced in response.

"Locked down . . ." It took a second to catch her meaning. "Holy shit, man! Did you have a vasectomy?"

"Christ, Marie," Ben muttered. "That's private."

"Danny's practically family," she said, giggling. "To be honest, I'm surprised you didn't tell him."

"Tell him what? That I had my manhood snipped?"

But things didn't add up. Surely, he would have taken extra time off and Danny couldn't remember that happening. "When the hell did you have this done?"

"Right after she found out she was pregnant with Hannah."

Danny thought back to that summer and remembered him being out for a medical procedure. "You said you had your knee scoped. You limped around on crutches for a week and wore a knee brace for a month." Ben didn't deny his accusations at all, instead he just shrugged his shoulders. "How the hell did you keep that a secret?"

"Michael," Marie blurted out. "I made him a giant pan of tiramisu."

"Of course you did."

Damn his brother and his fucking secrets. Before this last week, never had he realized his brother's silence could be so easily bought with baked goods.

THE EVENING WENT far better than expected and Bree enjoyed being more of a quiet observer than active participant. Sitting there, watching the three of them talk over each other, all trying to be the one to get the last word or the biggest laugh. It was what she'd missed for so long, the elegant simplicity of a dinner out with friends. Back when she was forced to leave behind her life in Columbia and move back in with her parents, never could she have imagined how isolating her life would become.

Having readied herself for bed, Bree opened the bathroom door to find Danny standing in the bedroom doorway opposite her, leaning one shoulder into the doorjamb.

"How do you like Marie?"

"I like her." Bree lounged against her own door frame, mirroring his stance. "I like both of them, as a matter of fact."

"I'm glad. Marie can be an acquired taste. A lot of the wives don't care for her."

"She mentioned something about lots of drama."

"There's a ton of it. Which is why I'm glad you like

Marie. She's very loyal and will do just about anything to help someone else if she can. But she's also pretty no-nonsense. Doesn't take crap from anyone. For those who try to backstab or screw her over, there's hell to pay."

"I'm not going to lie, Marie was a little intimidating at first." Danny raised an eyebrow in disbelief. "Okay. *A lot* intimidating. But once I told her the real reason we got married, she eased off. It's nice to see you have friends that are so protective of you."

He pushed off the door frame and moved closer, cutting the distance between them by half. With that small movement, the atmosphere suddenly shifted and the air crackled and hummed between them. Not too long ago she snuggled up against him and everything felt very platonic, comfortable. But now? Now he was staring at her with such intensity she found it difficult to catch her breath.

"Do you think I'm in need of protection?"

The low, intimate rumble of his voice scraped across her skin, electrifying every nerve. Years had passed since the last time her body had reacted to any man this way and she'd be lying if she said it didn't scare her.

She cleared her throat and reached for a safer subject. "Their kids adore you. The boys especially."

Danny smiled. "You sound surprised."

"A little, maybe."

"That I like them or that they like me?" He raised a finger. "Don't answer that."

He stepped even closer now, effectively trapping her between his body and the door frame. Danny wound a lock of her brown hair around his fingers, the smooth strands sliding between his forefinger and thumb. He scowled slightly as he studied it, like he was trying to decide if it was human hair or synthetic.

"Do you sleep in this thing?"

She tilted her head to meet his eyes, the back of her head resting against the doorjamb. "No." Her answer barely more than a whisper.

"Then why are you still wearing it?"

"I didn't want you to feel awkward." She couldn't look at him any longer. Instead, she stared at his chest, watched it rise and fall with each breath.

"Is that why you wore it all day yesterday and again today? Did you think I'd be embarrassed by you?"

He stood too close, asking questions she didn't want to answer. "People stare, Danny. They see someone my age with little to no hair and they just can't help themselves. I'm used to it, but—" That was a lie. She wasn't used to people staring and she never would be. It's not something she would ever get used to.

"But that doesn't explain why you're wearing it now when it's just the two of us."

With the side of his index finger he raised her chin, those dark blue eyes boring into her soul, his gaze too knowing, as if he could read every thought that crossed her mind. She loved that about him once, but it scared her now that she had no armor with which to protect herself. And whether he'd mean to or not, he'd break her heart again if she let him.

"If I tell you something will you promise to not find a

way to be offended?" One side of his mouth rose in a half smile, crinkling the skin at the corners of his eyes. "I hate this wig. *Hate* it. Reminds me of *Pretty Woman*."

"Are you suggesting I look like a hooker?" She smiled to show she wasn't upset. Actually, she was grateful for his honesty, especially since it explained things. In particular, his reaction from the morning before when he saw her wearing it for the first time.

"When I saw you in the grocery store and you were just wearing that ugly hat—"

"Now you're criticizing my hat, too?"

"—that was so much better. Because it was the real you."

"I'm sure that was a sight to behold since I was mad as hell."

He laughed a little at that, nothing more than a low rumble in his chest.

"Tonight at dinner, I couldn't see your face unless you looked directly at me. So many times, you laughed at Ben or Marie's story or smiled as you spoke to them and I couldn't see you." With both hands he pushed the heavy strands back and away from her face, just as one might draw back the curtains to let the morning sun in after a long, dark night.

"If you couldn't see my face, how do you know I was smiling?"

"Because I can hear it. Your voice takes on this whole other quality, one you couldn't fake if you tried."

"You're crazy."

"No, it's true."

Bree closed her eyes and turned her head away from him. His one hand went with her, his palm cradling her cheek. Her wig shifted slightly before she realized he had it in his grasp and meant to remove it.

"Danny, no," she pleaded, grabbing hold of his wrist to stop him.

"Stop hiding," he whispered, more of a request than demand.

To fight would be pointless, but still she held his arm in weak protest as the hairpiece slid from her head only to be tossed on top of the bathroom countertop nearby. Using the flat of his palm, he smoothed his hand over her head, caressing the baby-fine strands just as she did every time she removed the godforsaken thing. But his touch was far softer and warmer than her own and far more intimate than anything she'd experienced for years. Tears pricked the backs of her eyes and she fought like hell to contain them. But the dam cracked then crumbled, spilling those long, pent-up tears down her cheeks.

For some reason she halfway expected him to walk away, to declare it all too much and abandon her there. Instead, Danny pressed a kiss to her forehead, caressed her face, brushed away her tears with his thumbs, all the while whispering nonsensical words of comfort.

Only when she opened her eyes did she realize she clutched the front of his T-shirt with both hands. He couldn't have escaped if he wanted to.

"No more wig." He tipped her face upward to look at him. "Unless you really like it?"

"God, no." She choked out the words as she half laughed, half cried. "I hate the damn thing."

He laughed at that then wrapped her up in his embrace. "Good. Now you're on your way to that fresh start."

She relaxed into him, buried her face into his chest and let his warmth seep deep into her body. "I like the sound of that."

He held her for what seemed liked hours, but really wasn't more than a few minutes. Giving her time to soak it all up, like he knew it had been a very long time since someone just held her close. Finally taking her hand in his, Danny escorted her the short distance across the hall to the bedroom. Just inside the doorway he pressed one last lingering kiss to her temple, whispered good-night then left her to sleep.

Alone.

Chapter Eleven

JUST BEFORE 0600, Danny and Ben reported to One-Charlie's office. Their platoon leaders, Capt. JT Anthony and Sergeant First Class Calder "Bull" Magnusson were already there for their leader huddle. A minute or so later a loud, booming voice followed by laughter echoing down the hall alerted them to the arrival of fellow squad leader and platoon loudmouth, Jeff Gibson. Behind him was Tomas Rodriguez, the quiet intimidator of the group.

Once they were all settled, the captain got down to business.

"Due to the significant number of casualties A-Co suffered during the last rotation, Ruiz and Kozak are being promoted to squad leaders," Anthony informed them.

Damn. Danny hated that he was losing Kozak. Not only because he was a great guy, but also because he was always cool, calm, and focused under pressure. "Ice Man" was what he called him since nothing ever rattled him.

Both he and Ruiz had definitely earned their promotions to squad leaders, but that also meant both his and Ben's squads were now a man short.

Danny looked to Ben, who shook his head in disappointment. They knew what came next.

"Your brand-new, shiny privates, fresh from RASP, have already arrived from Benning. Lucky for you guys, they're both single without kids, so it should be a fairly simply transition. Bull will introduce you to them when we're done here."

Ben leaned toward Danny, keeping his voice low. "You know what I'm thinking?"

"Epic smoke session?"

"Absolutely." They both laughed and bumped fists.

He and Ben had developed quite a reputation in C Company as squad leaders who loved the physical challenge of regiment. As far as they were concerned, what better way to welcome their teams from block leave than with a morning run at a faster than normal pace, followed up by a series of flutterkicks and push-ups and pull-ups before finishing it off with a little friendly competition on the obstacle course. All before lunch.

Oh, yeah. This was gonna be fun.

"And people think I'm an asshole." This from Gibson.

"It's good to torture them," replied Danny. "The pain lets them know they're alive."

The captain finished going over the schedule for the week, which included fast roping insertion, extraction training, and a parachute jump planned for Thursday night. The following week C Company would travel the hour to Stewart where they'd spend the entire week doing live fire exercises on the various ranges, not returning until Friday.

Things were just wrapping up when Gibson took hold of his hand and lifted it into the air. "What the hell is this, MacGregor? Is this a goddamn wedding ring on your finger?"

Shit. He'd meant to stow it away in his ruck before first call. Now, four sets of eyes were zeroed in on him, awaiting an answer. He glanced over to Ben, who wore a smug smile. Clearly, he was enjoying this. Despite things not going exactly as he'd planned, Danny decided he might as well get it done and over with.

"It is."

"You're married? Did you know about this, Soup?" Gibson looked to Ben, who answered with just a nod of his head. "When the hell did you get married?"

"Friday." Danny turned to his platoon leader. "Are we done here? The sooner Soup and I can start breaking in the newbies, the better."

"Yeah, we're done," Anthony replied.

Danny rose from his chair, ready to make his great escape, only to be called back by the captain. "Give us a second, guys."

The rest cleared out and Bull closed the door behind him.

"I guess congratulations are in order," he said, offering his hand, which Danny accepted. He casually reclined against his desk. "I have to admit, I'm as surprised as everyone else given from what I've heard, you're the highest ranking member of 1st Batt's players club."

"Not anymore. Guess I'll have to pass that baton on to someone else."

"Not Gibson, I hope?" Anthony laughed, but soon turned serious. "Do you need some time off to get your wife settled?"

"No, sir. Got her all moved in over the weekend. She'll probably be draining my bank account and throwing out my shot glass collection by the end of the week." Which wasn't even remotely close to being true. But what was the fun in being married if he couldn't complain about his wife like all the other husbands around here.

"You still have a ton of paperwork that needs to be filed ASAP. To be honest, I'm not really sure what HQ requires these days. Seems like they change the policy every time I check."

But Danny knew. Once Bree accepted his offer, he called headquarters to get his ducks in a row. "I've got it all straightened out. Just have to make some photocopies and drop it all off at HQ by Friday."

"This is too important to put off until the end of the week. I'm not trying to be Debbie Downer here, but the last thing you want is for something to happen to you during training and your wife ends up dealing with a mountain of governmental red tape all because you delayed turning your paperwork in. Bull can oversee your teams when we start FRIES training this afternoon. When you and Wojciechowski have had your fun with the new recruits, get on over to HQ and get your stuff turned in."

Having been dismissed, Danny turned to leave.

"One last suggestion," Anthony said just as he opened the door. "Figure out a time and place to introduce the guys to your wife. Might as well get it over with."

Bull and Gibby were waiting for him in the hall and quickly fell in step as Danny headed for the squad bay.

"You're not getting off that easy," Bull began. "For all the years I've known you, you've somehow managed to avoid the gate honeys and the trap. You're our hero. Every time I turn around you're banging some hottie and instead of her going all crazy stalker on your ass or calling the commander, they just give you a kiss on a cheek and say thanks for a good time."

"Are you going somewhere with this?"

Now it was Gibson's turn to get in on the fun. "Why in the hell would you go and get married when you are actually living the life every man wishes he could have?"

"Gibby's got a point. Sex without commitment. No money drain. Blowjobs out the wazoo. You told me once the worst thing I ever did was get married. And you know what? You were right."

Danny felt bad about saying that. After all, Bull might have been hoodwinked into marriage before their last rotation, his wife suddenly miscarrying just weeks after their wedding. Only Bull had never seen any confirmation aside from a positive pregnancy test. And just last month a guy in Delta Company found an ad on Craigslist where a pregnant woman was selling positive sticks as a way for others to trap a guy into marriage. So now everyone questioned whether or not Bull's wife was telling the truth to begin with.

"What have you done with Danny MacGregor? The man who always says 'if the army wanted us to have a wife they would've issued us one,' " Gibby asked while shaking Danny's shoulders. "My only guess is that he must have met a hot piece of ass that wouldn't put out without a ring on her finger."

Danny pulled from his grasp and turned on him. "Watch it, Gibby. That's my wife you're talking about."

Bull's eyes widened in surprise. "Damn. He's serious about this. Who the hell did you marry?"

"My high school sweetheart," Danny answered. Although he'd never referred to Bree as that before, it felt right. "Any other questions? I've got to get my squad ready."

"In all the years I've known you, you've never once mentioned anything about a 'high school sweetheart.' " Bull added air quotes for emphasis. "And now you show up with a ring on your finger. Did you just walk up to her and say, 'Hey, let's get married?' "

Danny laughed. "Something like that."

"She must be one helluva woman to drag you into the depths of marriage hell," Bull said.

"Or a Siren."

They both turned to Gibby, speaking in unison. "A what?"

"You know, those beautiful women who sit on the shore," Gibby explained. "They seduce you with body and song only to make you crash your boat on the rocks? It's mythology."

Thankfully, Bull saved him from asking the question. "How the hell do you know about mythology?"

"I watch movies, jackass!"

Finally, the three went their separate ways and Danny caught up with Ben in the squad bay, still chuckling to himself as he prepared for their morning PT session.

"You're enjoying this, aren't you?"

"Of course I am."

"I'm never going to live this down, am I?"

Ben never even answered. Just burst into laughter as he walked away.

Damn. It was going to be a long day.

BREE WOKE MONDAY morning to find Danny already gone, the blanket he used left neatly folded on the couch with the pillow stacked on top. He'd forewarned her of his schedule, how he left early in the morning, often arriving well before sunrise. As to when he would return home, well, that was a completely different story. Life in regiment was far different than most other military units much less a typical 9-to-5 day job. There would be times he would be back for dinner and there would be times he wouldn't return home for days. So, true to his word, it really did seem she would have the place all to herself for the most part.

After breakfast she resumed her old routine, firing up her laptop to surf the net. There were no emails from old friends, no messages on Facebook. No job opportunities from LinkedIn. It all went to show she could get married, move to a new city and nothing would change if she didn't change. And the last thing she wanted was to get stuck in the same damn rut with a different view. Danny had gone out of his way to help her, turning his personal life upside down in the process.

She would not disappoint him.

He deserved better. She deserved better.

She closed down the computer, grabbed a knife from the kitchen, and headed into the spare bedroom. As music blared from the small speakers of her laptop, she got down to the business of unpacking. Danny had told her to make herself at home and she intended to do just that. No more cramming all her things into a ten-by-ten space so as not to impose on someone else.

The first box held many of her favorite books and a small collection of DVDs, which now filled some of the once-empty built-in shelves in the living room. The second contained home decor things from her place in Columbia. It hadn't been her intent for this box to be brought along, but one of the boys must have grabbed it by accident. Since it was here, why not put it to use? After all, Danny's bachelor minimalist decor could use not only a style update, but a splash of color, as well.

A chenille throw and coordinating pillows added life to the living room. Barely used pot holders and dish towels prettied the kitchen. Her plush bathmat and oversize towels added luxury to the boring bathroom. At the bottom of the box she found several picture frames of various sizes, all containing photos from the time she lived with her ex.

She wanted to destroy them years ago, but her mother convinced her not to, saying they were a photo record of someone once important in her life. It was a bullshit reason then and it was still bullshit now. Bree flipped over each frame, wasting no time pulling out the photos, tearing them apart with her bare hands, and dropping them in the trash.

That felt good. Freeing.

Surveying her progress in the living room, she enjoyed a sense of pride and accomplishment. In her opinion, it now looked homey without being overly feminine. No doubt she'd drastically improved its appearance, but the room needed more of Danny's things, too.

She headed into the spare bedroom again, this time stopping at his stack of boxes. Bree chewed on her thumbnail.

He said he had nothing to hide.

"Mi casa es tu casa," he'd said.

Surely he wouldn't get upset if she snooped around a bit in the hopes of finding things of his to put on display?

Before she talked herself out of it, she returned to the spare room and sliced through the packing tape on one of his boxes. She folded back the flaps to find a cornucopia of shot glasses stacked in long strings, not carefully wrapped in paper or any sort of packaging material. Which was odd, considering the organization of his underwear drawer. It also contained a dozen or so paperbacks, mostly Tom Clancy and Robert Ludlum, along with several old music CDs ranging from Eminem to System of a Down.

Surprisingly she hadn't come across any photos. But digital cameras had been the way to go for most of his time in the military so it only made sense she didn't find any. Of course she hadn't looked in this closet.

She pulled open the doors for the reach-in closet and found hanging there all alone his army dress uniform. A bow tie draped loosely around the neck of the hanger. Gold emblems on the sleeve displayed his rank for all to see. Unfortunately, she didn't know anything about the army and what it all meant. She'd have to Google it later.

Her finger traced the patches, the light blue braid looping one sleeve, his last name engraved across a plastic pin. Row after row of bright colored ribbons adorned the left front of his jacket, displaying his accomplishments. She once knew Danny better than anyone, but his uniform served as a reminder she didn't know much about the man who wore it now. On the shelf above sat a tan beret with yet another brightly colored insignia: a red lightning bolt slashing across a blue and green shield. Next to the beret were black dress shoes polished to a high gleam. And next to them a file box.

Bree lowered it to the floor and removed the lid.

Inside the box, on top of everything else, were a couple of flat jewelry boxes with the words United States of America embossed in gold lettering. Not giving much thought to it, she opened the first one, the hinges on the back tight from a lack of use. Inside was a bronze-colored star hanging from a red and blue ribbon with a "V" in the middle of it. Very regal-looking. She couldn't help but wonder if there was a medal like this to go with each ribbon. If so, then there would be a lot of medals hanging on his chest.

She closed the case and exchanged it for the second one. Again, the black case squeaked with newness and at first glimpse, her heart stuttered.

A Purple Heart.

Bree knew what this meant. Everyone in the country had to know what it meant and what had to have happened in order for him to receive it.

Her throat tightened to the point it became difficult to breathe. Yes, she knew there was a war going on. For a long time there were casualty counts every time she listened to the news. But her life in college and then after was so far removed from the war it never affected her. She knew Danny was in the military and her father had told her Danny's job was a dangerous one. But she told herself her father had a way of exaggerating, not to mention she'd done one hell of a job of hating Danny for the past decade. It wasn't until this very moment she had ever considered the possibility of losing him forever. He could have easily been just another casualty of war in the news.

Now, knowing he'd been wounded, that he came so close to losing his life, it shamed her. All these years he'd been fighting for his country and not once had she asked God to watch over him and keep him safe. A mistake she dared not repeat.

Bree said a quick prayer for Danny, for his friends in 1st Batt, and for all of those serving overseas.

She closed the medal case and tried to push the thought of him returning to war out of her mind.

Bree dug deeper into the box, thumbing through stacks and stacks of 4x6s. Most of the photos were of guys she didn't recognize, drinking beer in the desert. Then they were drinking beer on a boat. Then drinking beer in the woods. There were rude gestures and bloodshot eyes and big smiles. Few, if any, were appropriate to frame, but she pulled out the best ones that included Danny.

Beneath those she found an 8x10 photo with Class 09-02. This was just what she'd been looking for. A graduation photo, it would seem. The men stood tall in their uniforms, shoulders back, arranged much like a primary school photo. It took some searching, but she found a baby-faced Danny and Ben, both so young they couldn't have been more than nineteen or twenty at the time. She set it aside knowing exactly which frame it would fit.

Then, at the very bottom of the box, was a photo she recognized. One she had a copy of somewhere in the many photo albums at her parents' home.

It was taken of them at the beach the summer before they headed off to college. She and Danny sat side by side on the beach, the Ferris wheel in the background. Her long, sun-streaked hair blew in the wind while his arm was thrown casually over her shoulder. They were so young and in love. So unbelievably happy. And somewhere in a box of her own she had a million pictures as evidence that what they had was real.

But even so, this picture was special. The way she looked at him. The way he looked at her. Both so focused on the other it was as if they existed in a bubble. Nothing and no one else mattered.

Back when she believed their future included a lifetime together.

Until the bubble popped.

She smiled one last time at the photo and returned it to the box, burying it deep beneath all his other mementos. Just as he'd kept it.

ASIDE FROM THE one night when he arrived home to find Bree asleep on the couch, he hadn't seen her all week. That didn't mean he hadn't noticed she'd been quite busy. And for one brief moment, as he checked out the throw pillows and candles and fancy towels, he jokingly wondered if she had drained his bank account while he was away at work.

Then he noticed the framed pictures on the shelves, most of which were taken during his second deployment to Iraq. Which meant she'd gone through his things in order to find those. He waited for the feeling of violation that came with someone going through his personal items. It never came. Instead, he found it to be an incredibly sweet gesture.

Danny dropped his ruck inside the front door and called her name. Bree appeared in the hall, dressed in jeans and a plain top, the v-neck displaying a large expanse of soft skin. Her makeup was soft and pretty, and delicate dangling earrings framed her face. But the very best thing—no wig.

"Are you about ready to go?"

Upon the suggestion of his platoon leader, Danny had arranged for the guys to meet Bree at a local sports bar. Hopefully, after their long, hard week, they would be short on energy and Bree wouldn't find them so overwhelming.

"I don't know." She rubbed her hand over the fuzz on her head. "Maybe I should wear the wig. I mean, you have more hair on your head than I do."

"Is that all that's bothering you? I can take care of that." He scooted past her, heading for the bathroom, pulling off his shirt as he walked. "Give me ten minutes and I'll be ready to go."

He pulled a shaving kit from beneath the sink and removed the guard. Soon, the hum of clippers filled his ears as he made the first pass down the middle of his skull. Normally, Danny kept his hair longer on top with the sides and back short. But it was only hair and in the end didn't matter that much to him. If it made Bree feel more comfortable, all the better. After cleaning up, he stripped off his remaining clothes and hopped into the shower for just a quick rinse since they were short on time. Using one of the new towels he found hanging on the rod, Danny dried himself as he headed back into the bedroom, the plush white cotton heaven on his—

"Oh! Oh!" Bree immediately covered her eyes with her hands. "I'm sorry, I didn't realize you'd finish so quickly and I decided to wear the boots instead of the flats I had on."

"Nothing you haven't seen before, Bree."

"I know," she said, still refusing to uncover her eyes. Although she hid her face, the cut of her shirt revealed the flush of her skin, the color deepening with each passing second.

"And we're married now, Bree."

"I just—" As she blindly attempted to maneuver past, she collided with him instead, her palm meeting his wet chest. "Shit," she cursed under her breath.

Danny chuckled in response then stepped to the side, allowing her to run away. He quickly changed and found her waiting in the living room. This time, instead of covering her eyes, she couldn't look away.

Her eyes welled with tears and she tentatively reached out to touch him, her fingers trailing over his newly shorn scalp. "What did you do?"

Danny shrugged his shoulders. "It's not the first time I've done it. Not a big deal."

"Not a big deal, huh?" Bree smiled through the tears. "You shave your head for all the girls?"

He smiled but said nothing else. She could pretend she wasn't special, but for him she was the only woman worth any amount of trouble.

Chapter Twelve

THEY DROVE TO a sports bar located near the river, a place far enough away from HAAF that it wasn't a regular hangout for Rangers. As they made their way through the parking lot, Danny could sense her hesitation in the way she kept touching the hat on her head. He was so very proud of her for taking this step. Not only for meeting his friends, but for also being strong enough to go out in public without her wig. Danny held Bree's hand a little tighter, mostly for her benefit, but he needed a little reassurance himself. There would be no going back from this.

Barely inside the front doors, Gibby's voice boomed from the back of the bar. "There they are!"

His friends were a rowdy group to begin with. They would willfully say anything and everything to him, but at the end of the day they were all really good guys. In an attempt to keep the initial look of surprise from their faces and reduce the potential of staring, he had given Gibson advanced warning of Bree's condition.

Gibson met them halfway, smiling first at Bree then giving him a double-take. "Nice look there, Sarnt," he said, pointing to Danny's head. Then he turned and offered his hand to Bree. "Jeff Gibson. You must be the brand-new Missus MacGregor."

She smiled. "You can call me Bree."

"And *you* can call me anytime."

Jesus. That didn't take long. "Are you flirting with my wife, Gibby?"

"Why, yes, I am."

Thank goodness he was a short, ugly little fucker with big ears and beady little eyes. No way would Bree go for him.

Or would she?

"Now, Bree." Gibby took her hand from Danny's and looped it through his arm, escorting her back to where the others stood. "I don't know what this ugly bastard has on you. Obviously, MacDaddy must have blackmailed a beautiful woman such as you into marriage. Whatever it is, I can help. I've got a good friend in the 160th. Just say the word and he'll commandeer a real nice MH–60 and you and I can fly away into the sunset together. How does that sound?"

He guided her to an empty bar stool where she seated herself to face the group, much like a queen holding court.

"Wouldn't that be a lateral move?" Bree said, answering his question with a question. "If I'm going to all the trouble of dumping 'MacDaddy,' shouldn't I at least make it worth my while? Upgrade to a colonel or general, perhaps?"

A roar of laughter went up from the guys crowded around them as Gibby's mouth dropped open in astonishment. Danny had to pick up his jaw, as well, since his wife had just rendered Charlie Company's resident loudmouth speechless. Even better, she did it with the sweetest of smiles on her face. His earlier feeling of pride multiplied tenfold.

After an opening like that, the rest of the guys pushed forward, ready to meet the new Mrs. MacGregor. He introduced her to Capt. Anthony first, then Bull, Rodriguez, and Lucky. Several guys from his squad were there, as well, including Jenkins, his newest private. Ben came only to serve as a familiar face and left after the first beer, heading out with Rodriguez, who also had a family at home waiting for him. Soon after them, Anthony left so the enlisted guys could relax and let their hair down, so to speak.

His own brother, however, never responded to the invite.

LIKE ANY GOOD bodyguard, Danny never sat, choosing instead to stand just behind her. Occasionally, he would caress her back or rest his hand upon her hip. Maybe lean down to whisper something in her ear. She liked it, the intimacy, the closeness, although she feared making out his affection to be something it wasn't.

So she distracted herself with the conversation around

her, the men and their stories. Sometimes she found it difficult to keep up, especially when they kept calling each other different things, switching back and forth between last names and nicknames.

The guy sitting next to her, though, his name she could remember. Bull. Easily he was the tallest of the group with the looks of a Nordic god and baritone voice. He was also one of the few she'd noticed wearing a wedding ring.

"You're married?" she asked. He answered with a curt nod then drank down what remained in his glass. "What does your wife do?"

"Whatever she wants."

Oh. Definitely not the answer she expected. "I'm sorry."

Bull waved off her apology. "No, I'm the one that's sorry," he said, flagging down the waitress, ordering another Scotch for himself and a second glass of wine for her. A peace offering, she supposed. He folded his arms atop the table and turned to speak. "Word on the street is you two have known each other forever."

"We grew up together."

Having overheard her answer, Gibby jumped into their conversation. "Then you know Doc, as well?"

It took her a moment to figure out who he was talking about. "Michael? Yes, of course."

"This one here is a tight-lipped son of a bitch," Gibby said, pointing at Danny. "He's told us he's from Myrtle Beach, but that's it. It's as if he didn't exist before joining up. Not one story, nothing. And believe me, we've tried everything short of waterboarding."

"Oh, really? What do you want to know?"

Danny leaned closer to speak directly into her ear. "Bree," he said with mock warning.

She pushed him away with one hand. "I doubt I have anything interesting to share, since he joined the army after our first year in college."

"He went to college? Where to?"

"South Carolina. He had a baseball scholarship." The look of surprise on each of their faces was unbelievable. "You mean he's never told you about signing day?"

Danny muttered under his breath. "Here we go."

She turned to face him. "Just this one? I promise."

His hands settled on her hips and he whispered in her ear. "Let it be known there will be payback then." His warm breath on her neck sent a shiver down her spine. Payback might not be so bad, after all.

"All the hype started our junior year when college coaches and major league scouts came out to see him play in the state championship. So he was kind of a big deal in Myrtle Beach. By our senior year, several schools had offered baseball scholarships. But instead of just announcing where he was going and signing his letter of intent, he decided to make it a big production.

"You know how guys will pick up one hat out of three or four options and put it on their head? Well, Danny decided to do something different. There were a couple of reporters, some photographers, and a local TV station all waiting to see who he was signing with. Danny walks in wearing a hoodie and when the time came he stood up, unzipped his jacket and revealed his shirt. A shirt that said 'Got Cock?' across the front. He was so proud of himself. The paper cropped the photo to his neck. The local news ran a still photo and some old highlights. I'm convinced the whole reason he chose South Carolina was just so he could wear that stupid T-shirt."

It took a while for the laughter and the jabs to die down, but Danny took it well.

"Were you drafted?" This from the guy they called Lucky.

"Yeah," Danny answered. "White Sox."

Gibby, who'd clearly had more than his share, stood on the rungs of his bar stool, his finger stabbing the air over the table. "You could've played professionally!"

"Jesus, Gib. They draft just about anybody out of high school. And very few ever make it to the majors."

"But you got a scholarship!"

"Which I promptly lost my first year of school." A hush settled over the table. "I flunked out of school and they kicked me off the team. I wasn't drafted high enough to get a signing bonus. And what they pay you in the minors isn't enough to live on. So I enlisted."

Danny shrugged his shoulder in that "shit happens" kind of way and took another drink of his beer.

The guilt knotted her stomach.

She'd only meant to tell a funny story, not embarrass him in some passive-aggressive way. Or had she? After all he'd done to help her? He'd shown her nothing but kindness and this was how she repaid him? By retelling his failures to get a laugh from his friends?

The waitress delivered a tray of appetizers, and the

conversation at the table restarted on a different topic. But Danny remained silent behind her. He might try to sell it to them as not a big deal, but she remembered it all, just how big of a deal it really was. How it changed not only his life, but hers, too.

Clearly, he had the right idea all along. It was better to leave the past buried and forgotten.

WHAT AN ARROGANT little shit he'd been.

To hear Bree tell the story, it made him wonder why she'd tolerated his dumb ass for as long as she did. But she'd been there for almost every game, hair swept back into a ponytail, ball cap on her head, cheering him on from the stands. No matter if he was playing in the state championship or hanging out at the batting cages.

Now she stared into her glass, her thoughts likely lost in the past, back when everything changed for them.

It hadn't been as simple as he told them. Losing his scholarship was a major turning point in his life. He couldn't afford school without it. Which meant he couldn't stay in Columbia. She tried to talk him into getting a job, any job, so they could move in together. And then, after she graduated, she'd support him and he could go back to school.

She'd support him.

He couldn't remember them ever fighting before. But in a matter of days, everything between them crumbled.

This was why he never talked about his life before enlisting. During his time in regiment, he had stood shoulder to shoulder, fought side by side with some truly brilliant men. Even led guys with advanced degrees in mathematics and science and economics and engineering. It was difficult enough to earn the respect of your commanding officers, your peers, and later your subordinates without being known as the idiot who lost his full ride. So he'd kept it all quiet, determined to completely start over from scratch.

It was why he understood Bree's desperate need for a new beginning. On some subconscious level, it was probably why he proposed.

The waitress returned to the table with a round of Jaeger shots and the guys shoved one into his hand.

The men raised their glasses as Gibson began. "Here's to the kisses we've snatched—"

"Gibson!" he yelled, interrupting before he could carry on with that particular toast.

Gibby stopped midsentence. "Hooah?" Danny shook his head and looked toward Bree. Only then did the man come to his senses. He cleared his throat and began again as he held out the shot glass. "To Danny and Bree."

A smile returned to Bree's face, not nearly as bright as earlier ones, not quite as authentic, either. Instead, she put on her brave face.

And it killed him to know that the pain he caused long ago still cut so deep.

BREE DIDN'T MOVE when he shut off the engine. Too much wine. Too many people. Maybe it was all too much too soon. He'd best remember she still wasn't one hundred percent and make certain to not run her ragged. Not that he'd dare say that out loud. When he opened her car door, she still didn't stir.

"Bree."

Although he said her name no louder than a whisper, she jumped in surprise, those big brown eyes opening wide as she tried to figure out her surroundings. "Did I fall asleep?"

"Seems that way," he said, offering a hand to help her out of the vehicle. "Did you have a little too much fun?"

She placed her hand in his, so much smaller than his own with thin, delicate fingers. When she wobbled a bit on her heels, he steadied her with another hand at her waist.

"I'm sorry."

"For falling asleep? Not a big deal."

"No. About what happened at the bar. I'm sorry I told that story."

Shit. The last thing he wanted to do was rehash that again. He shifted her sideways so he could close the door.

"I need to apologize. You've done so much for me and . . ." She was still holding his hand when the first tear fell.

The need to comfort her overwhelmed him. He dabbed her tears away with his fingertip and pressed a kiss to her forehead. Using both hands she clutched the front of his shirt, burying her face into his chest. Unable to see her face, he could only assume a flood of tears followed, her body shaking from the force of it. Danny set his chin upon the top of her head and wrapped his arms tightly around her, one hand smoothing circles over her back.

She pushed away from his chest, but stayed within his embrace. Just putting a little space between them as she tried to catch her breath. "This isn't right. You're the wronged party here, not me. You should be angry with me, not trying to make me feel better."

"Maybe I'm holding you for purely selfish reasons? Maybe it's not about you at all and I'm just trying to make myself feel better?"

She froze in place. "Really?"

"No." He laughed and Bree took a playful swipe at his chest.

"Here's the truth. What I realized tonight is it's okay to talk about the past and my failed college career. If it hadn't been for me losing my scholarship, I'd never have enlisted. I wouldn't have become the person I am today or be doing the job I do. And I like who I am. So I'm glad that skeleton's out of the closet. Of course, you didn't need to have so much fun doing it."

Then came another round of tears she couldn't fight back.

Even with tearstains on her cheeks and reddened eyes, she was beautiful. He cradled her face in his palm. "Now, come on. I'm just teasing you. It's not a big deal."

Taking a deep breath, she put on her brave face and leaned back against the side of the car. She smiled, just a little, and sniffled through the remnants of her crying jag. She smoothed one hand over the top of his head. "I still can't believe you did this," she whispered.

His eyes drifted shut, relishing her touch as those delicate fingers stroked what remained of his hair and traced the shell of his ear. He could hear the scrape of stubble against her palm as she caressed his cheek. The warm press of her lips against his surprised him, along with the press of her body against his. Her lips were soft, her kiss tender, but uncertain, as well. Before he could react, she abruptly ended the kiss and looked away, somehow embarrassed by her actions.

"I'm sorry. I shouldn't have done that."

He wanted to take her by the shoulders and shake her, wanted her to stop apologizing. But she was still too fragile, too broken, for him to take such a hard line with her.

He whispered her name, but she didn't respond. Either she was ignoring him or was completely lost in her own thoughts as she chewed on the corner of her lip.

"Bree," he said with more force.

This time she looked up with those big brown eyes, her teeth releasing the plump flesh of her lower lip when something inside him just snapped. His hands went to her hips, backing her up against the side of his vehicle as his mouth came down upon hers. His chest and hips pressed into her softness, holding her captive, now giving him the freedom to take her face in both hands. Unlike before, Bree took what she wanted this go-round, her hands clinging to his neck, her body arching up to meet his. The edges of her fingernails bit into his skin as she pulled him closer. His mouth trailed along her jaw as he made his way to the tender spot just beneath her ear. The same place that always made her—

On a gasp, her lips parted and he, being an unapologetic asshole of the highest order, took complete advantage, covering her mouth once again, wanting nothing more than to taste her, to feel the warm, wet stroke of her tongue against his. Everything about their kiss was wild and frantic, just as he'd always remembered. A far cry from the polite press of lips they shared on their wedding day.

A bright flash from a car's high beams pierced the darkness and Danny pulled away from her.

"What's wrong?" she asked.

What wasn't wrong? For a moment he'd lost all of his self-restraint and was on the verge of taking even more while she was pressed up against his car in the parking lot. The only thing that could make this moment worse—

"Bree. Danny." His brother stood near the back of his truck, arms crossed, his posture and tone carrying that same air of superiority he'd displayed since Danny was a child. A tone that let everyone know he was in charge and planned to enforce the rules.

Except as far as Danny knew, they weren't breaking any. And even if they were, it wasn't any of Michael's damn business.

Danny held out his keys for Bree. "Why don't you head upstairs? I'll be there in a minute."

Bree looked to Michael then back to him. "I'd rather you come with me."

Danny turned his back to his brother, blocking him

out of their conversation. He took Bree's hand in his and dropped the keys into her palm. "I have a gut feeling Mike wants to talk to me in private. Okay?" he said, closing her fingers around them.

Reluctantly, she turned and walked away, occasionally looking over her shoulder as if she was checking to see if they were tearing each other limb from limb. Only once she'd reached the top of the stairs and clearly out of earshot did Michael start in.

"You do realize the two of you are playing with fire? Right?"

"You're blowing shit out of proportion." Danny folded his arms across his chest. "It was a kiss."

Michael narrowed his eyes. "Not from what I saw."

Of course he saw. "It was a kiss. That's it. Nothing would have happened."

His brother laughed but there was no humor in his voice. "I don't think you even believe what you're saying."

"This isn't for the long-term. That's what she wants, that's what I want. We agreed. But if something were to happen between us, it wouldn't concern you anyway." Danny started for his apartment but in an instant his brother's grasp forcefully turned him back around.

"The way you look at her, your feelings are written all over your face. And she's exactly the same way. She deserves better than this."

Danny pulled from his brother's grasp and started for his apartment. "For once, you and I agree."

Chapter Thirteen

GONE FOR A *run.*

She found the first note on the breakfast bar after she woke. Since it was part of his weekend routine, she didn't think much of it. A second note, saying he'd headed out to get the oil changed in the truck, he left while she showered. Nearly half of the day had passed and she still hadn't seen him.

Coward.

Bree grabbed the scrap of paper and channeled her frustrations by wadding it up into a little ball and throwing it at the trash can. Which missed, of course, because she never could play basketball worth a damn.

So what if kissing him wasn't the brightest of ideas, but it wasn't *that* big of a deal. They were adults. Who also happened to be married to each other. It's not as if they did anything wrong. And even so, they should be able to talk it out. Apparently, avoidance really was his way of handling things.

Just great. Barely into week three of their marriage and things had already gone to hell in a handbasket.

Not wanting to sit in an empty apartment all day, Bree picked up her phone and sent a quick text. Instead of a reply, she got a knock on the front door a few minutes later. "Wow. Do you always come running when food is mentioned?"

"I'm a growing boy," Michael said, smiling. "And eating with you sure as hell beats eating a PB&J all alone."

"Something tells me you wouldn't have to eat alone if you didn't want to."

"True. But too often the reward isn't worth the effort."

Michael had always been a straight shooter, but never lacked tact. "Are you saying women should put out just because you've bought us food?"

He scrubbed his face in frustration, a little growl escaping. "Good God, woman. Sometimes lunch is just lunch. And sex is just sex. Why do you women have to make everything so convoluted? I swear, it's the women who have far more expectations than men."

Now this was amusing. Bree folded her arms over her chest and reclined against the counter. "Enlighten me, please, Dr. Phil."

Michael shook his head and mumbled something along the lines of "smart-ass" under his breath. "I know there are assholes out there who expect sex if they buy a woman dinner. But there's just as many women who expect a long-term commitment if they put out."

Hmmm. Couldn't really argue with him on that point.

"My dad always said the key to any good relationship is open and honest communication." Then Michael laughed. "Of course that's never worked for me. Last woman I dated told me I was a little too honest."

Bree smiled at that. "I shudder to think what you said to her."

Even so, what she wouldn't give for a little honesty from his brother right about now. She grabbed a pen from the bottom of her purse and scribbled a message for Danny on a notepad.

"So where do you want to go?"

"Anywhere but here."

The smile left Michael's face, instantly replaced with one of concern. "Want to talk about it?"

"Not really."

Bree slung her handbag over her shoulder and headed for the door.

Out to lunch.

She left off the "with Michael" part. Of course he only knew that since he passed them on their way out and he was returning home. If he'd arrived home a few minutes earlier, would they have invited him to go with? Considering the conversation he'd had with his brother last night and the way he'd avoided Bree today, that was highly unlikely.

No point in moping around and waiting for them to return. Danny dusted off his riding gear, grabbed his mountain bike, and headed to a nearby park. Having the trail to himself gave him time to think, to figure out what the hell he should say to fix things with Bree. He needed to find a way to smooth things over so they could go back to living as roommates.

But deep down, he didn't want that. If he were honest with himself—

Danny shook the thought from his head. Get married. Get well. Get a job. Get a divorce. That was Bree's plan of action. Best stick to the plan. No good could come from someone going rogue and changing all the rules in mid-stream.

Carrying his bike over one shoulder, Danny climbed the stairs to his apartment. Both his and Mike's trucks were in the parking lot, which meant Bree should be home and they could talk. Just as he arrived at his door, laughter erupted in his apartment. Before he made it all the way inside, they went silent.

Bree sat cross-legged on the couch while his brother kicked back in his recliner.

"Hey there," he said, speaking directly to Bree. "Did you guys have a nice lunch?"

"Michael took me to this hole-in-the-wall with an honest-to-goodness low country boil, served on newspaper and everything."

Great.

He narrowed his eyes at his brother, who was smiling behind his beer. Beer from Danny's refrigerator. Michael knew damn well he'd just taken Bree out to eat at his absolute favorite place in all of Savannah without him. Asshole.

"Did you have a nice ride?" she asked.

"It was fine. If you don't mind I'm gonna hit the shower."

Since no objections were made, he stowed his bike in the spare bedroom and hit the bathroom. The moment he closed the door, their conversation started up again. He tried not to think about it. Two people who have known each other forever and are sitting in the same room would have reason to talk. Didn't mean they were talking about him. Or their marriage. But the silence happened a second time after his shower, this time as he crossed the hall into the bedroom. They didn't speak again until the door closed behind him.

So it wasn't all in his imagination.

Danny held his breath, one ear pressed against the bedroom door as he strained to hear their conversation. The last time he eavesdropped on someone's conversation he was in the middle school locker room, and the only reason he did it then was because he heard one of his friends mention Bree by name.

"Have you decided if you're going to see a doctor here or go back to Columbia for your follow-ups?" Michael asked.

Danny could tell Bree was answering him, but her words were spoken so softly, so low, he couldn't make out what she said. He had no idea her doctor was in Columbia. Had no idea that she'd have to do follow-up tests or scans or whatever else. It made sense once Mike mentioned it, but he'd never asked anything about her treatment. Danny had made a conscious effort not to. That first day in Myrtle Beach, Bree said she was tired of people always asking her about her cancer when all she wanted to do was put it behind her. So who was screwing up here? Him for not asking? Or his brother for prying?

Bree married him. Wore his ring on her hand. But he was clearly wrong to think that would mean Bree would talk about the important stuff with him.

ON MONDAY MORNING Danny waited for the last of his squad to come in. He pushed his sunglasses on top of his head and wiped the sweat from his eyes.

"What the hell has gotten into you?" Ben dropped his seventy-pound ruck on the grass and tried to catch his breath. "You know I'm all for busting these guys' asses, but we're not supposed to kill them. When you suggested a ruck march for morning PT, I didn't think we'd be trying to set a goddamn record."

"The pain reminds them—"

"Yeah, yeah. Fuck you. I've been doing this long enough to notice when someone's head isn't on straight." Ben jabbed a finger into Danny's face. "And your head isn't on straight."

Maybe he had a point.

Powered by anger and jealousy and a whole other list of emotions he didn't want to think about, Danny chose a grueling exercise that should have exhausted him to the point he would forget the taste of her mouth, her skin.

For his own sanity he needed to forget that kiss. How she tasted sweet like the cheap house wine she'd been drinking. How soft and warm and welcoming her body was as he pressed against her.

The sound of her laughter as she spent time with his brother.

Fuck. Right back where he started. In hell.

"So are you going to tell me what's going on or do I need to beat it out of you?"

Danny took a hard look at Ben. That wasn't a half-bad idea. A little hand-to-hand combat to burn off the excess adrenaline and testosterone coursing through his body.

Ben cracked the knuckles of his left hand. Then his right. That was when common sense came into play and Danny remembered how much this Jersey boy liked bringing the hammer. He didn't look like much, six foot nothing, buck eighty-five. His looks were deceiving, especially when he was in family-man mode, but he'd personally seen Ben level guys twice his size and not even break a sweat.

"Jesus, no. Last thing I need is to be fighting with you, too."

"Me, too? Are you fighting with Bree? What the hell are you two fighting about?"

"Not fighting, really. It's just—" Danny scrubbed a hand over his face. "Shit, man. What the hell have I gotten myself into? I just never imagined."

Ben laughed, caught his breath then laughed some more. Danny narrowed his eyes at him.

"What? You're surprised that a fake marriage would

end up as stressful as a real one? It's pretty funny, if you ask me. Look at it this way," he said, slapping a hand to Danny's shoulder. "You went from being a very confirmed bachelor to a married man in the span of what, two, three days? You've never even lived with a woman, much less kept one around for more than a long weekend. And now you're shocked to find out they can be moody as hell and you've got nowhere to run? Welcome to my world!"

Danny shook his head. "It's not all her fault. If anything, I probably started it." Ben gave him a look. One that told Danny he had zero problem beating down his ass for disrespecting a woman. "Okay, I did start it. And now I've got Mike all up in my business—"

Ben barked a laugh. "I should've known."

"Why would you say that?"

"Because if there's one thing everyone around here knows," he said, his finger circling in the air, "it's to keep a safe distance when the MacGregor brothers get into a pissing match. So what did he do now? Make a move on Bree?"

He gave Ben his signature "don't fuck with me" face.

"Shit, man. I was only joking."

"He didn't make a move on her. Not that I know of, at least. But it's like he's her confidant. Anything to do with her cancer and stuff she talks to him about. She doesn't tell me anything. She just shuts me completely out of one whole part of her life."

"Have you asked her about it?"

"No."

With the last of their men accounted for, Ben picked up his ruck and headed for the squad bay. "Then stop complaining," he shouted over his shoulder while walking away.

"I didn't want her to think I was hovering," Danny said, trailing after him.

Ben stopped abruptly and turned to face him. "The problem is you want to be everything to her. Yet you keep saying this is only a temporary deal."

"That's pretty much the same thing Mike said."

"As much as you really aren't going to like hearing this, I have to agree with your brother. So which is it? What's the status between you two relationship-wise? Have things stayed platonic or have you—"

White-hot anger coursed through him. "I swear to God," Danny said, getting in Ben's face, "if you ask me if I've fucked her, I'll break your fucking neck."

Ben held up his hands in surrender. "All I was going to ask was if you've had sex." He dropped his hands and stalked toward Danny. "Let me tell you something, MacGregor. I know how to be respectful to women. Don't forget I've been faithfully married to my wife since before I've known you, and you're the one who's been prancing around here for ten years like the cock of the walk."

Danny felt he'd been sucker punched and it took a few seconds for what Ben said to sink in. "Cock of the walk? What the fuck does that even mean?" Danny began to laugh, with Ben joining him.

"Hell if I know. I think I've been in Georgia too damn long." They went on their way to the squad bay. "Here's what I do know. You can't do anything about Bree right now. And to be honest, it's probably a good thing we're headed to Stewart for a few days. It'll give you guys a cooling-off period. Just send her a text. Tell her you're sorry. Do it before things get worse."

"You think I should apologize? Via text?"

"Trust me on this, Danny. In this case, something is better than nothing."

BEN WAS RIGHT.

He didn't have his head on straight. He needed to apologize to Bree but wanted to take his time and find just the right words to say.

After a shower and breakfast, Charlie Co. loaded up their gear and headed south to Fort Stewart for a week's worth of live fire exercises. For the hour-long ride he was lost in his thoughts, debating what kind of message he should send Bree. Some were too long. Some made him sound like a child. Others were too revealing.

Once they arrived, he lost himself in the repetitive training that required complete focus. Having a team member fresh from RASP meant his squad wouldn't run like a well-oiled machine. Instead, he and the fire team leader worked with Jenkins demonstrating each movement like steps to a dance. Afterward, they moved to the shoot house, putting those steps into practice. Then they did it again and again and again, before finally loading their weapons with live ammo. That was when the real fun began as they blew doors off the hinges and peppered targets. Once darkness had fallen, they put on their night-vision goggles and did it all over again in a green-colored world.

Finally, around 0300, after the brass casings were gathered and targets put away, after his weapons were cleaned and oiled and ready for the next round of training, he crawled into his sleeping bag. With his body tired and mind cleared, he finally decided on what was the right thing to say. He took his phone from his ruck and typed out a quick message to Bree.

I'm sorry.

ON FRIDAY BREE opened the front door to a pile of Danny's things on the floor. After kicking his boots and other gear out of the way, she closed the door behind her and carried the bags of groceries into the kitchen. Only once everything was put away did she realize the apartment was silent. No shower running. No music playing.

Was he here and avoiding her? Or had he just dropped his stuff and run?

They'd exchanged text messages throughout the week after she woke to find his two-word apology. Slowly but surely a conversation began and by this morning she believed things were resolved and the awkwardness was behind them. Which was why she decided to cook him a nice dinner. A peace offering of sorts.

She tiptoed down the hallway to the bedroom and found him sprawled across the bed. Sound asleep. Naked. The clean scent of his soap lingered in the air. She could only assume he'd taken a shower before yanking back the covers and collapsing face-first onto the mattress, resembling a starfish washed ashore. He didn't even bother with a pillow as he lay in the middle of his huge bed, his body angled from corner to corner, with only the top sheet tangled around his legs.

Damn.

She'd never get used to how beautiful he'd become. From his sculpted shoulders to his defined back, to the turned muscles of his arms and legs displaying power and strength even while completely at rest.

Just as God intended.

In college she wouldn't have thought twice about joining him on that bed. Running her tongue the length of his spine, starting between those two dimples low on his back and working her way up to his neck. But she wasn't that girl anymore, although there were plenty of times she wished to see her in the mirror again, if only for a day.

Bree closed the bedroom door, leaving him to catch up on some much-needed rest.

A couple hours later he emerged, sneaking up behind her as she worked in the kitchen.

"Something smells good."

She jumped involuntarily.

"Are you hungry?" Bree covered the sauce pot and turned to face him, nearly swallowing her tongue in the process.

He had dressed, kind of. Flannel pants hung low on his hips. An unzipped hoodie revealed a sculpted chest she'd imagined but not seen until this very moment.

Stubble shadowed his jaw and a line creased his cheek. If he hadn't shaved off most of his hair, he surely would have been rocking the sexy, rumpled look. Her gaze drifted to the hollow of his throat, his collarbones. She wanted to press her face against the tender spot where his shoulder and neck met and breathe deep, knowing that was where he always, *always* smelled the best. Of course her hands would need something to do. Like smoothing over the ridges and valleys before following the light dusting of hair that bisected his abdomen, circled his belly button and disappeared beneath the waistband of his pants.

"Do I need to change into something else?"

"Hmmm?" Her head snapped up to see the amusement in his eyes and smirk on his face.

He chuckled softly as he moved toward their small dining table.

The heated rush of embarrassment quickly followed. The oven buzzed, thankfully saving her from herself. She popped garlic bread in the oven and dropped the pasta in the boiling water. Hopefully, the heat and steam would disguise her flush. She stirred the pasta with vigor, but froze the moment the shuffle of papers registered in her head.

Shit. She'd pulled them out only to see how long she had until her next checkup. The last thing she wanted was for Danny to get an in-depth look at them. Because once he knew everything about her treatment, he wouldn't look at her in the same way ever again.

He stared at the papers in hand, his eyes scanning the cover page before finally looking up at her. "Everything go okay this week?" he asked, now holding the papers out to her.

She took them from him, shoving her medical records into an accordion file that held all of her personal documents. "Just fine."

He pointed to the folder in her hand. "Sure about that?"

Bree painted on her brightest smile. "Absolutely."

She hustled down the hallway and into the bedroom, where she stashed the folder in a cardboard banker's box. By the time she returned, Danny was in the process of setting the table for dinner. For a moment she believed that was the end of it. Only until he turned his attention to her.

Danny stood with his arms folded across his chest, watching her with such intensity.

"I promise, Danny. Nothing is wrong. My doctor in Myrtle Beach made sort of a CliffsNotes version of my medical records so I could see where I'm at as far as follow-ups for blood work and scans and stuff. I was just checking to see how much time I have until I need to schedule an appointment with someone local."

Several seconds passed before he finally spoke.

"I know you want breathing room. Need it, really. I promised you no hovering, but that doesn't mean you can't talk about what you went through, what you're going through, with me."

"I appreciate that." She smiled. "Really. I just . . . I'm tired of talking about it."

He nodded in understanding. "Okay. But I have one request."

Her insides twisted. "And that is?"

"If something changes and one day your doctor gives you bad news instead of good, I want you to tell me. And if there's good news, I want you to tell me so we can celebrate. Giving you space doesn't mean I don't care. Understood?"

"Got it."

But it became clear that reply wasn't enough. He cocked his head, raised an eyebrow, and just stood there, patiently waiting.

"Okay," she said. "I promise. Good news or bad news, I'll tell you."

He smiled in victory. "Thank you."

The remainder of the evening passed by quietly, with little chitchat during dinner or the movie that followed. They also kept distance between them, she sitting on the couch, he in the recliner.

Bree said good-night and headed for the bedroom, only realizing he'd followed along behind her once she reached the end of the hall. Afraid to say anything, she pulled her pajamas from the drawer as he disappeared into the closet. He returned seconds later; the pillows and blanket he normally used were bundled in his arms.

Just like that, things returned to the way they were her very first night in Savannah, with little said between them.

Chapter Fourteen

"NO WAY ARE you going to make it in time."

Danny's voice came from deep within the closet, rousing her from a light sleep. Bree rolled over to look at the clock and groaned. Not yet 6am on a Saturday. My, how the boy had changed. She remembered back when they were in college how difficult it was to drag his butt out of bed before noon. Of course in those days, he rarely made it to bed before the sun came up.

He exited the closet, dressed in his camo stuff head to toe. In his hands he held the tan beret with that brightly colored patch. "Better get moving. The traffic is going to be a nightmare. The parking will be even worse."

She pulled the pillow over her face.

"Come on, sleepyhead. Up and at 'em." Danny grabbed the pillow and tossed it across the room then yanked back the sheet, blanket, and comforter in one swipe. "Believe it or not, I still remember how long it takes you to get ready."

"That was when I had hair," she whined. "Lots of it, as a matter of fact." Bree climbed out of the bed and stomped her way to the bathroom, turning on the shower and giving it a chance to heat up. "If there's one perk to chemo, it's no hair anywhere."

When she turned around, he was right there, standing stock-still, his eyes zeroed in on her body.

It hadn't taken her long to commandeer one of his well-worn T-shirts. The traditional gray T-shirt with ARMY screened across the front was broken in to that point of unbelievable softness, and she couldn't resist swiping it. She'd worn it several times and he'd never seemed to be bothered by it. But now his eyes were practically burning a hole through the fabric.

"No hair anywhere?" he asked, quirking his eyebrow.

She laughed as she pushed past him and into the hallway, sliding open the louvered doors hiding away the washer and dryer. "My God, you are twelve."

And just as he often did when they were kids, he followed, right on her heels. Even leaned over her shoulder to whisper in her ear as she dug a fresh towel from the dryer. "I won't deny that."

She pushed past him a second time and headed for the bedroom to grab a change of clothes, only to find him blocking the doorway when she turned around.

"You're telling me you're completely bare?" His gaze skimmed her body, pausing momentarily somewhere below her waist before returning to her face. "Everywhere?"

She fought hard to suppress the shiver racing up and down her spine. "For now, yes. Having done chemo twice, it takes a little longer for things to grow back. Now, if you don't mind."

This time he stepped aside, allowing her to cross the hall and into the lone bathroom where she dropped her clothes on the counter. When she went to close the door, he was right there, resting his forearms high against the doorjamb as he canted toward her.

"I wanna see." Such childish enthusiasm in his voice. Not unlike a teenage boy wanting another peek of his best friend's stolen *Playboy.* Danny reached out, hooking a finger under the bottom of her T-shirt. More like his shirt.

"No." She laughed while simultaneously pushing his hand away and tugging the hem to its appropriate length.

What had possessed her to share such a thing with him? Oh, yeah. He implied it took her forever to get ready so this was her own damn fault. She'd dangled the proverbial carrot in front of his face and he was now in the mood to take a bite.

She started to close the door, hoping he'd take the hint. He didn't budge an inch, just stood there with a lazy grin on his face.

"Remember that time you shaved it all off?"

How could she forget? Every month the girls on her dormitory floor would gather in the rec room, giggling and laughing as one of them read all the polls and articles from that month's *Cosmo*. Just so happened that particular month was about personal grooming habits. And in one adventuresome moment, she took a fresh Lady Bic and proceeded to shave off every bit of pubic hair. Very carefully. The drastic change brought about this seductiveness in her. She felt more mature. Naughty. And Danny enjoyed the change even more than she did.

"I remember." Her words barely a whisper.

"Completely bare." His eyes were glazed, his mind trapped in a dreamlike state. "That was awesome." The smile on his face was not unlike that of the cat who ate the canary.

"Hardly. I regretted that decision for weeks to come."

For a few days she very much enjoyed the bareness. And his attention. But when it started to grow back, all the little hair follicles turned red and bumpy and itched terribly. At one point she found it difficult to concentrate in class, constantly dashing off to the restroom just so she could scratch herself in private. Never again would she do something so stupid.

"But still. I got to enjoy that then. Why not now? After all, I'm your husband now. Legal and everything." He waggled the metal band on his left hand in front of her. "Marriage should have its privileges."

She took several steps back until her rear bumped the bathroom vanity. "No." She fought hard to say it without smiling but she couldn't contain it. She repeated herself, hoping to sound more authoritative, sterner. At the very least she wanted to sound like she meant it. But her words of protest rang hollow even to her own ears. They both knew exactly how this little cat and mouse game would end; the only question that remained was when.

"Marriage isn't a good enough reason, especially since everyone knows your sex life pretty much ends once you get married."

He scoffed at her words, but she could see the wheels turning in his head. He was looking for another angle to play.

"Then how about you do it for your country? I'm a hero, you know."

She couldn't hold back the laughter this time and soon he was laughing along with her. Finally, she caught her breath. "I've missed this," she said, the words escaping before her brain caught up and stopped them.

He stared at her for a long time, a half smile on his face. "Me, too."

Then, as if he was embarrassed by the admission, Danny glanced at his watch and pushed away from the door frame with both hands. "All right. I've gotta go. And since there's nothing to see here . . ."

She pushed the bathroom door closed behind him and tested the shower to see if the water was warm. After quickly undressing, she took a good hard look at the reflection in the mirror. Completely bare. Everywhere.

What could it hurt anyway?

She grabbed the towel from the counter and quickly wrapped it around her. When she stepped into the hall, Danny was almost to the front door, keys jingling in his hand while his ruck hung from one shoulder.

"Hey, Danny." With his palm on the doorknob he turned around to face her. Bree waited until she had his full, undivided attention and then, when his eyes met hers, she grasped the tucked end of the towel and let it fall to the floor, leaving her standing there in all her naked glory. "Have a nice day."

His jaw dropped along with his keys. The rucksack also hit the floor as he prowled toward her.

Bree waggled a finger at him. "Nuh uh uh. You'll be late."

Danny clenched his fists and groaned in frustration before retracing his steps. He walked backward to the door, unwilling to take his eyes off her. "I'll get you for this, Dunbar," he growled. "Mark my words." He picked his things up from the floor, giving her a playful wink as he headed out the door.

Bree grabbed up her towel and walked into the bathroom, catching sight of her flushed skin in the mirror.

What had possessed her to do such a thing?

The giggle bubbled up from deep inside until she could no longer hold it in. One crazy little action and suddenly she felt more like her old self than she had in a very long time. Fun. Playful. Sometimes naughty. A little sexy.

Especially when Danny looked at her that way.

"Love the hair," Marie said, holding open the front door.

Bree smiled. "I found it at the party store and couldn't resist."

"Has Danny seen it?"

"Nope."

Marie laughed as she gathered the kids and their abundance of stuff. Within minutes they were all loaded up in her minivan and on their way to the parade.

Danny forewarned her that St. Patrick's Day took on a Mardi Gras vibe in Savannah. Each year, thousands of tourists dressed all in green invaded the normally quiet, historic city for one of the largest parades in the country. At first she was content to stay at home and avoid the whole ruckus. At least until she found out Danny would be marching in the parade, as that was tradition for the 1st Ranger Battalion.

So the day before she stopped at a local party store and found the amount of St. Patty's Day stuff to be truly astonishing. Stacks upon stacks of green bowler hats. Short and long wigs in varying shades of green. Beads. Boas. "Kiss me I'm Irish" buttons. You name it, they had it. Deciding a hat would look far better on her than green synthetic hair, Bree chose one with a black band and sequined shamrock. But as she made her way to the checkout she happened upon an amazing wig—a huge mass of bright red-orange spiraling curls styled in long layers. She pulled it from the clear packaging and tried it on, knowing immediately she had to have it. And, just for added fun, she topped it with a little rhinestone tiara, making herself an Irish princess.

Who cared if Ireland didn't have a royal family? Or that she was actually Scottish? Close enough.

The crowds were unbelievable. There were times when

Myrtle Beach would be crowded with tourists, and homecoming weekend in college was kind of crazy. But she'd never seen anything like this. People from all walks of life dressed in every type of green clothing imaginable. There were the socialite types, with their stylish clothes and fancy hats. Then you had men with huge beer bellies who painted their faces in green, white, and orange. And here she thought she was being edgy with her bright red curls.

They parked in a church parking lot and still had to walk several blocks to the parade route. While Marie wrangled the twins and argued with a disinterested Leah, who spent most of the time with her head down, staring at her phone, Bree took the easier task of pushing the stroller with an adorable Hannah. Dressed in a green tutu and coordinating headband, she was quite the little flirt, smiling and babbling at all those who passed by.

On Bull Street they found several other regiment wives. After the brief introductions, she and Marie unfolded their chairs and settled in. There seemed to be an endless number of high school marching bands and crepe paper floats, along with bagpipers wearing tartan kilts.

"Is that all you brought?"

It took Bree a moment to realize Marie was talking about her small crossbody purse. "Should I have brought something else?"

"Figures Danny wouldn't tell you about the tradition. All along the parade route women rush out into the street and kiss the troops. Kissing bandits, they call us. By the time they reach the end, the guys are decked out in green beads, green leis and covered in lipstick."

Bree shook her head. "I didn't know. I don't have anything like that."

"That's okay. I have plenty." Marie pulled a bag from the storage compartment of Hannah's stroller. "As a matter of fact, I order it in bulk from an online party store."

"I do have lipstick, though." Bree pulled a pale pink lipstick from her bag.

Marie pushed her hand away. "No way. That won't do. Put it away." From her purse she pulled out a black tube and removed the cap, revealing a Crayola-red lipstick. "If you're going to do it, you have to do it right."

A block away, 1st Battalion rounded the corner and began making their way toward them. Unlike the other groups, they kept coming and coming, a massive sea of camouflaged uniforms and tan berets.

"How many guys are there?"

"The entire battalion?" Marie paused to smooth the bright red color over her lips. "About six hundred or so."

"How am I supposed to find him? I'll never be able to find him."

Marie placed a hand on her arm. "They march as companies so that makes it easier. Also those who are staff sergeants or higher walk along the outside. They say it's to keep an eye on the younger guys, but I think it's so they get the most attention." Marie laughed. "Even so, we try to sit in about the same place every year, so they'll be looking for us."

According to Marie, after the flag bearers came the battalion commanders and other officers that were part of HQ.

"Michael will be in with this group."

"Wouldn't that be weird? Kissing my brother-in-law?"

"No. A lot of times the mothers will come and kiss their sons on the cheek along with their buddies. Just a way to show someone is thinking of them. But if you're going to do it, you need this." She handed her the tube of bright red lipstick.

"Last time I wore this color was for a dance recital when I was nine."

Marie laughed. "I'm afraid I left my bright blue eye shadow at home. So this will be all you get."

Since the one thing they didn't bring was a mirror, Bree let Marie put the lipstick on for her. Satisfied with her work, she gave Bree a little push, sending her into the street, strands of beads dangling from her hands. She spotted Michael, green beads hanging around his neck and an abundance of smeared red lip stains on his face. She called his name and gave a little wave, unsure if she should run into their formation or just wait at the sidelines. Thankfully, Michael came to her and leaned down, offering his cheek. "Nice hair."

"Why, thank you," she said, draping another strand of beads around his neck. "Looks like I'm not the first one to get ahold of you."

"Afraid not," he said with a smile. "But you're the only one I'd go to willingly."

"That bad, huh?"

Mike simply nodded as he retook his place within the battalion.

Bree laughed as she made her way back to Marie. "Well, that was fun."

"See? I told you."

Row after row of men in tan berets marched past. Although Marie said she'd tell her when, Bree couldn't help but scan the many rows of men marching past, looking for Danny.

"Here comes Charlie Company." She took one more look a Bree. "You need to reapply."

"Oh, no. Surely I have enough."

The words had barely escaped her mouth when Marie grasped her chin and came at her with the lipstick for a second time.

"Hon, you need to load it up. Mark your man. Let all those other women out there know Danny MacGregor is definitely taken. And before I forget." Marie pulled a long green feather boa from her bag. "Give him one of these while you're at it."

"I'm not so sure about this. What if Danny doesn't like it?"

Marie shoved it into her hands. "He's gonna love it. I promise."

Then just as Marie said, Bree spotted Danny walking along the outside of the formation. By the look of his face and the amount of beads around his neck, he was just as popular as his brother, if not more.

"Come on, Bree." Marie grabbed her hand and darted into the street. "It's go time!"

LIKE SEVERAL OTHER times already that morning, a woman burst from the crowd and ran up to him. But like any good husband, Danny kept his eyes straight ahead and continued marching forward while the kissing bandit tried to have her way with him. It was all in good fun. Any other year he fully appreciated each and every one of the women he encountered along the way. But this year was different. This year there was only one woman he wanted.

Especially after that little stunt this morning. Calling his attention and then dropping her towel. Even after all these years she still was, by far, the sexiest woman he'd ever seen. It took every ounce of his self-restraint to not chase her down, throw her over his shoulder, take her back to bed, and run his mouth all over her.

As C-Co neared Olgethorpe Avenue, Danny's eyes scanned the crowded sidewalks in search of Bree, knowing she'd be sitting with several other wives. A blur of orange and green raced up to him but he kept this one at a distance.

He held up a hand while still looking over her head to the crowd. "Not now, sweetheart. How about one of the other guys?"

"Danny?"

For the first time he looked at the woman's face and realized it was his wife. "Oh, my God," he said, pushing the fire-colored curls back from her face. "I didn't even recognize you."

She raised a brow, giving him a skeptical smile. "And yet, you still called me 'sweetheart.' "

Shit.

Momentarily stunned, he wasn't sure what to say. But

the time he found the words to apologize she was laughing at him.

Danny narrowed his eyes at her. "I'll get you for that."

"Promise?" Bree smiled and draped the feather boa around his neck, following it up with a quick peck to his lips.

But a peck was far from enough.

Before she got too far away, he took hold of her hand. With a swift tug and a graceful spin, she was back in his arms. All sparkle and smile. A mischievous glint in her eyes with those crazy orange curls. This was the girl he fell in love with all those years before. So goddamn beautiful, his heart ached.

"Dan—" His name became an unfinished gasp.

With one arm wrapped about her waist, another at her neck, he brought his mouth to hers, bending her backward, making escape impossible. She relaxed not only into his embrace, but his kiss. The crowds around them erupted, an uproar of hoots and wolf whistles and applause as he took his time and deepened the kiss. Even his brothers-in-arms cheered him on as they continued marching past. When air became necessary, the kiss ended, leaving them both dazed and smiling as they tried to catch their breath. But he wasn't done with her yet and placed quick pecks upon her jaw, her neck, leaving a trail of faded red lipstick on her skin, marking her for all to see.

She squirmed in his arms. "I know what you're doing," she said, laughing and pushing at his shoulder. "Knock it off!"

"Consider this payback."

Finally, Danny righted her back on her feet and took a good, long look at her. Her eyes sparkled. Her skin flushed beneath the smear of lipstick. But it was her laugh that resonated deep in his soul.

God, he had missed that sound.

"Having fun?" he asked.

"Too much, I think." She walked alongside him for several feet, using her fingers to wipe some of the lipstick from his face. "You're a mess," she said, giggling.

"That's okay. Leave it." He took hold of her fingers and kissed them before letting her go. "Let it serve as a warning to all the others."

Chapter Fifteen

As much as he hated to admit it, he'd missed his bed. His great, big, girlie bed. Yes, it had the softest, thickest mattress known to man. And he'd spent a shitload on the pillows alone. But after spending days, weeks, sometimes months living and sleeping in the crappiest of places on earth, Danny thought he'd earned a nice fluffy bed to come home to. Deserved it, really. Then he did the gentlemanly thing and offered it to his wife while he slept on the couch.

Such an idiot.

Knowing Bree would be in the shower a good ten, fifteen minutes despite her lack of hair anywhere, Danny stripped down to his boxer briefs and collapsed onto the bed. Hands tucked behind his head, he settled in and closed his eyes. Although the room was quiet, his mind was far from still. Images of Bree shuffled in his mind like a slideshow.

Bree wearing his T-shirt.

Bree in a towel.

Naked Bree.

And if that wasn't enough, curly red-headed Bree with bright red lipstick on her gorgeous mouth. It was a look that made him instantly hard as he imagined her leaving a trail of red lipstick on his body as she worked his way from his mouth, down his chest, below his waist to his—

The bathroom door opened and Danny cracked one eye open to see light stream across the hall and into the bedroom, illuminating Bree's path. Damn. He was just getting to the good part. But this was nice, too. A cloud of steam followed in her wake, carrying with it the same scent that had come to permeate every nook and cranny of his once stale apartment. He loved the smell, whatever it was. A blend of something citrus and sweet reminding him of lemonade and sugar cookies. But most of all, it always made him think of Bree, of her bright smile and sparkling eyes and freckles dotting her nose.

"Do you want me to turn out the light?" she whispered.

Danny closed his eyes and groaned, knowing his time in the big, comfy bed was nearing its end. "Nah. I'm getting ready to hop in the shower."

But he found it impossible to move, much less make any real effort to get up.

Her hands punched and smacked the down pillows, fluffing them, before the bed dipped to his left as she climbed in. Although his eyes remained closed he could tell from her movements she was stretching out alongside him, the scent of her so very close now, bringing her warmth, as well. In his mind they were lying on a sandy beach somewhere instead of a crummy little apartment in Savannah.

"This bed is big enough for the two of us, Danny," she whispered again, jolting him from his momentary dreamlike state. "There's really no need for you to sleep on the couch."

Good God. Her words were a song from heaven. An invitation from an angel.

Or maybe the devil's temptation.

"I don't mind the couch."

Damn liar. He didn't sound convincing even to his own ears.

"It's up to you. Offer still stands."

The bed shifted again and he sensed her rolling onto her side, most likely facing away from him. Within the minute she rolled over once again, punching her pillow, sighing loudly, obviously restless. If she'd let him rest in peace just a few minutes more, he'd get out of her way and let her have the entire bed to herself. Or maybe all that tossing and turning was an attempt to chase him off sooner rather than later.

"What does this mean?" she asked.

He had no clue in hell what she was referring to so Danny cracked open one eye and turned to face her. If she was baiting him into that dreaded minefield of relationship analysis, he was out of here.

"Your tattoo," she clarified.

Definitely dodged a bullet. Small talk about his tattoo he could handle.

"Which one are you talking about?" He really wasn't in the mood for chitchat, but it allowed him a few more minutes to close his eyes again and relax.

She shifted again, this time close enough the mattress dipped beneath his back. Then he felt the tip of her finger upon his skin, alighting every nerve in his body as she traced the inked script on his inner biceps.

"It's Latin, right? What does it say?"

He was having difficulty remembering. Her scent, her warmth, her touch, all of it wreaking havoc on his brain. Not to mention the sudden blood loss to parts farther south.

As she reached the final letters of his tattoo—*aut inveniam viam aut faciam*—she paused only a moment then worked her way from the end back to the beginning.

He cleared his throat before forcing the words out. "It means 'I shall either find a way or make one.' "

She repeated the words several times as if committing them to memory. "Where is it from?"

This time he opened his eyes to find she was sitting upright, her legs crossed beneath her as she looked down at him.

"It's not from anywhere, really. Hannibal said it."

Her brow crinkled. "Hannibal? As in Lecter?"

Danny chuckled and rolled onto his side toward her. "No, not Hannibal Lecter," he said. Of course, she mirrored his position and lay down, facing him with a sweet smile on her face. He couldn't help but smile back.

Stupid bastard.

Instead of fleeing for the door like he should be doing,

he furthered their conversation. Initiated closeness. Mere inches separated their bodies, their faces. Even in the half dark of the bedroom, he noticed the spark in her eyes, bright with curiosity.

"It's a quote from Hannibal, the military commander. During the Second Punic War, he marched his troops and war elephants over the Pyrenees and the Alps—"

She placed her palm on his biceps. "Wait a minute. War elephants?"

"The military used elephants not only to transport food and weapons, but they trained them to attack front lines and trample the enemy."

She sat up a bit, her eyes going wide. "That sounds horrific."

Danny shrugged. "That's war."

The words were barely out of his mouth and he wished he could take them back. Even if they were the truth. The last thing he wanted to do was scare the wits out of her. In the future he'd need to find a balance between the truth and a lie. Maybe sugarcoating things just a bit would be the best option. The last thing he needed her doing was worrying about him when she needed to focus on herself, on getting stronger.

"Are you going to finish the story?" she asked.

Only then did he realize he'd been silent too long.

"Are you going to interrupt me again?" Bree narrowed her eyes, making him laugh. "Okay. So the Romans were prepared for an attack from the sea and had soldiers waiting for them along the Mediterranean coast. That's why Hannibal wanted to attack from the north and take the Romans by surprise. But to do that, he had to move his troops over the mountains. His superiors told him it couldn't be done. Because of the harsh conditions he lost a lot of men and most of his elephants, but the idea worked. It exposed Italy to a northerly attack. Now he's considered one of the greatest military strategists ever."

Her eyes drifted back to the tattoo, her fingers tracing his skin once again. "That makes sense, I guess." Her lips quirked, as if holding back a smile. "For a second there I was worried you tattooed quotes from a fictional serial killer on your body."

She shifted slightly and her tank top inched higher, revealing a sliver of skin above the waistband of her pajama bottoms. His fingers itched to touch her, to stroke her warm flesh beneath his palm. His mouth watered from want of tasting her, to sample her sweetness, to roll her body beneath his and lick every inch of her skin.

Her finger now grazed a scar near his collarbone, still pink and raised in its newness. "What's this from?"

"A tree."

Bree laughed. "You're so full of it."

"Nope. It was a tree. We were training in the woods at night, wearing night-vision goggles. I tripped, landed on a branch from a freshly downed limb. Straight in, straight out. Damn lucky, considering. If you don't believe me, ask Mike. After all, that scar's his handiwork."

"Did it hurt?"

"Like a son of a bitch. Of course my ego took the brunt of that beating. The guys still give me a hard time about it every time we train in the woods."

She lifted her hand to his face, tracing the faint line on the underside of his chin. "Now this one, I know," she said, smiling as she ran her finger along the scar he acquired at the ripe old age of nine. "You were such a little show-off."

"That's what I get for trying to impress a girl."

His dad had given him a brand-new bike for his birthday. The first one he'd ever had since all the others had been handed down from Mike. Although he'd only had it a few hours, he was determined to be popping wheelies by the end of the day. Didn't matter the bike was too big for him; he was going to do it. And he did. Popped one wheelie and then another. Then she came out of her house and he called out for her to watch him. That was when things went a little sideways and he face-planted into a neighbor's mailbox.

"And this?" Her finger trailed the no longer perfect line of his nose.

He smiled. "Officially? Caught an elbow in the face during a pickup game of basketball."

She raised a brow. "And the truth?"

"Got into a bar fight with a bunch of trash-talking jarheads while on leave in Florida."

Bree shook her head in disbelief. "Always the troublemaker."

The last was the scar across his eyebrow. "That's from a rock."

"First a tree, now a rock. I'm not sure I believe you this time."

"To be honest, I don't really know. Only that we were

on patrol, going house to house in this little village at the base of the mountains. An IED exploded and kicked up a bunch of rocks, debris, shrapnel. Took seven stitches. My eye was swollen shut a couple of days, but nothing permanent."

At least not permanent for him.

What he didn't want to tell her was the blast killed one man and resulted in two others losing multiple limbs.

Her eyes filled with worry and Danny held his breath, hoping what he said was enough to satisfy her curiosity. She opened her mouth to say something then closed it again as if she thought better of it. Their own little version of "don't ask, don't tell."

THERE WAS MORE to the story. From the tension in his body and hurt in his eyes she could only assume the worst. If he chose to talk about it she would listen, but she refused to push. She learned long ago, forcing him into a conversation only garnered a ton of aggravation instead of answers.

"Believe it or not, of the three, the tree hurt the most," he said, the right corner of his mouth lifting almost into a half smile.

That was a tactic she recognized. Making light of a situation as a means of distraction was classic Danny MacGregor behavior. Did he assume she'd forgotten all of his old tricks? Hardly. The more things changed, the more they stayed the same.

But her heart still ached to comfort him, so Bree

pressed a gentle kiss to that faint line slashing his brow. The physical scar might be less noticeable than the rest, but instinct told her the emotional scar ran far, far deeper. She moved on to the other battle scars, a brush of lips across his imperfect nose, another pressed to the small scar on his chin. She caressed his cheek, the day-old stubble prickly against her palm. Dark blue eyes stared up at her and she found herself silently willing him to say something, anything.

What she received in return was more silence, so she let it go and whispered good-night.

She placed a hand upon his chest only to use him as leverage as she rolled back to her side of the bed. Instead, he trapped her hand beneath his, keeping her there. This time when she met his gaze, everything shifted instantly. What began as comfort gave way to want, which quickly transformed to an undeniable need. Beneath her palm his skin was hot, his muscles rigid. His pulse pounded in the hollow of his throat and she was struck with the overwhelming urge to press her lips to his skin, to feel his blood hammer beneath her lips and taste the salt of his skin on her tongue. Before she talked herself out of it, Bree pressed her mouth to his neck.

His hand moved to her hip, strong calloused fingers digging into her flesh through her flannel pajama bottoms. When she nipped at his flesh with her teeth, he'd had enough of her teasing and pushed her onto her back. It didn't matter that he was so much stronger than her; she fought to pull him completely on top of her, wanting his body to blanket her own.

Instead, he trapped her hands beneath his, giving her only a little of his weight where his hips rested upon hers.

God, she had missed this. The heat and ache and want. She missed surrendering control, his mouth covering hers, his tongue winding hotly around hers. For the first time in a very long time she was desperate to have a man inside her. Not just any man, though. She wanted Danny. For as long as he would have her. If only a week or a month or a year, it didn't matter to her. A broken heart was well worth the price of feeling alive.

His mouth trailed down her neck to her shoulder and she scrabbled for purchase, her nails scraping across skin. When he countered with a frantic move of his own, grasping the hem of her T-shirt and shoving it upward, she gasped in surprise.

Then, just as quickly as it began, it ended.

Danny lowered her shirt back into place then distanced himself by sitting back on his heels. "Dammit." He shook his head, his breath rushing in and out of his lungs. "I'm sorry."

Bree tried to catch her breath as she propped herself on her elbows. "You didn't do anything wrong, Danny."

"The hell I didn't." His head hung from his shoulders while he roughly scrubbed one hand across his face. She reached out for him, wanting to reestablish that powerful connection. Instead, he practically leaped off the bed to avoid her touch and raced from the room. "I'm gonna sleep on the couch."

Oh, hell no. He was not getting off that easy.

She climbed off the bed and followed, hot on his heels.

"Why are you running away?"

Danny threw his pillow and blanket on the loveseat and headed into the kitchen. "Because you don't want this, Bree."

"I don't? Well, that's shocking and offensive all at the same time. I'm a grown woman, Danny, not the little girl you used to know."

"Believe me. I know that." He yanked open the refrigerator with such force she was surprised he didn't pull the door from its hinges.

"I can make up my own mind about what I do or do not want."

"I agree." Still refusing to make eye contact, he pulled out a beer and slammed the door shut.

"Then what's the problem? We're adults." Right now though, it took every ounce of her self-restraint to not stomp her feet and wave her fists like the little girl she used to be. "We can have sex if we want to. And it doesn't have to mean a thing."

Danny popped the can open and stared into the top, in no hurry to take a drink. "You deserve better than that."

Argh. She wanted to scream. And she would have if it hadn't been so late at night and she didn't want to disturb the neighbors. The man was so unbelievably frustrating, she wanted to strangle him.

She stomped off to the bedroom and grabbed one of his hoodies from the closet, throwing it on over her pajama top. Then she slipped on her shoes and grabbed her purse.

"You can take the bed," she spat. "I'll sleep on the couch when I get back."

That got his attention and finally he looked at her. "Where are you going?"

On the way to the door, she grabbed the car keys from off the breakfast bar. "For a drive. I need some air."

"Bree, please don't go. I'm sorry."

She stopped at the door and turned to face him. "Sorry for what, Danny? For not desiring me? For not taking advantage of the situation even though I want you to? I can hardly blame you for that. You're a good man. Maybe too good."

Bree opened the door, only to have it slammed shut again and stay that way as Danny pressed one strong hand against it. Her gaze trailed from that hand to his wrist, along the flexed muscles in his forearm to his shoulder, finally, turning enough to see his face. She couldn't tell if he was angry or hurt or something else altogether.

"What the hell are you doing, Danny?"

"Not letting you go."

Chapter Sixteen

DANNY PUSHED HER against the door, trapping her there with both hands. "You think I'm a good man? I'm not." He slid his hands from her shoulders, over her breasts to her hips, finally filling his palms with the sweet curves of her ass. He lifted her from the floor, leveraged her back against the door and pulled her knees up to his waist. "You think I don't want you?" He ground his erection into the warm heaven between her thighs. The sound of her sharp inhale made him crazy, driving him to do it over and over only to hear her make the sound again and again.

"I've been walking around in a fucking daze because you're in my head so much. I can't think of anything else other than spreading your legs wide and tasting every inch of you or of burying myself deep inside you." He buried his face in her neck, trying to regain some semblance of control. "Jesus, I was so lost in the thought of you this past week I'm surprised I wasn't shot during live fire training."

"You're joking." Her words were hot and breathy on his skin as he bit the tender flesh beneath her ear. "Please tell me you're joking."

"Not even the slightest bit."

She must have believed him this time, grasping his face with both hands as she ravaged his mouth. And he was lost. In her warmth, her touch. Her fingernails scraped across his neck and scalp. With his hair cut so short, she couldn't grip it in her hands so she took hold of his ears instead. Her tongue stroked and tangled with his, allowing him a taste of her as she slid her hands down his throat, across his collarbones, alternating between smoothing over his skin and clutching at his flesh. She broke the kiss and retreated just enough to catch his lower lip between her teeth. Her bite was far from gentle, sending a shock of electricity throughout his body and awakening every nerve.

"Not here," he groaned. With his hands cupping her bottom, he stepped away from the door and headed for the bedroom.

Wrapping her arms tight around his neck, she pressed herself against him, leaving no space between. "I was looking forward to the door," she whispered. She caught his earlobe between her lips, flicking it with her tongue as he walked them down the hallway.

"So anyone walking past would hear? No way."

With his luck, someone would show up wanting something. Like his brother, for instance. The guy who had the shittiest timing in the world. The same guy who had taken every opportunity to remind him how this thing between him and Bree was a huge fucking mistake.

Although they had the apartment all to themselves, he kicked the bedroom door shut behind them. Blocking out Mike. Blocking out the whole rest of the world. In here, it was just the two of them, where nothing and no one could ever come between them.

With her still in his arms, he climbed onto the bed, walking on his knees until he reached the middle, setting her there.

She hastily reached for the zipper pull on the hoodie she'd commandeered from his closet minutes earlier. He pulled her hands away from the fastener, holding them at her sides beneath his. While he'd held her against the door, she had him at the disadvantage. Now it was his turn.

Danny leaned in but purposely avoided her lips. He kissed her cheek, her jaw. Grasping the zipper pull between his fingers, he eased it down, taking his damn sweet time. He didn't need to look in her eyes to see her impatience. He could practically feel the frustration rolling off her in waves. But without knowing what the future held for the two of them, it was better to believe they might only have this one chance. He absolutely refused to rush, sliding his hands into the sleeves at her shoulders, his palms smoothing over her flesh as he pushed the fabric from her arms.

"Danny, please." Her chest rose and fell heavier with each uneven breath.

He placed a kiss upon the tender skin at the hollow of her throat. "In a hurry? Have somewhere you need to be?" A soft moan escaped her mouth as his lips skimmed across her collarbone to the lacy strap of her tank top.

"Absolutely not," she replied. He curled his fingers around the fabric, pulling it over the cap of her shoulder, his mouth tasting the newly revealed flesh. "But it's been so long."

A thrill ran through him knowing that. He wasn't stupid enough to think she hadn't been with anyone else in the past ten years. But a part of him deep down inside liked the idea of being her first of sorts for the second time in her life. As if that made any damn sense.

Danny grasped the hem of her tank top and she followed his lead. Bree raised up her arms as he lifted it over her head and tossed it to the floor. Almost instantly, her hands folded over her belly.

"Maybe this wasn't such a good idea, after all."

She was trying to hide the long scar he'd seen only minutes before. The same one that had sent him running from the room. Not because he found it ugly. Instead, it served as a reminder of all the pain she'd already suffered and he feared adding to it. Then she chased after him. Strong. Determined. Ready to fight. Suddenly, that scar resembled one of his own. A sign of strength instead of weakness. Just like him, she'd been battle tested and wounded. And just like him, she'd pushed her way through and made it to the other side.

And his heart could no longer resist her.

"I disagree," he whispered against her lips. "I think

you were absolutely right the first time. This is a very good idea."

She squeezed her eyes shut, refusing to look at him. Taking hold of her hands, Danny kissed the center of each palm then guided her to link her hands around his neck. Leveraging his weight on his hands, he eased her back until she lay flat on the bed. With each kiss, each breath they shared, she relaxed beneath him.

He moved down her body, nuzzling the soft underside of her breast. She gasped the moment his teeth scraped her taut nipple then sighed softly when he laved it with his tongue. That hadn't changed. Those were the same sounds she made years ago and his body recognized each one. He eased his way down her body, tasting her skin as he went. He ran his tongue just above the edge of her plaid pajama pants, before hooking his fingers into the waistband. She lifted her hips from off the bed, allowing him to pull her bottoms down then off her legs, revealing nothing, or everything, depending upon how one looked at it. She'd gone commando and he couldn't help but smile to himself. He settled between her knees, pressing chaste kisses to her inner thigh, her hip, to the rosy pink scar marring the pale skin of her stomach. Every muscle in her body tensed. And not in a good way.

He pressed up on his hands to meet her eyes. She was almost scowling, her forehead wrinkled, and a little crease had appeared between her brows. "Want to tell me what's going on?"

"What makes you think—"

"Christ, woman." He smiled. "The smoke alarms are

about to go off because the gears in your head are grinding so hard."

She dramatically flung one hand over her face, covering her eyes. "Just so you know, it may not happen."

He waited for her to elaborate, but she never did.

"It? As in orgasm? Why would you think that?"

She huffed in frustration. "After the first round of treatment, it was . . ." She uncovered her face, her gaze searching the ceiling as if the right word was hidden within the 1970s acoustic popcorn. "It was difficult. And I haven't gone for a test run after the second round of surgery."

"Not even solo?"

"Really?" Her head snapped up to look at him. "I lived with my parents. Who were *always* right there. And because of the cancer my mother felt she had the right to invade my privacy whenever she damn well felt like it."

He chuckled. "Wouldn't have stopped me."

"Oh, God." She closed her eyes and her head fell back to the bed.

Her laughter subsided and soon the smile disappeared from her face. Even through the darkness, he caught sight of the single tear that slipped down her cheek.

"To be honest," she whispered, "I kind of gave up hope."

Shit.

He could barely wrap his head around what she was saying. It wasn't that she merely gave up on self-pleasure. She gave up on the idea of intimacy and love and sex. He might have given up the dream of a woman to love and cherish the rest of his life. But Bree . . . she gave up on living.

And fuck if that didn't nearly kill him.

He fought the urge to pull her into his arms and comfort her, to hold her until she let all the sadness go. But if he did that, she'd be pissed. She'd find a way to twist it, interpret his care and concern as pity and then she'd be right back in that same place.

Instead, he took everything he really wanted to say and everything he really wanted to do and put it in a kiss. A gentle press of his lips to hers, until she slanted her mouth against his and took him deeper, allowing him to taste her as he stroked her tongue with his. He trailed his lips across her jaw, down her neck, making his way to her shoulder. But as he moved lower, she tensed beneath him.

"Do you want to stop?" He raked his fingertips over the soft skin of her belly, large, sweeping motions from one side to the other, her muscles quivering beneath his touch.

"Not at all. I was just trying to lower expectations."

He ducked his head, smiling against her skin as he pressed a kiss to the crease at the top of her thigh. "For you? Or for me?" His fingers trailed lower, stroking, teasing the bare flesh he'd been fantasizing about the whole damn day.

"Both of us, I guess?"

"Sounds like a challenge to me." He pressed her legs wide, his mouth hovering over her center. Close enough that when he spoke his breath fanned across her skin, but far enough away she didn't get any of what she really wanted. "You're forgetting two very important things."

"And those would be?"

"One." He pushed one finger carefully inside her, inciting a soft gasp from her lips. With slow, smooth strokes, Danny studied her face for any hint of pain or discomfort. "At one point in time I knew your body almost as well as my own. Or have you forgotten all those 'lab sessions' we used to have?"

Bree half smiled, half giggled. "Maybe that was true in high school, but things are different now."

She was fooling her damn self if she truly believed he didn't remember all of her little sounds. The gasps, the sighs of pleasure, the soft moans. Those sounds haunted his dreams for years after he left. He wouldn't forget those any more than all the things he did to make her crazy. And if what turned her on now did differ from ten years ago, well, he was bound and determined to figure it all out. Again.

"Not so different," he said, continuing to pump slowly. Her eyelids fluttered. Her breathing slowed. Her body arched slightly into his touch. "And the second thing . . ."

He added a second finger and again her breathing hitched, followed by a long, soft moan. God, that sound. It took every ounce of his self-control to not strip off his boxer briefs and enter her in one hard thrust. But this being her first time in who knows how long, he needed to keep things at a careful pace. Despite her inner muscles clenching around his fingers. Despite the sounds she made whenever he stroked that special place inside her.

She wasn't completely ready for him, and without a doubt he'd hurt her if he jumped the gun.

"And?"

His head snapped up to see she was looking directly at him. The fact she was following the conversation meant he wasn't doing his job very well. Especially since he was aroused to the point of pain and had completely forgotten what he was going to say in the first place. He took a slow, measured breath, fighting to retain his control.

"What's the second thing?"

He needed to overwhelm her senses. Needed to get her out of her head if he was going to achieve his goal.

"The second thing is Rangers never quit."

The sound of her laughter was music and torture and humiliation all at the same time. "Oh. My. God," she said, laughing. "That's *so* damn cheesy. I can't believe you just said—"

Her words ended on a gasp as he fastened his mouth to her clit, sucking, licking, biting, showing absolutely no mercy. He couldn't hold back now if he tried, spurred on by the taste and smell and feel of her until he had her writhing beneath him. Her feet skidded atop the comforter, unable to gain any traction, her hands fisted in the sheets. She tried to squirm away, but he held her firmly in place, living out the fantasy that had been playing on repeat in his mind for the past few weeks.

When her extensive vocabulary was reduced to the breathless, repetitive exclamations of his name, God, and fuck, in that exact order, he knew she was on the edge. He increased the thrust of his fingers, sucked hard upon her flesh and within seconds her body went taut, bowing off the mattress. Her head fell back, her mouth open wide in a silent scream. He held her there, seeing her through to the very end until she finally collapsed into a quivering heap, a light sheen of sweat covering her body.

He pressed a kiss to her stomach and another over her heart before she pushed him away as if her nerves were far too sensitive to tolerate any more. He stretched out alongside her, his head resting on his hand with a smug smile of satisfaction on his face as they both attempted to catch their breath.

"You deserve a medal for that," she said without opening her eyes.

Danny chuckled. "That would definitely make for an interesting ceremony when the commendation was read, but I'd accept it with pride."

She turned to look at him now, a half grin on her face. Bree took hold of his hand and limply twined her fingers with his, resting his hand upon her chest where he could feel the racing of her heart. "As great as that was, I want to feel you inside me."

"You're sure about that?"

He held his breath, waiting for her response.

"Absolutely." Her half grin now expanded into a full-blown smile. "For the first time in a very long time I feel alive and I don't want it to end."

"OKAY, THEN. I'LL be right back."

Looking like the cat who ate the canary, Danny

pressed a quick kiss to her lips before rolling off the bed and racing to the bathroom.

His quick exit was a good thing. Because if he hadn't rushed out of the room, she likely would have told him that birth control was unnecessary. Then, wanting to understand, he would have asked a lot of questions. She'd have no choice but to tell him everything then. Which would likely lead to one of two outcomes: either he'd look at her with pity, which would make her want to strangle him, or he'd run away out of some screwed-up fear of hurting her. Either way, everything would stop and their opportunity would be squandered.

Instead, she wanted the thrill and the heat and feel of him inside of her, surrounding her. She wanted to lose her mind and pretend the last several years hadn't happened. Pretend the surgeries and chemo and cancer never happened at all. If only for a short while, she wanted to feel beautiful. Sexy. She wanted to feel like the girl he loved ten years ago.

He returned just as quickly and tossed the small foil package onto the bed next to her.

She raised a brow. "Only one?"

Danny shook his head and smiled. "Be nice," he teased.

Bree settled in, tucking her hands beneath her head as she watched him strip out of his boxer briefs. Of course he made a show out of it, turning, bending, and flexing. He was absolutely stunning and he knew it. Part of her found it impossible to believe this was the same boy she once knew. Gone was the good-looking athletic teen, replaced with a man who rivaled Adonis. She giggled as he crawled up the bed wearing nothing more than a smile as he straddled her body, bracing his weight on his hands. He lowered his head as if to give her a kiss, but quickly pulled back to look at her, a mischievous glint in his dark blue eyes.

"Who's not being nice now?" she asked while running her hands from his wrists, up his arms. His eyelids drifted shut as she touched him, taking her time to admire all the hard curves and ridges of his muscles, all that strength and power on display. Her palms swept over his shoulders and behind his neck, bringing his mouth down to hers. This time he didn't pull away; instead, he kissed her tenderly, taking his time and thoroughly tasting her. Her hands drifted to his chest, his abdomen.

"You're shaking," he whispered.

She hadn't noticed it until he pointed it out. But now that he said something, she realized her hands trembled against his stomach.

He spoke against her mouth. "Just like our first time together, except I was the one shaking back then."

She pushed him away, just far enough to meet his eyes. "I don't remember that."

"Oh, I do." Danny chuckled. "I was scared shitless. And I had a million and one thoughts running through my head."

Bree narrowed her eyes. "Like what?" She didn't quite believe him because even as a teen he had exuded confidence.

"What if I put the condom on wrong? What if it tears?

What if she gets pregnant? What if I don't know what the fuck I'm doing? What if I hurt her? Even worse—" he paused for dramatic effect "—what if she laughs?"

She caressed his cheek, his jaw. Touched the dimple in his chin with the tip of her finger. "And you said the wheels were turning in my head."

He smiled at that. "I'm just struck by the odd similarity between then and now."

Bree leaned up to kiss his lips. "I promise not to laugh."

When she took his erection in her hand, his eyes drifted shut in ecstasy as she began to stroke him with a gentle caress. His breathing became ragged as she teased him, never giving him exactly what he wanted. And in doing so, she was swamped with long-forgotten feelings of lust and desire, even amusement, that she was capable of making such a strong and powerful man tremble beneath her touch.

"Oh hell, no," he groaned, carefully removing her grip. "A man only has so much self-control. And after your little stunt this morning, I've been on the verge of blowing a gasket all day. Not to mention the torture of the past few weeks. If I let you do that, history will definitely be repeating itself."

"What are you talking about?"

"How that first time it was over before I even got inside of you." He dipped his head, licking the tip of her breast before sucking her nipple into his mouth. Just as she arched into his attention he released her flesh with an audible pop. "Thank God for teenage libidos and quick recoveries."

"You totally did not." She giggled. "Did you?"

Not one ounce of embellishment as he stared at her with those dark blue eyes.

"Of course I did. I was sixteen and you were in my bed. Naked. Then you said, 'Do it now, Danny!' and I totally shot the mother lode." She laughed out loud at his impersonation of the teenage version of herself. He leveled a finger at her. "You promised not to laugh."

She clasped her hands over her mouth and fought to contain her laughter. Her eyes watered, her lungs burned.

"Keep laughing," he said, playfully chastising her. "You're going to hurt his feelings." Danny nodded to his erection and she burst out laughing all over again. But just to be on the safe side, she decided to give "him" a little encouragement. For the second time, Danny avoided her hands and rolled off her, settling against the pillows. He grabbed the foil packet and quickly sheathed himself then guided her to straddle him, his erection thick and hard beneath her.

"How did I not know that happened?"

His hands cupped her small breasts, his thumbs brushing their peaks. "Because I distracted you with lots and lots of foreplay," he whispered.

She thought back to that rainy, summer afternoon. How just like this evening he'd knelt between her legs. Suddenly, it all became abundantly clear. "And all this time I thought you were a born giver."

"I was a teenage boy desperate to lose his virginity," he said, smiling. "The first time I was a giver out of necessity. Not that I regret it one bit."

He leaned forward, wrapping her in the security of his arms, the dusting of hair on his chest tickling her breasts. Bree rose up on her knees and took him inside, a few tentative glides as she eased herself down, both of them moaning in satisfaction once he filled her completely.

She buried her face into his neck, breathing through the touches of pain and discomfort. Danny pressed kisses to her forehead, the side of her face. His fingers traced the gutter of her spine in long, soothing strokes.

"Are you okay?"

She could only nod in response. Everything she was feeling, the sensations of fullness and completion, the emotional intimacy and physical connection, all of it nearly overwhelmed her. Not until this very moment had she realized how much she missed being with a man.

But Danny wasn't just any man. He was the first man she'd ever loved. Perhaps the only man she would ever love.

Ten years might have passed, but their bodies remembered everything. The action. The reaction. The give and take. She rocked with him, Danny guiding her hips in slow and measured strokes, handling her with care as if she was fragile. It was a gentleness she appreciated at first as her body adjusted to him, but now she craved more. And as frustrating as it was for her, it had to be even worse for him. His jaw flexed and clenched with such force, she wouldn't be surprised if he cracked a few teeth before they were through. She tried to increase the pace, but he held her firm, his fingertips digging into her flesh.

"I won't break, Danny."

"I know that," he growled.

Still, he continued with his maddeningly slow pace.

Well, he wasn't the only one to remember things from their past. She remembered what drove him wild, what would make him lose control.

Bree grabbed his head, her nails digging into the tender flesh at the base of his skull, and kissed him hard, her tongue thrusting, winding hotly around his. She sucked his bottom lip into her mouth and bit down, nearly drawing blood. Then she finished him off by giving his lip a good tug before releasing it.

"Christ Almighty." In the blink of an eye, Danny tightened his grip and rolled them both until she was on her back, her hands now pinned to the mattress beneath his as he loomed over her, his eyes black with desire. She was unable to hide her satisfied smile.

"Is this what you want?" he asked through gritted teeth as he gave one good thrust.

"God, yes. A million times yes."

He kissed her back with that same intensity and she wrapped her legs around his waist, lifting to meet each of his urgent thrusts.

"Harder," she pleaded.

He groaned as if in physical pain, but gave her what she wanted, what they both wanted, hooking his arms behind her knees so he could drive deeper into her.

"Fuck, Bree. I'm close," he said, his breathing hot and labored on her neck. "So fucking close."

She knew he wanted her to come again, but she likely

wouldn't. And it didn't matter. He'd already given her so much. "It's okay, Danny," she whispered. "Let go."

With her blessing he increased his pace and raced toward completion, finally driving hard into her once, twice, as he came with a strangled groan. His body shuddered against hers as he murmured a string of expletives in her ear. Something else that hadn't changed. She smiled against his cheek and held him there, pleasantly surprised when a small tremor of bliss eased through her.

Danny pressed a kiss to her temple, brushed the tip of his nose against hers, finally resting his forehead against hers.

"Everything okay?" he asked, his words coming out in a winded rush. "I didn't hurt you, did I?"

Bree shook her head. "Not at all. It was perfect."

She sealed her reply with a kiss, an answer that was truth and lie all in one. Yes, he hadn't hurt her physically. But she couldn't help but fear that while her heart was fine for now, it was only a matter of time before he would shatter it into a million pieces.

Chapter Seventeen

DANNY SAID TO hell with his early-morning routine. He silenced his alarm and ignored his buzzing phone, choosing instead to sleep late. Actually, Bree slept late and he just watched her sleep, entranced by the quirk of her brows and flutter of her eyelashes as she dreamed. Occasionally, her lips would move as if she was speaking to someone, then soften into a smile, leaving him to wonder who she was dreaming of.

Instead of disrupting her sleep, he snuggled deep beneath the covers, relishing the warm press of her skin against his and the sound of her soft, restful exhales. It was the first time in a very long time that had happened, waking up next to a woman in his very own bed.

Before, when the army required him to live in the barracks, going back to the woman's place to hook up or splurging on a motel if he had the cash was the norm. Even after moving up the ranks and being allowed to move off post, it was a habit he stuck to, and the women he encountered never knew any different. In those early years he'd grown accustomed to sneaking out under the cover of darkness and avoiding awkward morning-after conversations and messy entanglements altogether. Just because he moved into his own place didn't mean that part of his life needed to change.

Then he proposed to Bree. Inviting her not only into his life and his apartment, but into his bed, too.

Not once did he consider just how much he would love being around her again. Hearing her laugh. Seeing her smile. Walking into his apartment after a long day or even longer week and having someone there to greet him. The fact they could no longer ignore the magnetic pull that existed between them wasn't surprising. What was surprising was that they'd fought their undeniable attraction this long.

He'd never intended for them to be more than platonic roommates. Yes, he'd teased her about enjoying all the benefits of marriage, but he hadn't meant anything by it. He was determined to help her no matter what. Of course, his father always said the road to hell was paved with good intentions.

After Bree finally woke that morning, they lazed around in bed for a bit longer then spent the morning puttering around and running errands together like they'd been married a lifetime. By late afternoon they found themselves downtown, walking along the river, feasting on corned beef sandwiches and listening to live music.

The beer line moved at a snail's pace despite the smaller Sunday crowds. Having enjoyed the parade and a lot of what Savannah had to offer, most of the tourists had packed up their belongings and headed home. Danny looked back to where Bree stood only a few feet from a music stage, her head bopping in time to the beat, a wide smile on her face. As if she sensed he was watching her, she glanced over her shoulder in his direction and when their eyes met, her eyes sparkled and smile widened. She raised a hand and waggled her fingers at him, igniting a warmth that slowly spread throughout his body.

God, she was adorable.

Despite her terrible dance moves and ugly plaid golfer's hat. Proving once again, without a doubt, he was completely and totally in love with her.

Of course, he'd always loved her. That had never changed in the past ten years, no matter how much he tried to deny it or push her from his mind. And now he was in deep.

"What'll it be?"

The guy working the beer truck stared down at him, eyebrows raised in question. It took a second for Danny's mind to shift gears. "Two Guinnesses, please."

"Sure thing," the man replied, shaking his head as he turned away from the open window.

Only after he pulled cash from his wallet did he see his own reflection in the glass and the big goofy grin on his face. No wonder the beer guy was looking at him like he was nuts. His reflection was that of a lovestruck teenager. And in a way, he felt like one.

Danny exchanged bills for drinks then eased his way

back through the crowd to where Bree stood. He snuck up behind her, pressing a quick kiss to the exposed skin just above her collar. She jumped and skittered a few steps away, before turning to see it was him.

"Jesus," she said, clutching her chest.

He chuckled. "Who'd you think it was?"

"I don't know. You just took me by surprise."

"I see that." Danny handed her a beer. "Try one of these."

Bree held the translucent cup in front of her face, eyeing its contents suspiciously. "It's black."

"It's good. I promise. Have I ever steered you wrong?"

She narrowed her eyes at him. "I don't think you want me to answer that."

Danny laughed. Clearly, he forgot who he was talking to. "Yeah, that was a loaded question. But just do me a favor and try it. If you don't like it, I'll get you something else. Promise." After using his index finger to make an X over his heart, Bree took a cautious sip. And then another. "What do you think?"

"Definitely doesn't taste like the watered-down tap beer I used to drink in college."

He smiled. "No, I'm sure it doesn't."

This time she took a real drink from the plastic cup, the thick foam clinging to her upper lip.

Before she had the chance to swipe it away, he took care of it for her. With the tip of his tongue, Danny licked away the foam then sucked her top lip into his mouth. And since he was already there and breaking all of his rules about PDAs, he followed up with a proper kiss.

"I tried calling you this morning."

Having recognized the voice, Danny took his sweet time pulling away from Bree and answered without turning around. "Decided to sleep in."

Bree's skin blushed from having been caught midkiss. "Clearly, I'm a bad influence," she said to his brother. "I didn't have my fill of corned beef yesterday and was determined to get some more before the weekend was over."

Finally, Danny turned to face him and watched as Michael's gaze traveled from Bree to him, then to their joined hands, his disapproval evident. Bree cracked under his brother's scrutiny and handed Danny her beer. "I have to run to the ladies' room."

What a chicken shit. But he'd let her run away if it saved her some embarrassment.

And right on cue, his brother started in as soon as Bree was out of earshot. "Still playing with fire, I see."

"Still using the same old metaphor, I see." Danny took a long drink of his beer and turned his attention to the stage.

God, he hated that saying. Playing with fire? If Mike wasn't careful Danny'd go all literal on his ass and light him on fire. A little lighter fluid. A match or two. Whoosh.

Mike folded his arms across his chest and stepped in closer, attempting to use his two additional inches of height to intimidate him. It worked for a while when they were kids. Now, not so much. "If things between you and Bree continue this way, it will end badly, Danny. You do realize that, don't you?"

"How so?"

"Because what I just saw sure didn't look like just friends or roommates or whatever you want to call it today. Unless things have changed between you two?"

For the life of him, he couldn't figure out what the hell Michael's problem was. Couldn't his brother see how happy Bree made him? Did Michael really want him to be miserable the rest of his damn life? Because now that Bree was back in his life, living with him, loving him, it was easy to see just how mediocre the past ten years had been. The army, he loved. The guys he stood shoulder to shoulder with, he loved. But something was always missing. He wasn't a complete idiot. He always knew exactly what it was, who it was, that was missing. And maybe he never gave himself the chance to try to find it again with someone else. But when you love someone the way he loved Bree, well, it was pretty fucking obvious to him she was irreplaceable.

Maybe he was stupid to fall so deeply into her, knowing this arrangement between them was temporary. But how many people would kill for a second chance? People easily say they'd give a year of their life for ten more minutes with the one they loved. He understood that. And although he knew his heart would be ripped to pieces when she walked away from him, no way could he ever regret these weeks or months that he'd have her one last time.

To keep from saying something he would regret, Danny shook his head and drank down the remainder of his beer in one shot. Then he stacked Bree's plastic cup inside his and drank down half of hers for good measure.

"Here's how I see it," Michael began. "For the first

time in I don't even know how long, you skipped your run. Usually you're the one to wake my ass up after you've crawled home from wherever the night before. So for you to suddenly change all your routines and ignore my messages, it was a little surprising. And then I got to thinking. In your whole life, you've only put one person before everyone else."

"You say that like it's a bad thing. Most people would find my actions toward Bree admirable."

"Most people don't know how self-destructive you can be."

Danny swallowed down most of his anger and looked across the crowd to see Bree making her way back to them. He and his brother had fought for as long as he could remember, and the last thing he wanted was for Bree to get drawn into their mess.

"You know what, Mike? Why don't you relax a bit? Come down off that fucking high horse of yours and have a beer with me and Bree. Enjoy the nice weather, the food, the music. Appreciate the fact that we're not in some Third World hellhole eating sand for dinner. If you can't do that, if you can't enjoy the moment, then get lost. Because the last time I checked, I don't answer to you."

AFTER A LONG day of crowds and loud music, Danny and Bree left behind the chaos of River Street and made their way toward Forsyth Park. Moonlight streamed through the gnarled branches of large live oaks, casting ghostly shadows on the ground. Spanish moss hung from the limbs and billowed in the breeze, only adding to the ambiance.

As far as weekends went, this one had been nearly perfect. Sure, it started out a little rocky, but the following day was filled with playful banter and lots of laughter. Even if they hadn't had sex the weekend would have been great. But with sex? Holy good God. It was like ordering the most decadent brownie sundae only to have it arrive with two cherries on top and extra sprinkles. Then to wake up this morning alongside Danny felt very, very good. And so very right. Like this was how their lives should have been all along.

As they wandered along downtown, Danny never hesitated to introduce her to the regiment guys they ran into along the way. The older guys were unable to hide their surprise when he referred to her as "my wife," while the younger ones didn't appear to find it all that shocking.

But his mood notably shifted after they saw Michael. Where he was flirty and affectionate before, holding her hand, kissing her neck, wrapping his arm around her shoulders and pulling her snug against his body, there was so much distance between them now he might as well have been half a world away.

The soft glow from cast-iron lampposts guided them directly to the park's famous fountain where a few others meandered around. For the most part they had the park all to themselves and the revelry along the river seemed so very far away. Danny pulled his hands from his pockets and rested his forearms atop the iron fence circling the fountain.

Bree stared up at the moon. Heard the call of birds and crickets and whatever else was out there in the dark. Finally, she braved the silence between them. "You've gone quiet. Everything okay?"

Danny shrugged his shoulders and shook his head. From her angle, it was difficult to tell what he was trying to say. Maybe even he didn't know. "It's fun that they dye the fountain water green for St. Patty's Day, but it's far prettier without it."

The swift change in topic nearly gave her conversational whiplash, but he'd said more in that one sentence than he had in the past hour. So she rolled with it.

"You were right when you told me it's beautiful here," she said, keeping the conversation neutral. "So different from Myrtle Beach. I can see why you live here."

He huffed a laugh. "Didn't have much of a choice."

"Really?" She turned to face him, but his gaze remained on the fountain in front of them.

"I requested 2nd Batt. They're based at Fort Lewis. Washington State. But the army sent me here instead. Guess they didn't realize or didn't care that I was trying to run away as far as possible. The idea of one day running into you with someone else, maybe even married and with kids . . ."

Without warning, their conversation headed the wrong way down a one-way street. He turned to face her, running the palm of his hand from her shoulder to wrist. Any other time she would find the action comforting, soothing even, if it wasn't for the sinking feeling in the pit of her stomach.

"You didn't do anything wrong, Bree. I know it sounds cliché to say it wasn't you, that it was all me, but that's the truth. I really fucked up when I lost my scholarship. And in my mind, I not only fucked up my future but yours, as well." He removed his hand and turned back toward the fountain. "You deserved better than to be stuck with a screwup for the rest of your life."

For ten years she believed she was the only one to feel the pain of heartbreak and disappointment. That he'd run away to find excitement and adventure because his life in South Carolina, his future with her, was lacking. Not once had she considered he'd left out of embarrassment of losing his scholarship and guilt from ruining their future plans.

But for him, joining the army had been the right choice. She could see that now. Hell, anyone could see that. There had been times today when he would spot one of the younger guys from his company and would take a moment to give them a bit of advice. "Have fun, but not too much fun. Don't let all your hard work go to waste because of one stupid mistake. Play it smart. Keep an eye out for each other." He'd learned a hard lesson all those years ago and he was determined to keep them from doing the same. Proof that he wasn't the screwup he believed himself to be.

"How did Mike end up in the same battalion?"

"Luck mostly. With each school I made it through—Airborne, RIP, then Ranger school, I'd call him up and rub it in. Used to say he was too much of a pussy to pass them." He laughed. "And I'll be damned if sometime while he was in med school he changed his paperwork."

Bree shook her head in disbelief. "You two were always competitive, but that's taking it to a whole new level. Did he request Hunter? Is that how he ended up here?"

"It's different for officers. Whereas there are a bunch of infantry spots, there's only one battalion surgeon." He smiled then. "I'm not sure how many asses he had to kiss to get in here when the other guy left, but I'd imagine he'd say the line was long and distinguished."

"Does it bother you he's here?"

He shrugged his shoulders, looking so very much like the boy she knew so long ago. "At first it did. But after our first deployment together, he told me he was proud of me, of the job I do. I think that's what I was looking for the most when I left South Carolina. In Myrtle Beach I'll forever be known as the screwup. Here I'm respected. Or at least I think so." He peeled himself from off the fence and offered a hand. "Hate to cut this short, but I've got an early morning tomorrow."

She slipped her palm in his, watched as his fingers tightened around hers. For a split second she thought he'd pull her in close, wrap his arm around her shoulders as they made their way to the car. But he didn't. The space between them had narrowed, but there was still so much distance between them. And she knew she wasn't the only one to feel it.

When they reached the Tahoe he opened the door and held her hand as she climbed in. The nighttime traffic crawled as they headed home and the last of the tourists left town. Laying her head back against the seat, she stared out the side window, the steady stream of headlights and taillights nothing but a blur as they passed. Then, without really thinking, she asked the question that had circled her brain for years.

"How long before you left Columbia did you enlist?"

She turned her head toward him, awaiting his answer. At first Danny only shook his head, his reluctance to answer obvious even in the dark. Finally came her answer. "Three weeks."

He didn't elaborate. Didn't dance around the subject or make excuses. Just answered with straight-up honesty. Instantly, tears burned her eyes so she turned to look out the window once again, not wanting him to see if a tear or two happened to slip free.

Three weeks. For three long weeks he'd planned to leave her, not once hinting during those twenty-one days their lives would soon change forever.

Bree took a deep breath and discreetly swiped away a single tear from her cheek, the pain in her chest no different than it was ten years before.

DANNY SAT ON the edge of the loveseat, elbows on his knees, his head hanging. In less than a matter of hours, his brother's prediction had come to fruition. He'd hurt Bree. Badly.

God, how he wanted her to rail on him. To yell and scream, even slam a door or two. Anything that would vent her frustrations and give him his just deserts all at the same time. Instead, she quietly slunk off to the bathroom like a poor abused dog only wanting love.

"Fucking idiot," he whispered, his fist meeting his forehead with each word. Before his fist met his skull a third time, the warm touch of her hand stopped its progress.

Danny opened his eyes, her bare feet appearing in his line of vision first. He raised his head to look at her, all squeaky clean and fresh from the shower. The sun had kissed her cheeks over the past two days, giving her a healthy glow. She was so beautiful. So kind and loving. Far more than he ever deserved. At the very least he could give her the whole truth.

"I was driving around aimlessly one day," he began. "Just trying to figure out what the hell I was going to do."

Bree dropped hold of his hand and stepped back, placing herself just out of his reach. She stood with her arms crossed over her chest, protecting herself as best she could. "Go on," she whispered.

He remembered that day just as clearly as if it had been yesterday. The crowds of people wandering campus as finals neared. The bright sun and cloudless sky of an early-arriving summer. Never in his life had he felt so lost. Not even after his mother had died because at least then he had his father and his brother. And Bree. But this time he wasn't a little kid anymore and was far too old to have others cleaning up his messes.

"Student loans weren't an option since I'd flunked out. And no way could I ask my dad to pay for school, not after what I'd done. Partying. Skipping class. I was more concerned with being the life of the party than a student. My first go at adulthood, of making my own decisions, and I royally screwed it all up. I stopped for gas at a corner convenience store and as I stood there pumping gas, I noticed a recruiting office across the street and thought 'I can do that.' It wasn't anything I spent a lot of time thinking about."

Her eyes widened in surprise. "You just walked in a recruiting office out of the blue and signed up?"

"As crazy as it sounds, that's exactly what I did. I walked in the front door with no plan and walked out a couple hours later with an 11B contract, not really knowing what the hell that meant. I didn't have an Airborne option or a Ranger option. I just took what they had and by some small miracle lucked out later on with the rest." Her head tilted to one side, those dark brown eyes studying him closely. She took a step closer to him, but remained just out of reach. "For three weeks I tried to find a way to tell you that I was leaving. And every time I planned to tell you, I chickened out. Part of me believed that if I told you I'd enlisted in the army, you'd ask me to stay. And if you'd asked me to stay, I wouldn't have been able to say no. And I feared in the long run everything would get to be too much and we'd grow to resent each other."

She moved closer now and he placed his hands on her hips, bringing her to stand between his knees so he could rest his forehead upon her belly. He heard her soft sigh and felt her body shift. Then, in his peripheral vision, he saw her hands hover over his shoulders, hesitating. Letting his head fall back, he looked up at her.

"That's probably what would have happened." She

chewed on the inside of her lip, then, using her index finger, carefully stroked the furrow between his brows until his face relaxed and his scowl was gone. "We were eighteen and in love. And I was selfish. I just assumed that us being together would always be enough to make you happy. But if there is one thing I've learned over the years it's that you can't rely on someone else for your happiness." Her gentle touch drifted from his face to his scalp, where she smoothed her hand over the short stubble on his head. His eyes drifted shut, relishing the feel of her touch. "I don't want you to think I'm angry at you anymore."

He opened his eyes and stared into those dark brown depths. "But you were."

"Of course." The corner of her mouth lifted in a smile that contradicted the sadness in her eyes. "I might have even hated you once."

"But now?"

"Now?" She took a deep breath and exhaled like the weight of the world had lifted off her shoulders. "I can't hate you. I was never very good at it even when I put all my effort into it. But remembering how things once were between us is still bittersweet. And thinking about what might have been, that's what hurts."

Danny wrapped his arms about her waist and hugged her close to him. He understood exactly what she was saying. Despite the army training him to not second-guess himself, to avoid contemplating what-if, to only act and react, he would forever second-guess his decision to not tell her he was leaving.

Her palm smoothed from his neck to his shoulder, her fingertips raking the length of his arm until finally reaching his hand. She clutched his fingers with hers and tugged on his hand.

"It's time for bed."

He opened his eyes and looked at the pillow and blanket he'd retrieved from the closet only moments earlier. With a gentle hand she lifted his chin so his eyes met hers and leaned over to press a tender kiss to his lips. She whispered against his mouth, "No more sleeping on the couch."

Danny nodded and rose to his feet, following his wife to their bed.

Chapter Eighteen

"Our parents were very much against us dating because I'm Catholic and he's Jewish."

Bree smiled and took another sip of her sweet tea as Marie gave a dramatic retelling of how she and Ben first met.

"We snuck around. A lot. Climbing out bedroom windows. Climbing in bedroom windows." Marie smiled wide. "We found out I was pregnant the summer after I graduated high school. So we packed the few belongings we had into his rusted-out Camaro and eloped without telling anyone. It was all very Romeo and Juliet. Without the buzzkill ending, of course."

"Of course."

Marie shook her head. "God help us if our children break half the rules that Ben and I did."

They didn't hesitate to laugh out loud, since they had the screened porch of the small Savannah café all to themselves. Marie had called only an hour earlier, wanting to take advantage of having a sitter for Hannah and finishing her client meeting earlier than expected. She suggested this place since it was off the beaten path. Meaning, the tourists hadn't found it yet and they wouldn't have to wait an hour for soup and a sandwich.

"When did things change for you and Danny?" Marie asked as the server placed their food in front of them.

"Which time?"

Marie stabbed at bits of her salad. "The very first time. You've known him your entire life, right? How did you suddenly go from childhood friends to boyfriend and girlfriend? Did he pass you a note in class? Check the box 'yes' or 'no'?"

Bree smiled at the image Marie painted. And while she remembered her friends receiving similar notes in school, it just wasn't Danny's style. "No notes. It all happened in seventh grade, after Brady Miller asked me to the winter dance."

"Oooh. Making Danny jealous way back in your middle school days, huh?"

"It wasn't like that. He thought dances were stupid, but I wanted to go. About thirty minutes into the dance, I see him standing with a group of his friends and he's just staring at us. Next thing I know he's dancing with April Wentworth."

"Bitch. I hate her already." Marie waved her fork. "Continue."

"Actually, she was a very sweet girl. I think she works for Doctors Without Borders or something like that now."

"Ugh. A do-gooder. Even worse."

"I went to the bathroom and when I came back, Brady was dancing with April. I didn't know what to do and I couldn't face my friends, so I stood far away from everyone else, trying to decide if I should wait to see what happened next or just go ahead and call my mom to come get me. Then Danny found me. He took me by the hand and led me into the middle of the dance floor."

She could still remember how he placed his hands tentatively at her waist. How she rested her sweating palms on his shoulders. They swayed in place, unable to look at one another in the eye, much less speak. When the song ended, he took her by the hand and led her off the dance floor to a place far away from where their friends gathered. There, in a darkened corner of the gymnasium, Danny stole her first kiss.

"And then he kissed me." Even all these years later, the memory caused Bree's cheeks to heat. "We never talked about it, but from that point on we were together."

Marie giggled softly and went about her lunch. "I gotta hand it to him. I knew Danny was smooth, I just never realized he was *that* smooth. And at such a young age."

"Huh?"

"You said that April girl ended up with your date. Bobby. Billy—"

"Brady."

"That's it," she said, flinging her fork from side to side. "Anyway, the do-gooder ends up with Brady. Danny gets you. Everyone goes home happy, right?" Marie raised both hands in the air. "He pulled off the switcheroo!"

They were still giggling when Marie's cell phone rang and she excused herself to answer it, leaving Bree alone with her memories of a thirteen-year-old Danny. So hesitant. So sweet. Far different from the take-charge man he'd become. Which segued into thoughts of what he did to her last night. And then again before he left long before dawn this morning. She could still feel the burn of his stubble upon her skin. On her breasts and belly. Between her thighs. Especially between her thighs. He'd taken his sweet time, determined to be very, *very* thorough.

"Sorry about that," Marie said, interrupting her thoughts. "It was Hannah's sitter reminding me she has to leave in an hour." She plopped back down into her seat, but instead of digging into her lunch, she watched Bree, studying her. Not unlike the first time they met and she had a million questions she was dying to ask. "I have to say something is different about you today."

Bree shook her head. "Nope. Same old me."

"There's something."

"Everything's the same. Nothing has changed." Bree cleared her throat and took a long drink of her tea. "The humidity must be really high today." Using the square of linen, she fanned her face just the tiniest bit. She needed air. Desperately. And instead of hot soup for lunch, a big bowl of ice cream. With lots and lots of hot fudge and whipped cream. Which reminded her she needed to stop at the store on the way home since they'd used all of it over the weekend. Only not on ice cream.

"You slept with Danny!"

Bree's head shot up to find Marie narrowing her eyes and pointing with a salad fork.

"What would make you say that?"

"You're smiling at that bowl of tomato soup," Marie said, laughing. "No one smiles at soup! And now you're blushing!"

She didn't need to look in a mirror to know that Marie told the truth as the heat of embarrassment intensified and burned through her. She probably looked like the beet on Marie's plate.

"My, oh my. How things change. Three weeks ago you were polite and sweet and giving me the 'Oh, he only married me so I could have insurance' spiel. And now you're wriggling around in your seat like your panties are on fire." She leaned across the table in a conspiratorial manner. "So? How was it? And don't you dare say 'fine.' "

"But it was fine."

"Liar!" Marie slammed the palm of her empty hand on the table. "The recollection of fine sex doesn't make a girl squirm in place. It doesn't give you that 'I've had mind-blowing sex and multiple orgasms' glow."

Bree glanced to the door leading inside to make certain no one was eavesdropping. "Okay. It was hot. Scorching, even. It's amazing we didn't set the fire alarms off. Happy now?" Bree stirred her soup hoping it would cool. "But it's no big deal. It's just sex."

Marie snorted. "And you believe this?"

"Why does it have to be something more? Michael and I were talking about this the other day. Sometimes lunch is just lunch and sex is just sex."

"I have no doubt Michael believes that. But you?" Marie pointed at her using her salad fork. "You and Danny have a history. A very long one. And from what you've told me, at one time, the two of you loved each other. You can't just forget it."

"We are not in love."

Marie arched a well-manicured eyebrow. "Are you sure about that?"

"Absolutely. We have a deal. We're just two consenting adults having sex." Bree paused, no longer able to hold back the smile on her face. "Lots and lots of sex."

GOD, HE HATED getting home this late.

Danny laughed to himself as he climbed the stairs to his apartment, thinking of all the other times before he didn't give a damn what time he crawled home. But after the weekend they'd spent together and Bree's little send-off this morning, he'd found himself almost counting down the minutes until he could get out of there. So it was only right karma bit him in the ass and one cluster-fuck after another delayed his leaving.

When he walked into their darkened apartment, he thought for sure he'd find her sound asleep already. Instead, light streamed from the closet keeping the room from being plunged into total darkness, and he found Bree propped up against a stack of pillows, playing on her laptop.

"Hi," she said, her voice soft and sweet. "Have you had dinner?"

"Not yet."

He quickly undressed, leaving his clothes in a heap on the floor. Her eyes followed him as he rounded the bed and closed her laptop, taking it from her.

"Are you hungry?" she asked.

He placed her laptop on top of the dresser and climbed onto the end of the bed. "Starving." In one swift move, he grabbed both her ankles and tugged until she was flat on her back. A few seconds more and he'd divested her of her panties. "Don't mind me. I'll be done in a minute," he said, nibbling and biting his way up her thighs. "All you need to do is lie there."

Bree giggled and squirmed beneath him as he buried his face between her legs. She bent her knees, opening herself wider to him. But the moment her slender fingers clutched his head, he pulled away, purposely leaving her to dangle on the edge.

"You're so mean," she said breathlessly as he climbed up her body.

"Payback, baby," he chuckled. Danny grabbed a foil packet from the nightstand but didn't rush to open it. "Seems to me someone has a short memory."

Only this morning, after thoroughly feasting upon her and bringing her to orgasm, did she give him a pat on the cheek, whisper her thanks and roll over, pretending to go back to sleep.

"I was just playing," she whined.

"Mmm hmm." He pushed up the soft cotton T-shirt she'd commandeered from his drawer, exposing her breasts.

"I'm sorry," she begged.

He barely flicked one taut nipple with his tongue. "Sure you are. Now."

"I made you brownies."

Danny shifted to her other breast, this time blowing a gentle stream of air over the tip.

"With white icing."

That got his attention. She'd made his favorite. He raised his head to look into her eyes.

Bree smiled a little Cheshire cat grin and wrapped her arms around his neck, her fingertips gently stroking the back of his head. "With sprinkles," she whispered.

Danny shrugged. "Okay."

Her laughter bounced off the walls as he licked and sucked and kissed her throat, her ear, only going silent when he finally covered her mouth with his. Within minutes he was buried deep inside her, savoring the tight warmth surrounding him until he reached the point he had to move.

He'd forgotten how much fun it was to have sex with Bree. Teasing and laughter combined with the hot glide of sweaty bodies and sweet taste of her mouth was nothing short of intoxicating.

All those times he mocked his friends for rushing home to their wives; if what they had was even half as good as what he and Bree shared, well, he got it now. And he wasn't certain how he'd ever go back to living without her.

As they lay on their backs trying to catch their breath, Danny's stomach growled, causing her to laugh.

"Dear God. We need to feed that thing." Bree pushed up on one hand and pulled down her shirt. "Come on. There's some leftovers in the fridge."

After a quick pit stop in the bathroom, he pulled on his boxer briefs as he made his way to the kitchen. Danny stopped short at the end of the hall, his breath catching in his chest. What an image she made as she reached in the refrigerator, the hem of his T-shirt rising just enough to reveal the bottom swell of her bare ass.

And just like that he was hard again.

Bree shoved the refrigerator door closed with her elbow and piled an insane amount of food on the counter. As he considered spreading her out across their small dining table, his stomach grumbled a second time. Clearly, round two would have to wait.

"How was your day?" she asked, pulling a single plate from the cabinet.

"Good. Yours?"

"Good," she answered. "I had lunch with Marie. She offered me a job."

That took him by surprise. Mostly because Ben hadn't said a thing about it. Of course, he probably didn't have a clue. "Doing what?"

"Bookkeeping. Answering the phone." She sliced his sandwich in half, garnished it with a pickle and handful of chips before handing it to him. "She's really busy right now and needs an extra hand. I'd also watch Hannah while she meets with clients or goes to a job site."

"Kind of overqualified for that, aren't you?"

"Yeah. But I like Marie and it'll get me out of the house. I wanted to talk to you first, though, before I give her an answer. Just to make sure you'd be okay with it."

"Why wouldn't I be?" he said around a mouthful of roast beef.

"I don't know. Because she's married to your best friend? You've already given me so much and maybe there are some things you want to keep separate."

"Doesn't bother me a bit."

"You're sure?"

Danny smiled. "Absolutely. Are you sure you're ready for this?"

She took her time, waiting until she returned everything to the fridge and rinsed the knife she used before answering him. "It'll be good to dip my toes in the water. A full-time job would likely be too much too soon."

"Kind of a win-win for both of you, then."

"Something like that."

Having finished, he rinsed his plate and waited patiently as she uncovered the brownies. "I almost forgot. I've got something for you." Danny rushed back into the bedroom and from the front pocket of his ACUs pulled out the folded piece of newspaper. He unfolded the picture taken the moment he bent her over his arm and kissed her during the St. Patrick's Day parade. Using his fingertips, he carefully pressed the creases from it.

"I'd like to take credit for finding it, but really it was hanging in my locker when we came back from lunch. And of course, the guys loved giving me a ration of shit over it."

"Oh, my God. I didn't realize there was a photographer there."

"Neither did I." He moved next to her, so he could look at it again while he finished his brownie. "It's a good-looking picture, though."

"It almost looks like that old photo from Times Square at the end of World War II. Except for the bright red wig."

"And the squid."

Bree looked at him like he was nuts.

"It was a navy guy in the original photo," he explained.

She shook her head and hung their picture on the refrigerator using a magnetic bottle opener. "I wonder if I can get an actual print of the picture."

"Wouldn't hurt to ask."

Bree wrapped her arms around his neck and pressed her body close to his. She whispered her thanks and placed a soft kiss to his lips. His hands skimmed down the back of her T-shirt until he reached bare flesh. Cupping the soft swells of her ass, he gave a quick squeeze then lifted. He smiled when she instinctively wrapped her legs around his waist, locking her ankles behind him.

"Thank you for the brownie," he said then walked his wife back to the bedroom.

Chapter Nineteen

BREE ROLLED ONTO her stomach and pulled the pillow over her head, pressing it tighter to her ears in hopes of drowning out the sounds of the helicopters flying overhead. She should have followed the news reporter's advice and purchased earplugs, but she didn't want to use them out of fear of missing a knock at the door or her phone ringing. After all, her husband was out there somewhere in the darkness, jumping out of airplanes and attacking a fictional enemy. Although it was just a training exercise, the risks were very real.

In the past month alone, three men had died during training exercises. Two airmen died when their plane crashed off the Florida coast. The other, a soldier in Arizona, died when his parachute failed.

With each news report her anxiety reached new heights despite Danny's assurances. Again and again he would tell her, "This is what we do. We train and train and train to avoid mistakes. Sometimes accidents happen, but in regiment those accidents are rare."

So she smiled and nodded in understanding, trying to pretend everything was okay. Meanwhile, her insides were twisted into knots.

She wondered how military wives handled the stress day in and day out while their loved ones fought a war far from home. Did they trick themselves into believing their husbands were off on a business trip? That the most dangerous decision they faced was whether or not to submit that $200 bar tab with their expense report?

Once the nighttime invasion of Savannah was complete, she finally fell into a deep sleep, only to be woken again a couple hours later. She and Danny traded only a few text messages before they signed off, but still the alarm clock sounded way too soon. For the first time in five weeks, she wished she didn't have a job to go to. Of course, she quickly remembered what it was like to wake every morning and know that it wasn't going to be any different than the day before. Or the day before that one. And so on and so on . . .

She hefted herself into the Tahoe, careful to not spill coffee down the front of her freshly pressed shirt. Yes, she was a little overdressed, considering she never left Marie's house and rarely came face-to-face with another adult aside from the UPS man. But ironing a shirt and wearing tailored pants made it feel more like a real job than just a part-time assistant slash babysitter.

As she navigated her way through the streets of Savannah without the use of GPS, she was surprised at how quickly she'd settled in. Here she was driving around in Danny's truck like she owned the thing, feeling more and more like one half of a real couple. Depending on how late he got home, they'd spend the evening watching either baseball or a movie. Occasionally, they went out to eat. And on the weekends they'd do the tourist thing and explore old forts and wildlife preserves, places even Danny hadn't visited in his ten years living here.

True to his word, marrying Danny had provided her life with new meaning and purpose. He'd rescued her from the rut, just as promised. Although it was nice to settle in, she needed to focus on the long-term and made a mental note to contact a few of her former coworkers to see if they knew of any jobs coming down the pike.

Like every other day, she arrived at Ben and Marie's a little before nine. No longer did she bother to ring the doorbell. Instead, she let herself in the house just as Marie instructed, so she wasn't left standing on the front porch in the event Marie was busy upstairs with Hannah. Bree shouted a quick hello and before she could even close the front door, Marie came racing downstairs, looking frazzled.

"Thank God you're early." Bree followed a hurried Marie through the living room and into the kitchen. "There's been a major water leak at the Belliveaus' house and of course their hand-scraped hardwood floors were just installed yesterday. I need to get over there and assess the damage for myself. For now if you could just keep an eye on—" Marie stopped short and swore under her breath.

In the high chair sat a giggling Hannah, her face, hair and hands coated in a thick pink substance. Yogurt, maybe? The dogs gathered at her feet, jumping and dashing around as she chucked tiny handfuls of Cheerios in their direction.

The phone in Marie's hand buzzed once again, but instead of answering she laid it upon the kitchen island and grabbed a small broom and dustpan from under the sink. Before she could begin cleaning up, her phone was buzzing again. Clearly, someone was quite impatient this morning.

"Go do what you need to do. I can handle this," Bree said, holding out her hands in silent request for the broom and dustpan.

"I didn't hire you to be a housekeeper."

"Doesn't matter. You hired me to help you out around here. I'm helping out."

"But this is a huge mess. Hannah's a huge mess. And you're so nicely dressed."

They both looked over at the little girl who continued to giggle and clap her hands as the dogs bounced around her. "I need to give her a bath before I go."

"I can get it. Really. I'll wash. Hannah will wash. It'll be just fine."

"At least change your clothes first. There's a load of T-shirts and shorts in the dryer. No sense in ruining your nice clothes." Reluctantly, Marie handed over the broom and dustpan. "I don't know how I'll repay you."

Bree waved her off. "Stop worrying and get going."

After squashing a few more protests, Marie was finally out the door, leaving Bree to assess the damage. Hannah stared at her with wide brown eyes as if she just realized her momma had left the building, and Bree braced herself for the tears that surely would come. Instead, the baby smiled again and threw another handful of cereal at her waiting crowd.

The kitchen was a disaster. Breakfast dishes were piled in the sink. A gross mix of sticky stuff and pet hair coated the floor around the high chair. But there was a smiling child in the middle of it all, and the mess no longer mattered as much.

Just as Marie had said, Bree found an assortment of T-shirts to change into, but only one pair of skimpy black running shorts in the entire load. They were identical to the ones Danny wore with 1st Batt's scroll on the left leg that looked sexy as hell on him, but were so short and so thin they were damn near indecent.

A plastic bowl clattered on the kitchen tile, followed by an impatient scream. Sounded like someone had had her fill of fun so Bree quickly changed her clothes and hightailed it to the kitchen. After several minutes of struggling with the high chair, she finally managed to remove the tray and give Hannah an initial wipe-down. The dogs had done a pretty good job with the floor cleanup, so mopping could wait.

They headed upstairs where she searched the bathroom to find the necessities as the tub filled. Like most teenage girls, Bree had a few babysitting jobs here and there, so she wasn't completely inept. But still, it'd been nearly fifteen years since she'd bathed an infant, and she was definitely out of practice.

"Ready for this?"

Hannah stared up at her with huge brown eyes, her little tongue thrusting against her lips. What a sticky, adorable mess she was. So cute it made Bree's chest ache.

Bath time took longer than expected. Mainly because Bree didn't have the heart to end Hannah's fun. Instead, she spent the next half hour watching Hannah splash and play and babble nonsense at her collection of miniature rubber ducks.

The dull ache in her chest transitioned into a painful throb. Holding someone else's child would be the closest she'd ever come to motherhood. She'd never have a baby grow inside her, feel it turn and kick and let its demand for cupcakes or ice cream be known. She'd never hear a small voice call out for her in the middle of the night when they were scared and needing to be held. She'd never hang a dozen stockings over the fireplace and chase children back to their rooms because they wanted a peek at Santa.

For months her head told her heart that a life without children would be even better. That she'd have the freedom to go where she wanted, when she wanted. No responsibilities to tie her down. Her life was her own and she could do with it what she pleased.

But now that she held this little bundle of sweet smells and soft skin and baby's breath in her arms, her heart knew she was a damn liar. A spontaneous trip to the Bahamas or nice furniture or more disposable income would never fill the hole left behind when the doctors took her second ovary along with her uterus.

"Is everything okay?"

She'd been so lost inside her own misery and hadn't heard Marie return home. Bree swiped the hot tears from her cheeks and quickly rose from the rocking chair, handing a sleeping Hannah off to her mother.

"Bree."

"I'm okay. Just really tired. I can't sleep with those damn helicopters buzzing around all night."

"Are you sure that's all it is?"

"I'm sure. How's the Belliveau house?"

"Fine. There was a leak from a new fixture in the kitchen, but it was tiny. Not the flood it was described to be," she said, laying Hannah in her crib and covering her with a blanket. "Why don't you go home and try to get some rest."

"But what about—"

"I can handle things from here on out now that crisis has been averted. So go on." Marie waved her hand, shooing her from the room. "Go get some sleep before the sun goes down and those men of ours start invading the damn town again. As a matter of fact, I might do the very same."

Maybe Marie was right. An afternoon nap might be the very thing she needed to shake the funk she was in. Bree gathered Hannah's bath towels and yogurt-covered pj's and headed downstairs for the laundry room. After changing back into her own clothes, she grabbed her handbag from the counter.

"I'll see you in the morning," she said to Marie as she passed by her on the way out.

"All right. And Bree—"

After fishing her car keys out from the bottom of her purse, she turned to look back at her friend.

"Just so you know, I cried at the drop of a hat with each of my kids. Any chances you're pregnant?" The look on Marie's face was so hopeful the tears were an indicator of something to celebrate.

She mustered the best smile she could under the circumstances. "Afraid not," she said, stopping in the doorway. "I'll see you in the morning."

Bree closed the front door behind her and could only hope that tomorrow things would be better.

GOD, HOW HE loved airfield seizure training. It was, after all, the 75th's specialty. Need to topple some foreign government? First things first: send in the Rangers to parachute behind enemy lines in the dark of night and take over their airfields. Which was made all the more interesting if the assholes' Spidey-senses started to twinge and they decided to park every damn vehicle they could find on the runways to prevent the military planes from landing. Like that would stop them from coming anyway. He could still remember the day when he found out hot-wiring cars would become an essential part of his military training.

Then there were the night jumps out of a C–17 while loaded down with a shit ton of equipment. For many of the guys, the airborne component was a necessary evil. Despite their fear of heights, they sucked it up and jumped because all the best jobs in the military required it. But for him, the sweet build of anticipation made his insides tingle from the moment he hooked on to the static line and made his way to the door, followed by a brief moment of terror when he bailed out into the pitch-black sky. Then, once his parachute was fully opened and untangled, a sense of peace washed over him as he floated to earth.

The only thing he didn't like—the landings. Controlled crash would be more accurate. And if there was a call for a medic through the headset, well then, that sucked. Because it meant someone had likely jacked an ankle or knee if not something worse. But if you were one of the lucky ones who made it to your feet, that was when the real fun began with explosions and gunfire and dirt bikes racing around and every fucking kind of aircraft imaginable circling the skies above you.

Goddamn, he loved his job.

In the past three days he'd managed maybe seven hours of sleep. And just like every other guy in 1st Batt when they'd go op-tempo, he'd survived on three things: adrenaline, caffeine, and Copenhagen.

As he made his way to the mess hall along with the other guys for lunch, he saw his brother for the first time all week. He sped up to catch him. "Any word on Rodriguez?" His fellow squad leader had been one of the unfortunate ones the night before when his left foot found a hole in the ground upon landing and his ankle rolled over on him.

"Not yet. Sent him for an MRI. Best guess is an ATFL tear."

"Damn. Surgery?"

"Nothing broken but it looked pretty nasty. I'd be surprised if he didn't have surgery."

Which meant Rodriguez would be out of commission not just weeks, but likely months, until his rehab was complete. Looked like Osweiler could get his first shot as squad leader sooner than he expected.

"How does Bree like her new oncologist?"

The question took Danny by complete surprise. He knew she'd have follow-ups. They'd discussed that much. But when he promised not to hover, he honestly thought she'd at least keep him in the loop without requiring him to press the issue. Obviously not. And yet, Michael was once again in the know.

He schooled his expression as best he could. "We haven't had the chance to really talk this week. Just a text message here and there."

Michael's eyes narrowed as if he knew damn well Danny was lying to him. Thankfully, his cell phone buzzed in his pocket, distracting him for the moment. "I'm needed in the clinic," Michael said as he read the screen. He slapped Danny on the back of his shoulder as he headed off. "I'll catch up with you later."

"Sure thing."

He watched his brother walk away as he stood there feeling as if he'd just been smacked upside the head with a two-by-four.

She'd promised. Bree had looked him in the eye and promised to keep him informed, whether there was any news, good or bad.

For the past five weeks they'd been sharing not only a bed, but their lives together, too. He'd made a point to be open and honest with her, to answer all of her questions. He'd explained why he'd left without saying goodbye ten years before and why he didn't like returning home to Myrtle Beach. To regain her trust, to make himself worthy of her, he knew he had to be completely forthcoming. So it grated to learn she hadn't done the same. And to pour salt into an old wound, she'd entrusted her secrets to his brother instead.

Danny took a deep breath and scrubbed a hand over his face, trying to rein in his anger. He pulled his cell phone from his pocket and fired off a text message.

Just checking in. Everything going okay this week?

All through lunch he kept checking his phone for a reply. By the time he had to stow his phone away in his locker, he still hadn't heard from her. Night had fallen before he had a chance to check his phone again. Still, he found absolutely nothing.

Chapter Twenty

Bree dumped her plate and napkin in the trash and grabbed a second bottled water from a nearby ice chest. Spending the day at Charlie Company's family picnic really wasn't her idea of fun at the moment, especially since Marie was at home with Hannah, leaving her with no one to chat with. And yet, at the same time, she was secretly grateful since the past two days she'd submersed herself in a stack of invoices and payables, effectively avoiding any lingering questions from Marie.

She really needed to find her way out of this funk. She'd survived lows before, often with a dash of anger, but this was different. This time it lingered.

Far away from the wives and girlfriends and little ones running wild, Bree found a shady spot beneath an oak tree. A group of boys gathered around Danny as he held a baseball and showed them different grips then adjusted their fingers once they took the ball in their hands.

He ruffled their hair, adjusted their caps. Demonstrated how to position their feet to make a pitch. He called out warnings to innocent bystanders and chased down errant throws. He was so good with them. Patient. Her entire life she'd known he'd be a good dad someday.

"Hey, there."

Bree shielded her eyes from the sun to see Michael standing next to her. "I didn't realize you'd be here today."

He shrugged then plopped down on the ground next to her. "Haven't talked to you in a while. I saw you sitting over here by yourself and thought I'd say hi." From the look on his face, her gut said this would likely end up being more of a therapy session than friendly conversation. "So, how are things going?"

She turned her attention back to the ball field. "Fine as always."

Michael chuckled. "Now I know something is wrong. No woman I've ever known has used the word *fine* and meant it."

Bree blew out a breath. "Honestly, it's taking a great deal of effort to not bite your head off right about now."

"That's to be expected."

"I know that," she snapped. "Doesn't mean I have to like it."

She glanced at her phone for the time, wondering how much longer they'd be here. What she really wanted to do was go home, crawl into bed and just be left in peace and quiet.

"Earlier this week I asked Danny how your appointment with the oncologist went." Michael reclined back on his elbows. "It was pretty obvious you hadn't told him anything about it."

"There's nothing to tell. Just normal screening stuff. You know that."

"That's the problem, Bree. I know that, but he doesn't. The less you tell him, the more scared he gets."

Now he was getting dramatic. "You don't know that."

"Did he do something? Say something to make you so upset? I have no problem kicking his ass if he's hurt you in any way—"

"He didn't do anything. I'm just having a hard time right now, that's all."

"You might as well tell me what the problem is," he said, plucking at the long grass with his fingers. "I've got all day and nowhere to be."

"You want to know what my problem is?" She waited until his eyes met hers then directed his attention to two little girls practicing cartwheels. "That is my problem. And that." Directing his attention to a woman pushing a stroller. "And that." Finally pointing at Danny as he helped a young boy with his swing.

He sat up straight now. "If that's how you're feeling at the moment, then why are you here torturing yourself? Danny knew there'd be a ton of kids—" Michael swore under his breath. "Have you told him anything, Bree? Anything at all?"

Hot tears burned her eyes and a heavy dose of guilt settled squarely upon her chest.

"My brother went above and beyond for you and this is how you treat him?"

Out of answers, she popped up to her feet and headed for the parking lot.

After spending the last few minutes hitting fly balls to a group of boys, Danny glanced over to where Bree and Michael had been sitting only to find them gone. As much as he hated to admit it, he hoped his brother could succeed where he'd failed and get Bree to socialize a little bit. He hated seeing her so down and if Michael could cheer her up, then so be it.

But then, out of the corner of his eye, he caught sight of the bright pink shirt she wore. And by the time he realized she was headed for the parking lot, he noticed Mike jogging to catch up and slinging an arm over her shoulder.

Enough with this bullshit. He was tired of being on the outside looking in. Tired of their whispered conversations about her diagnosis, her ongoing treatments. Tired of them making him look like a fool.

This ended. Now.

He dropped the bat on the ground and followed after them. A large SUV blocked his view as he approached, but the moment he rounded the back of the vehicle, he got one hell of an eyeful. Bree in his brother's embrace, her face buried in his chest while Mike stroked her back.

In his head he knew nothing remotely sexual was going on, but fuck if his heart didn't give a damn. The idea she would accept comfort from his own brother instead of confiding her fears and insecurities in him, instead of telling *her husband*, temporary or not, made him want to rage.

Everything slowed. Blood rushed in his ears. His heart pounded in his chest. The fury inside reached the point he could no longer contain it.

After three quick steps and in one swift motion, he pulled Bree away from his brother's arms and swung with his opposite hand. Danny's fist connected with his brother's face, the crunching of bone against bone louder than Bree's screams.

But he didn't stop with the single blow. Danny threw another and another until Michael retaliated and connected with punches of his own. The first shot connected with Danny's mouth and he welcomed the grinding of teeth and copper taste of blood from his freshly split lip. Adrenaline surged through his veins and in that moment he felt invincible.

"Jesus Christ! Knock it the fuck off before you're both court-martialed!" came a voice from behind them.

Ignoring the voice, Danny charged ahead, dropping his shoulder, pounding into his brother's torso as if he were a tackling dummy. Although Michael had squared his body to prepare for the attack, the momentum still knocked him to the ground. Each throwing multiple blows until Bull hauled Danny to his feet and dragged him backward by both arms.

Seeing the opportunity to sucker punch him, Michael hopped to his feet and swung.

"Get your fucking head on straight, Danny!" he yelled.

Gibby stepped between the two of them and placed

his hands on Michael's chest to put some distance between them.

"I'm not the one cozying up to another man's wife!"

"I wasn't doing anything with Bree!"

"What the fuck are you even doing here? Don't you know better than to fraternize with lowly enlisted men?"

"You're right. My mistake," Michael said, raising his hands in the air. "I was just leaving."

It took more than a few deep breaths for Danny to settle himself down. Bull waited by his side, more likely than not to ensure he didn't find any more trouble.

His hands still shook from the adrenaline coursing through his body and only once his heart rate and nerves settled could he even bear to look at his wife. Except by the time that came about, she was gone. And so was his truck.

Shit.

He'd truly fucked up this time.

HOURS PASSED BEFORE Gibby returned Danny to his apartment. Before they even pulled into the parking lot, Danny knew the Tahoe wouldn't be there. He'd tried calling her cell phone several times, but each time it went straight to voice mail.

As he climbed the stairs he wondered what he would find. Would her things be gone? Did he embarrass her enough, make her angry enough, that she'd packed up all her belongings and left town? He opened the door to their darkened apartment and made his way down the hall, peeking in the spare bedroom and then the one they shared. At first glance it didn't appear she'd left him. At least not yet.

He wanted to try her phone again, but pride stopped him. Ten attempts already. It was her turn now.

A quick shower helped with his disposition although his mood darkened a bit when his phone showed he hadn't missed any calls. Fixing things with Bree obviously would have to wait until she gave him the time of day. Of course, that wasn't the only fixing needing to be done. Danny grabbed a bottle of Jack Daniel's from atop the refrigerator and headed out across the courtyard.

A sharp pain shot from hand to elbow as he knocked on Mike's front door. He was shaking his hand to ease the discomfort when the door opened.

"Still hurts, huh?" his brother asked, holding an ice pack to his own cheek.

"Not so much."

"Liar."

Mike pushed the door open wide in silent invitation.

Without asking, Danny went into the kitchen, took two glasses from the cabinet, and walked back into the living room. Setting them both on the coffee table, he poured a healthy amount of Jack into each glass then slid one across the wooden top in Mike's direction.

His brother stared at him through narrowed eyes then finally reached for his glass.

Danny followed suit and swore silently when the first sip of bourbon set his busted lip on fire. He pressed a finger against the wound to temporarily ease the ache.

Thankfully, the burning eased and numbness quickly followed.

"Your mouth okay?" Mike asked before taking a drink of his own.

"Yeah. You?" Danny pointed to his brother's bruised cheekbone.

Mike touched the corner of his eye, the swelling evident when he pressed with his fingertips. "Barely felt a thing. You hit like a goddamn girl."

Danny laughed. "Who's the liar now?"

Ignoring him, Mike went to the kitchen, pulled a plastic grocery bag from a cabinet, and filled it with ice. "I'm going to assume nothing is broken in your hand, not that you'd let me or any other doctor look at it anyway. Do me one favor? Amuse me and put this on your hand."

Reluctantly, Danny took the bag from him. But before he obliged the good doctor, he opened the bag, removed a few pieces of ice, and dropped them into his glass.

His brother shook his head and dropped in the chair across from him. "Good Lord, you are a lazy ass."

"Resourceful is what I am."

They shared a laugh, but the silence quickly returned. Danny pulled his phone from his pocket and set it on top of the table. No messages. No missed calls.

"Anything from Bree?"

Danny shook his head. "You haven't heard from her, have you?" He hated the desperation in his voice. Even more, he hated the possibility she'd called Mike while steadily avoiding him.

"No, I haven't." Mike scooted forward in his chair, his

elbows resting on his knees. "Danny, surely you know there's nothing going on between us."

"I know, I know. Temporary insanity, I guess. I just feel like she's intentionally shutting me out of her life."

"She is."

He said it so matter-of-fact-like, it struck him with the same force as the earlier blow to his face.

"Believe me when I say I've been asking her to talk to you. There's a lot going on in that head of hers that's no fault of yours."

"So you tell me."

"Come on, Danny. You know I can't do that. But you two need to have a good, long talk. That's what I was telling her in the parking lot. Had her convinced, too, not that it'll do much good now." Michael relaxed back into his chair. "Let me ask you something. What do you think life was like for her after you left? And I don't mean years later. I mean the days and weeks and months afterward."

Truth was, he hadn't thought about it. Hadn't wanted to think about the pain he might have caused. And luckily for him, the army was willing to oblige him with weeks on end of physical and mental exhaustion. It wasn't until that block leave almost a year after enlisting that he even considered what her life was like.

"Tell me."

"Bree was a mess after you left. You absolutely crushed her. So the fact she's finding it hard to trust you again isn't all that surprising. Not to me, at least."

Fuck. Danny twisted his neck from side to side, the

vertebrae popping loudly, but the tension and pressure in his spine remained.

"I've monumentally fucked everything up, haven't I?"

"Yeah, you have." Michael reached for the bottle of Jack and refilled his glass.

"Jesus. Did lying even cross your mind?"

Mike laughed. "Nope. But the thing is, there is plenty of time to fix it. And you do want to fix things with Bree, right?" Danny nodded. "So what the hell are you doing sitting here?"

Once again, his brother was right.

As Danny rose to his feet, he drank down the remaining bourbon and made his way to the kitchen where he left his glass and tossed the ice-filled bag in the sink.

"We're okay, right?" he asked once he reached the door.

"Never were anything but, little brother."

Halfway out the door, Mike called his name. "You've forgotten something," he said, holding up the bottle of Jack.

"Keep it. It's the least I owe you."

BREE SPENT THE first hour after leaving the park driving aimlessly around Savannah, but then found herself on the two-lane highway to Tybee Island. And just like she used to do after moving back home with her parents, she made her way to the beach, the sand and surf calling to her.

She stared at the waves coming ashore, thinking back

to what Michael said. Somewhere along the way, she came up with the crazy idea she could protect her heart by not talking about her cancer with Danny. She convinced herself he'd never look at her the same way if he knew the whole truth. But in hindsight, maybe her subconscious was punishing him in a passive-aggressive sort of way. By not talking about her cancer, Danny's imagination was allowed to run wild. Which was nothing short of cruel to a man whose mother died of cancer when he was only five.

When darkness fell, she stood up and dusted herself off. The time had come to face her husband.

She slid the key into the lock, but the door opened in front of her before she could turn the bolt. Danny's face was bruised, his lip swollen on one side. Upon first glance she couldn't tell if he was welcoming her home or barricading her entry. Without saying a word he finally stepped to the side.

With the door closed behind her, she dropped her purse and keys on the coffee table and fell into the recliner. Danny took a seat opposite from her on the loveseat and cleared his throat. "I think you should know I've already apologized to Mike. I owe you an apology, as well."

"Danny—"

"Please," he said, raising a hand. "I don't honestly believe there's something going on between you two. I just . . ." His shoulders lifted to his ears, his hands suspended midair as he struggled to find the right words. "I don't know what I was thinking. I just snapped. And I'm sorry. Really, really sorry."

In return, she quickly accepted his apology.

Danny closed his eyes and carefully scrubbed a hand over his face, his knuckles cut and bruised. He hung his head, the palm of his hand skimming over the top his head to rub the back of his neck. She'd seen him tired from physical exhaustion, but this was different. He looked emotionally drained, beaten down. And when he lifted his face and looked at her with those deep blue eyes, she saw a hint of fear for the very first time since they'd moved to Savannah.

"I met with an oncologist this week," she began. "More of a get-to-know-each-other kind of thing than anything else. He drew some blood and we went over my medical history. Everything is good."

The breath he'd been holding whooshed from his lungs. "That's good. Really good." The right corner of his mouth lifted in a half smile, the relief evident on his face.

How she'd get through the rest of the conversation she didn't know. Only one thing was for certain, she wouldn't be able to look him in the eye. Instead, she stared at her folded hands and distracted herself a moment longer as she scraped at the chipping nail polish on her thumb. Secretly, she hoped he'd ask what he wanted to know. But he promised not to pry into her life and ask a bunch of questions. And for two months he'd kept his end of the bargain despite his worries. He wouldn't suddenly change now.

"I'm sorry for avoiding you this week. I've had kind of a tough time the past few days, but it's not because of anything you've done or said."

"You don't need to explain yourself."

"But I do," she answered swiftly so as to not let herself off the hook.

She told him how she'd been left to care for Hannah earlier in the week. How although she'd been around her for weeks it was the first time she'd had to do more than just listen out for her on the baby monitor. She told him how she bathed her and dressed her and held her in her arms as she rocked her to sleep.

"You want a baby," he said, just plain and simple.

A half laugh escaped her, although the conversation was far from amusing. "I'd love one, but can't have one. Ever." Her eyes met his and Danny dipped his head, silently encouraging her to go on. "With the first diagnosis they removed one ovary. With the second, they removed . . . everything. Not only will I never carry a child, but I couldn't find a doctor who would harvest my eggs so I could use a surrogate later on if I wanted to."

"You could always adopt."

"Adoptions are expensive and agencies want guarantees. The last thing they want to do is give a child to someone who has a higher than average chance of dying. They want a doctor to sign a piece of paper saying I'll never have cancer again. That will never happen." Her lip trembled and the tears slipped down her cheeks before she could stop them. She straightened her spine and swiped the tears away with the back of her hand. "It's done. I've accepted it. And honestly, I'm grateful just to be alive. But every once in a while, there's a selfish part of me that wonders, why me?" she said, hiccupping the words. "Why didn't I get to be one of the lucky ones who has it all?" Bree covered her face with both hands, now unable to control the flood of tears.

Within seconds she was being lifted from the chair, one strong arm cradling her back, another beneath her knees. She thought he intended to carry her to bed, like he'd done so many times before. Instead, Danny took her place in the recliner and settled her across his lap, guiding her head to rest against his shoulder. At first she resisted, not wanting his pity. But he held her prisoner in his arms, unwilling to let her go.

Even before their conversation, before the picnic, she was so very tired and now, even more so. Within a matter of seconds she gave up the fight and Danny loosened his hold as she relaxed into his embrace.

"You go ahead and cry all you need to," he whispered against her temple as he began to gently rock the two of them. "I've got you. And this time, I'm not going anywhere."

Months of pent-up anger and sadness and resentment, feelings she had shoved down deep as she tried to move forward with her life, all came rushing out in a flood of tears. True to his word, he stayed with her through it all. Never rushing her through her grief, never asking if she was almost done. Instead, he rocked her well into the night, stopping occasionally to dry her tears or kiss her cheek. By the time she'd cried herself out, she felt physically drained but lighter somehow. The weight she'd been lugging around by herself for so long was now gone and she could finally move forward.

She placed her hand on his chest, felt the strong, steady beat of his heart beneath her palm. "Thank you," she whispered.

"You don't ever have to handle it alone. No matter what, I'll always be here for you. Okay?"

Danny smiled when she nodded in understanding and placed a delicate kiss to her lips. Tightening his hold once more, he rose to his feet and carried her to bed.

Chapter Twenty-One

The stack of clothes and shoes and other essentials piled on the bed far exceeded the size of Bree's weekend bag. Of course, if Danny would just tell her what his plans were, it'd be far easier to pack. She did know that it'd be somewhere relatively close since his company was on call and not allowed to travel farther than two hours from HAAF, so a weekend on a Caribbean beach, sipping fruity drinks with little umbrellas in them, was out of the question.

Surely, he wasn't dragging her to some golf resort?

Bree laughed to herself. That definitely sounded like something Michael would do, but Danny, not so much. A nice weekend of lazing around, being waited on was more his style. Maybe a nice dinner and afterward take in some sights and live music, too.

Things between them had improved dramatically in the past two weeks since she let down her guard and told him all of her secrets. There still were, and likely always would be, moments of sadness, but nothing like the heavy weight pressing upon her before. And taking Danny's advice, she shared with Marie, as well, just so anytime she wept while watching TV commercials or had a craving for ice cream or had a touch of stomach flu, Marie wouldn't jump to the assumption Bree was pregnant. And knowing she wouldn't have to dance around the subject of having kids or adopting in the future made living life far easier.

From the bedroom she heard the turn of the dead bolt and heavy footsteps on the entryway tile, followed by him calling out her name. Bree quickly tossed in the delicate lingerie she'd purchased the day before and zippered the suitcase closed in a rush.

"How's my birthday girl? All packed and ready to go?"

She spun around to face him. "Hey, there."

A smile stretched his face, revealing the dimple in his cheek. "Whatcha hidin'?"

"Nothing," she said, trying her best to project a look of wide-eyed innocence.

Clearly not buying it, he stalked toward her instead. "I have ways of making you talk."

Bree placed her hand flat on his chest and narrowed her eyes. "You have your surprises, I have mine. And you're the one who started this whole thing to begin with."

"Fair enough." He pressed a quick kiss to her lips, followed by a second and third. "Let me take a quick shower and then we're outta here," he said while grasping the back of his shirt with one hand and pulling it over his head in one smooth motion.

Her hand, however, remained in place a moment too long.

"Want to join me?"

Bree forced her gaze from the warm, damp flesh beneath her palm to his face.

Danny lowered his voice and waggled his eyebrows. "I could use help washing my front."

"Whatever." Bree pushed off his chest, putting a little distance between them. "Hurry up or we're going to be late."

Danny laughed and gave a little swat to her behind as she maneuvered past him. "You don't even know where we're going!"

She shot him a look of irritation over her shoulder then smiled just before he disappeared into the bathroom, happy that they'd found their playful groove once again.

In the other room her laptop dinged with a new email as she double-checked the contents of her handbag. Wallet. Lipstick. Phone and charger. From the bottom of her purse, she pulled out a foil packet and with a smile, tossed it on the kitchen table. Not that it was taking up any room, just that it was completely unnecessary now.

When she first suggested they go without using a condom, he resisted temptation, citing the fact that while he'd always been sure to wear one, he hadn't been exactly a Boy Scout, either. Despite the annual physicals provided by the military, he chose to have an additional checkup completed by someone other than his brother. And when the results came back good, they celebrated. Which was very, *very* good.

The shower shut off and she turned just in time to see Danny streak across the hallway, all the while carrying the towel and dripping water all over the carpet. It still amazed her how quickly he readied himself and she knew she had only a matter of minutes to wrap everything up.

Recalling her email dinged earlier, Bree decided to check it one last time before they headed out. More than likely it was a promotional email from Target or iTunes or Macy's because Lord knew they loved to email her every single day, but in case it wasn't—she stopped short at seeing a familiar name in the window and clicked open the message. Her eyes scanned the screen and once she reached the end, unable to believe what she'd read, Bree started over at the top and read it a second time.

"Ready to go?"

Danny stood at the door wearing a blue button-down shirt and chinos, an overnight bag in each hand.

"Yeah. I just need a second." Ignoring the look of concern on his face, she closed out her email and powered off the computer. Needing a moment to steady herself, she took a deep breath and carefully hung her handbag over one shoulder.

With one little email, everything had changed.

Their overnight bags landed on the floor with a dull thud and Bree looked up to see Danny prowling toward her. Panic twisted her gut, fearing he'd somehow caught a glimpse of the email. "What's wrong?"

"Nothing," he said, taking her face in both of his hands. "Just remembered I forgot something."

"I thought we were in a hurry," she whispered the moment before his lips touched hers.

"Never in too much of a hurry for this."

True to his word, Danny took his time, the first brush of his lips against hers soft and tender then progressing to more playful and demanding. When he pressed her lips open and stroked her tongue with his, she melted into him, forgetting all her previous worries about the email. She rested her hands upon his chest and soaked all of him in. The steady beat of his heart beneath her palm. The heat of his body and minty scent of his breath. Then, without warning, he backed away.

A little dazed and a lot confused, she looked up to see a cocky grin and mischievous glint in his eyes. "Now it's time to go."

WITHOUT A DOUBT, Danny had big plans for the weekend. Ones that included telling Bree how much he loved her, how he wanted to ditch the temporary part of their arrangement and remain husband and wife for the rest of their lives.

The black velvet box he'd kept hidden for days was burning a hole in his pocket, but he was determined to do this right. That day in her backyard when he first suggested they married, she'd said she'd always dreamed of a romantic proposal. Of how she'd always thought there would be flowers and dinner and a man getting down on one knee. And in all his smart-ass glory, he said he'd have to leave it to the next guy. Only now, *he* wanted to be the next guy. He wanted to be her only guy. So tomorrow night Bree would get the marriage proposal she'd always wanted.

As Danny pulled into the private lot of the historic Savannah hotel, Bree clapped her hands and squeed. "Are we staying here?"

"No," he deadpanned. "I was just checking to see if they could watch our bags for us."

Bree rolled her eyes and hopped out of the Tahoe before he shifted into Park. With her cell phone at the ready, she began snapping pictures in every direction, oohing and aahing about the ivy-covered walls and the iron fences and the hanging baskets overflowing with brightly colored blooms.

He'd make fun of her if he wasn't secretly relieved. The last thing he wanted was for Bree to be disappointed they weren't going farther than fifteen minutes from home or staying in one of the modern properties along the riverfront.

"We can't stay long," he said while retrieving their bags from the back of the truck. "We have somewhere else we need to be."

She lowered her phone and turned to face him, her smile alone worth every dime he was shelling out this weekend. "What all do you have planned?"

"Wouldn't be a surprise if I told you."

Within the hour they'd boarded a riverboat dinner cruise and were sipping umbrella drinks on the boat's top deck as they cruised east on the Savannah River, heading for The Waving Girl and old Fort Jackson. Many times in the past ten years he'd seen these boats cruising the river, and each and every time he wondered what kind of man would spend any amount of money on something so cliché. Which was the same thought he always had about the horse-drawn carriage rides. And the four-star bed-and-breakfast hotels.

And now he knew the answer.

Although it was late when they returned to the hotel, Bree was in tourist mode once again, having charged her phone a few additional percent on the short drive back. This time she snapped pictures of the room's interior since they'd only made it as far as the downstairs parlor when they checked in earlier.

Danny watched in amusement as she scurried about the room, taking pictures of the claw-foot tub, the antique plates and vases decorating the fireplace mantel, of the four-poster bed and the creepy portrait that hung above the headboard, all the while ignoring the obnoxious beep of her phone as it warned her of its imminent death. Leaving the best for last, she stepped out onto the balcony to admire the small courtyard garden below, complete with cast-iron fountain, now beautifully lit by the full moon.

With one final beep, her phone died. Bree whispered a curse and lowered her arms.

"Are you done for the night?" he asked from the doorway.

She sighed in disappointment. "I really wanted a

picture of the garden. Everything about it is perfect right at this very moment."

He made his way across the balcony, the old wooden floors creaking beneath his feet. "I guess a mental picture will have to do for now." But as far as he was concerned, to hell with the garden. This was the picture he wanted to sear into his brain, of her silhouette in the dark, of the moonlight highlighting the side of her face and neck.

Danny skimmed the back of his finger against the softness of her shoulder, just a ghost of a touch, really, before sliding beneath the spaghetti-width strings of her dress that crisscrossed her back. Her breathing became more labored as he stroked and teased her skin. When he leaned forward to press a kiss to her nape, the cell phone she'd been holding clattered to the floor.

They both reached for it at the same time, but his arm was longer. "I've got it," he said, picking it up and shoving it in his pocket. Taking her now-empty hand in his, Danny guided it back to the railing in front of her, wrapping her fingers around the wood. "You just hold on to this."

"Danny . . ."

"The only way we can be seen is from the courtyard and we'll hear anyone long before they could see us."

"If you say so." Her soft giggle transitioned into a contented sigh as Danny picked up where he left off. He pressed delicate kisses against her shoulder, traced her neck with the tip of his nose. When Bree's head lolled to one side, he took her earlobe between his teeth, testing the tender flesh before soothing it with his tongue.

With one hand he caressed her breasts through the soft fabric of her dress, the tips pebbling beneath his palm. His other hand coasted along her side, across her hip, where he felt the thin ridge of a waistband and texture of lace. Bree had always been a practical girl when it came to her underthings, but tonight she was wearing something different, something special. He drew up the skirt of the dress with his fingertips until it gathered at her waist so he could sneak a peek.

"Holy shit," he whispered.

The soft white lace she wore provided far more coverage than a traditional thong, but was cut in a way to expose more of her bottom, leaving the sweet curves of her ass cheeks on beautiful display.

Suddenly, he found it difficult to breathe.

Bree looked over her shoulder at him. "You like?"

"What do you think?"

In an instant he'd hauled her over his shoulder and carried her into their room, kicking the French door closed with his foot perhaps a little too hard. But he sure as hell wasn't going to take the time now to see if he'd broken it. He set her on her feet at the foot end of the bed, only long enough to lift the dress over her head before spinning her around and bending her over the mattress.

Laughing, she attempted to roll onto her back, but he quickly stopped her with a hand. "But I want to touch you," she complained.

"You can. Later."

Silently she agreed, remaining just as he wanted even after he removed his hand. Danny quickly went to work on his clothes but just as he loosened the last button on his shirt, he looked up to find the old judge or ship's captain, whatever he was, staring at him. Judging him.

Bree noticed him freeze up. "What's the matter?"

He pointed to the antique portrait above the bed. "His eyes are following me."

Danny pulled his arms from the sleeves and, grabbing one of the corner posts, hoisted himself up to walk across the bed.

"What the hell are you doing?" She laughed.

"I can't work like this. Damn thing is creeping me out." He hung his shirt from the top edge of the frame, straightening the fabric to make sure it stayed completely covered. He removed his hands and stepped back, watching to see if it would remain in place. Completely satisfied with his temporary solution, he climbed down from the bed.

"Now . . ." Danny swatted her ass, eliciting another giggle from her. "Where were we?"

He leaned over her, pressing his chest to her back as he started over at the top, kissing her neck and shoulders. With hands and mouth he savored every inch of her skin, working his way south until once again he'd reached that lacy white fabric. He smoothed his palm over the swell of her ass.

"Damn, Bree. These are nice. They're making me kinda crazy. Make me want to . . ." And before he second-guessed himself and before she could stop him, he leaned over and nipped her left cheek. Her yelp of surprise lengthened into a soft moan as he soothed the mark with his lips and tongue while his fingers provided an additional distraction between her thighs.

"Danny, please." Bree pushed herself up on her toes, exposing herself even more to him. "Please."

Within seconds he removed the remainder of his clothes and in one swift motion pulled the white lace from her body. He fisted his length, using the time to take a mental picture of his own so he would always remember her in this moment: open, exposed, her hands twisted in the comforter as she pulled herself higher onto the bed, begging him to fill her.

He entered her with one hard thrust, forcing Bree to stifle her cry in the sheets.

Danny froze. "Fuck, Bree. Are you okay? I'm—"

She turned her head to the side. "Don't stop. Don't ever stop."

Only then did he begin to move, determined to keep himself in check. But he was fighting a losing battle, especially since days before she'd taken that final barrier of latex and effectively tossed it aside. Now as he leaned over her, blanketing her writhing body beneath his, he covered her hand with his. Bree grasped hold of his fingers, twined and clenched them between hers, nearly cutting off the circulation to his fingertips. The antique bed and hundred-year-old floorboards squeaked beneath them as she cried out his name, begging and pleading with him to take her harder, faster, and the urgency within him rose up with a vengeance. Fighting for his last bit of control, he reached between her legs and roughly stroked the small bundle of nerves there. She buried her face into the mattress, muffling her screams as her body went taut and seized around him, catapulting him into his own release. Completely spent, he collapsed on top of her, his face resting against her sweat-slicked skin.

He was still trying to catch his breath when Bree began to squirm beneath him.

"Can't breathe," came her muffled voice.

Shit.

Danny stood up and quickly rolled her over on the bed. She gazed up at him with glassy eyes and soft smile as his hands skimmed over her face, down her neck, across her hips, checking for any visible injuries. "Are you okay? I know better than to get so rough with you."

With slow, languid movements, she rose from the bed and wrapped her arms around his neck, leaning the full length of her body against his. "Oh, no, I'm good." She lifted her chin, wanting a kiss, to which he happily obliged. "As a matter of fact, I'm very good. The people downstairs might not be too happy, but—" she lifted one shoulder "—who cares?"

God, she was beautiful. And sexy. And fun. She made him laugh. And go a little crazy. But he wanted nothing more than to keep that smile of satisfaction on her face for the rest of his life.

He swept her up in his arms and carried her the few steps to the side of the bed before drawing back the covers. She climbed into bed while he did those routine things that had to be done, like shutting off the lights, double-checking the doors were locked, and putting both their phones on the chargers.

"I hope you don't have anything big planned for tomorrow. I might need to spend the day recovering."

He climbed into bed beside her and pulled the covers up around their sweat-cooled bodies. "Nothing that requires you to do more than just lie there."

She arched a brow and smiled. "That sounds perfect."

Bree hummed in contentment as she settled against him, and the three little words he longed to say were poised on the tip of his tongue. But he bit them back, determined to save them for the next day.

As her body went lax and her breathing softened, Danny held her tighter, inhaling her delicious fragrance of lemonade and sugar cookies mixed with the heady scent of sex. He pressed a kiss to her cheek, to her temple, and nestled her beneath his chin.

Tomorrow he would tell her he loved her. Tomorrow he would get down on one knee and ask her to be his wife for the rest of their lives. If he'd waited this long, he could easily wait another day. All he needed to do was relax and stick to the plan, and everything would be perfect.

He closed his eyes, and like a kid on Christmas Eve, wished for tomorrow to come faster.

Chapter Twenty-Two

THE OBNOXIOUSLY LOUD ring of Danny's phone startled her awake. Bree cracked open one eye to read 6:38 on the digital clock and rolled over to face him. "You really aren't going for a run this morning, are you?" The words weren't completely out of her mouth before he threw back the covers and leaped out of bed.

"I have to go," he said, pulling his shirt down from where it hung on the portrait above the bed.

Holding the bedsheet to her chest, Bree leaned up on one elbow. "Go where?"

He continued to dress in the same clothes he wore the night before. "I have to report to HAAF within two hours."

"Two hours?" She was finding it impossible to make her brain function on so little sleep. All she could do was repeat everything he said.

"Listen to me. I need you to get dressed." He marched

across the room and grabbed up her suitcase from the luggage rack then returned to drop it on the foot end of the bed. "I'll need you to drop me off at HAAF, but after you can come back here."

Bree pulled out a T-shirt and pair of shorts from her overnight bag as he turned and headed into the bathroom. "Where are they sending you?"

Not bothering with a bra, she sat up and pulled the T-shirt over her head then slid off the bed to finish dressing. And of course, he returned the moment she was bending over to pull on her white lace thong, giving him more than an eyeful. Danny swore under his breath and she smiled at the teasing thought of that visual.

But he didn't smile back, his face tense and hard as stone. And that worried her. Even during times of stress or anger, they'd always found a moment of levity. Not this morning.

"You didn't answer me." When he stared at her questioningly, she repeated her earlier question.

"I'm sorry," he said, shaking his head. "Even if I did know, I wouldn't be able to tell you."

He was quiet the fifteen-minute drive home and once they arrived she could only stand frozen in the middle of the apartment, watching him rush from one room to the next as he gathered his things.

With his bag ready to go and sitting near the front door, he disappeared into the spare bedroom only to return with a stack of papers. Taking Bree by the hand, he asked her to sit at their small table then placed a sheaf of papers in front of her.

He opened the manila file, beginning with the first stack of papers clipped together.

"You shouldn't have any problems with the Tahoe, but if you do, here's the most recent maintenance records. The tires are fine. Just so happened I had the oil changed last weekend so all should be okay for a while. But if anything happens with it, any problems at all, call this guy." He scribbled a name and phone number on the top page. "Tell him you're my wife and he'll take care of everything for you."

She craned her neck to read his handwriting upside down. "Who's Doug Murray?"

"Retired army. Former Ranger. He's an older guy who helps take care of things around here while we're deployed. Don't worry, you can trust him."

He closed the folder and moved to the second file. "I've updated all my paperwork and named you my beneficiary."

"Danny—"

"This is the business of war, Bree." He reached across the table and took her hand in his. "As much as I dislike discussing it, it has to be done. You've worked in financial planning. You know this is important. The car payment is automatic deduct. Same with the rent and utilities. There's plenty of money in checking that nothing should ever bounce, but in the event something happens, I've given you power of attorney so you'll be able to deal with the bank. All the login, password and account information is in this file."

His thumb swept across the backs of her fingers a few

times until he focused on her ring. Carefully, he centered the setting on her finger with the pad of his thumb. "I've also signed a living will, giving you medical power of attorney, too."

Bree pulled her hand away and placed it in her lap. She didn't want this responsibility. Didn't want to be the one to make life and death decisions for him. Didn't want him put in a position where a living will was even considered a necessity.

"Shouldn't you list your dad for that?" she asked. "Or Mike, even? He'd be the better choice since he's a doctor. He'd understand things far better than I would."

He got up from his chair, she assumed to walk away from the conversation. Instead, he came around to her side of the table and crouched down beside her.

"I know you don't want to do this, but you're my wife, Bree."

She could feel the tears building but fought hard to hold them at bay. She needed to be strong even if the thought of putting this information to use was heartbreaking. It took several seconds before she could swallow down the fear and speak without her voice breaking. "I'll do it."

He smiled, patting her thigh. "I guess that covers everything. Time to go."

As they made their way through the parking lot, a cool breeze gusted and a misting rain began to fall, the weather now matching her mood. Dreary. Dismal. Driving to base took less than five minutes, but felt like an eternity. Like everything was happening in slow motion, yet passing too quickly at the same time. After parking, he turned the engine off and stared off into the distance.

"Be sure to always have your cell phone charged and with you. HQ has your number in case of emergency."

They climbed out of the truck and Danny grabbed his bags from the back. As they walked toward the gathering area, he handed her the car keys.

"How long will you be gone? I'm not asking for specifics," she quickly added when he gave her the side eye. "Just your best guess."

Danny shook his head. "There's really no way of knowing. Could be a week. Could be a couple of months. I promise we'll celebrate your birthday as soon as I come back."

Bree swore under her breath. Unfortunately, not so low he didn't hear her.

"What is it?"

She shouldn't have put off telling him about the email.

"You planned such a beautiful weekend for me, went to all that hard work. And I didn't want to say anything to ruin it. But I only have a week to decide and you don't know when you'll be back."

"A week to decide what?" He stepped directly in front of her, bending his knees just enough to bring his eyes level with hers. "Bree? A week to decide what?"

"That friend of mine in Greensboro offered me a job. If I want it, I have to be there by the end of the month."

In an instant his face went blank, making it impossible to get a read of what he was thinking or feeling.

"And what do you want?" he asked.

What she really wanted was for him to ask her to stay in Savannah, to be his wife forever. But that wasn't what they'd agreed upon all those months ago, and it wasn't fair to have this discussion now that he was headed off to God only knew where.

"It's a really great job," she heard herself tell him. "An opportunity like this may not come around again." But she'd turn it down, no regrets, if only he said they might have a future together. She stared into his eyes, hoping to see a flicker of disappointment, anger, something. Instead, nothing.

"Well . . ." He shrugged his shoulders. "It's all been leading up to this. If it's a job you really want, you should definitely take it."

"What about the—" She didn't want to say it, much less think about it. The moment she'd dreaded for weeks was now coming to fruition. Her eyes burned. Her chest ached. And she wondered if Danny could hear her heart shattering into a million pieces.

Once again, Danny came to her rescue. This time finishing her thought.

"You want to know about the divorce?"

Bree nodded.

He dropped his bags on the ground and stepped in close, his voice low so only she could hear. "Don't file anything while I'm gone. Okay? I'll handle everything."

Something about his tone sent a shiver down her spine. He must have noticed, now trying to chase the chill away by furiously rubbing the thin cotton covering her upper arms. "Why do you want to wait, Danny?"

She held her breath, hoping he'd say he wanted to forget their agreement. That he wanted her to stay with him forever. Instead, he looked at her with those deep blue eyes, his expression devoid of any and all emotion. The fun, charismatic Danny was gone, with only the hardened soldier remaining.

"This way if something happens to me you'll still have the insurance coverage you need. You'll get survivor benefits. I'll die knowing you're taken care of, no matter what."

The tears she'd been holding back all morning finally broke loose.

At the thought of never seeing him again, Bree collapsed against his chest, her fingers clutching the front of his uniform. She hung on for dear life, afraid if she let go she'd crumble to the ground. Danny wrapped his arms around her, his hold so tight she found it nearly impossible to breathe.

They remained that way for several heartbeats until they heard his name called from a distance.

"I'm sorry, but I have to go," he said, removing the grip she held on his clothes. He kissed her fingers before taking her face in both of his hands. He pressed one more kiss to her forehead, another to the tip of her nose, and finally one last tender touch to her lips.

Danny picked up his bags and took a few steps back, taking a long look at her as if committing her to memory. "Good luck in North Carolina, Dunbar. Kick some ass up there." And then that trademark smile appeared like a ray of sunshine, the rarely seen dimple creasing his cheek.

"Just so you know," he called to her, "you'll always be my favorite wife."

With one last wink, he turned and walked away, not bothering to look back.

BREE RETURNED TO the bed-and-breakfast alone. She packed up her things, canceled her spa appointment, and checked out of the hotel. She was hardly in the mood to enjoy a massage, let alone celebrate her birthday. The owners of the bed-and-breakfast were lovely, boxing up the birthday cake Danny had special ordered along with a bottle of champagne. She also received a rain check for her spa day and two nights' stay, the owners encouraging her to come back and celebrate his homecoming instead. Only problem with that idea was she'd likely be living in Greensboro by the time he returned stateside.

For now, instead of going home, she drove to Marie's, putting off the inevitable task of facing their apartment alone.

As she climbed the steps of the front porch, she gathered a few items left scattered across the yard by the boys. She rang the doorbell once, to which the dogs barked in response. She waited and waited then rang again, wondering if Marie and the kids were out back and didn't hear the bell.

Finally, a shadowed silhouette approached the leaded glass door. When it opened, Bree was taken aback by the woman standing in front of her. Marie wore yellow gloves and carried a mop bucket in one hand. Her eyes, red and swollen, told Bree all she needed to know. She walked inside and closed the door behind her.

"He left me one hell of a mess this time," Marie said, marching through the house to the downstairs guest room they were remodeling. "Dust all over the damn place. I swear, I could clean for days and still not get all of it."

Bree followed behind her, along with the dogs. But the house was silent. No telltale signs of cartoons or video games blaring. No music playing, either. The only sounds to disrupt the silence were that of rain against the windows and Cosmo's nails clicking on the wood floors as he trailed behind them.

"Where are the kids?"

"Leah went to a friend's house after we got back. The boys are at a birthday party. Hannah is next door. Ben and I planned on hanging wallpaper today but—"

On a mission of some sort, Marie marched down the back hallway until she reached the small bedroom facing the back of the house. For years it had been their staging area, a workshop of sorts as they remodeled the house room by room. With the rest of the house complete, the time had come for its face-lift.

Several weeks before, Marie had shown her a sketch of her vision. Crown moulding banded the top of the room. Bright white plantation shutters covered the windows, matching the wainscoting wrapping around the lower half. Unlike the rest of the house, which was contemporary in style, this one was to be unabashedly feminine. The wallpaper a delicate floral and soft chenille fabrics on the four-poster bed. It screamed traditional Savannah, with a view into the backyard of the small rose garden and ivy-covered wall.

She held her hands up momentarily before they dropped limply to her sides. "Now this all gets put on hold. Again." Marie grabbed the sponge from the bottom of the bucket and dropped to her knees, scrubbing away the fine layer of construction dust from the baseboards. "Sometimes I get so tired of it all. Of our things being put on hold. Of him missing their first steps. Missing their birthdays. And dance recitals.

"I knew what it meant when he enlisted. I knew he'd be absent a lot and I'd have to handle things on my own. And I'd like to think I've handled it all just fine, you know? The house hasn't burned to the ground and I haven't lost one of the kids yet, so I think I'm doing a pretty good job. But still there are days when I think it'd be easier to just—"

Her words came to an abrupt stop and Marie sat back on her heels. She shook her head as if trying to rid the word she wanted to say from her thoughts. "I don't know what I think."

As the tears began to fall, Marie looked in disbelief at the room around her.

Then it all became clear.

This was what Danny had warned her about. That even the strongest fortress had a weak point and could crumble to the ground in a moment's notice. This woman, whom Bree thought was the strongest woman she'd ever known, a woman who wrangled four kids and ran her own business and handled any crisis with ease, had moments when she, too, broke down and cried, wanted to give up.

Bree sat down next to her on the wooden floors and wrapped both arms around Marie's shoulders. For those first few seconds Marie held stalwart and rigid. Then her arms embraced Bree and they cried together.

They cried for the husbands they would miss. They cried out of anger at their leaving. But most of all, they cried in fear they might never return.

WITHIN NINETY MINUTES of his arrival at Hunter Army Airfield, the transport planes were loaded and Charlie Company went wheels up. Early in the flight, Lucky made his way around the C-17, handing out sleeping pills so the guys could manipulate their sleep cycles and hit the ground running the moment they landed.

On his previous deployments, Danny found it fairly easy to quiet his thoughts and fall asleep without the use of meds. He'd just pop in some earplugs and visualize the tide coming in while watching the sun rise over Myrtle Beach. But that wasn't going to work this time since he'd been gutted by the woman he loved just before boarding.

Everything about the weekend had been going according to plan. Right until his cell phone went off. Instead of being on a godforsaken plane headed to Africa, he should be enjoying the day with his wife.

Their evening was to include a candlelit dinner with

champagne and birthday cake, followed by a late-night ghost tour by horse-drawn carriage. Somewhere along the way, when the mood was just right, he'd tell her he loved her and that he didn't want their marriage to ever end. And of course, in his head, she always agreed. Maybe even say she'd hoped from the very beginning he'd change his mind. Then she'd laugh a little, and cry a little, but only because she was so, so happy. And then they would return to their room and make love for hours on an antique brass bed covered in rose petals.

What a fucking idiot he was.

He'd spent weeks planning what he hoped would be a romantic birthday weekend she'd never forget only to find out Bree had spent that same time applying and interviewing for jobs hundreds of miles away.

Karma, he supposed.

It was for the better he hadn't proclaimed his love. That he didn't tell her how over the past few months she'd become as important as air to him. How after a long week of training he couldn't wait to get home, wrap his arms around her and hold her tight. How he couldn't believe he was so damned lucky to get a second chance at happiness with her. How he looked forward to spending the rest of their lives together.

And now? Well, he didn't want to think about that.

Danny popped the two little pills into his mouth and finished off his bottle of water. He screwed the plastic cap back on and stowed the empty in his ruck. His stomach rumbled with hunger, but he ignored it, knowing the meds would kick in faster on an empty stomach. After all, the sooner he fell asleep, the sooner he'd forget he no longer had a wife to come back home to.

He squirmed for a bit, trying to find a comfortable position. He propped his feet up then put them back on the floor. He tried leaning all the way over, nearly resting his head on his knees. Then he shifted sideways in his seat, hoping he didn't wake up eight hours later with a massive crick in his neck.

Finally settled, Danny closed his eyes. And, much like he did almost ten years earlier on his first deployment, he thought of Bree.

Her beautiful smile. Her contagious laugh.

Those big brown eyes. The little crinkle between her brows when she was mad.

Her ice-cold feet. The warm flush of her skin.

The arch of her back. The scrape of her nails.

Soft moans. Breathless gasps.

Warm mouth. Full lips.

Tender kisses.

Wedding kisses.

Wedding rings.

I do.

Forever.

Always.

AFTER THEIR TEARS had dried, Bree and Marie decided to commemorate her birthday as best they could, starting with the cake and champagne Danny had ordered. Each armed with a fork, they ate straight from the box. And with each bite, they felt a little bit better.

Hours later the late-afternoon sun broke through the rain clouds and the silence disappeared as each child returned home. The neighbor keeping Hannah brought her home after her nap. Leah returned home after the movie, no longer in the mood to spend the night with friends. The boys burst through the front door in a ruckus with noisemakers and goodies and loud stories of how one boy smacked another in the head while taking a whack at the piñata. Within a matter of minutes the Wojciechowski house had returned to its normal chaotic routine with siblings fighting and children laughing and dogs racing wildly through the house.

As darkness fell and the house eased into nighttime routines, Bree said good-night.

"Are you sure you don't want to stay the night?" Marie asked at the door. "I know sleeping on the twin bed in the nursery doesn't hold the same appeal as my soon-to-be guest room would, but it still beats going home alone to an empty apartment."

Bree shrugged her shoulders. "I have to go home sometime."

Marie nodded in understanding. "Just so you know, you are always welcome here."

"I know," she called out as she headed down the front steps. "I'll see you Monday."

For the short drive home, she pulled one of Danny's favorite CDs from the holder strapped to the sun visor and slid it into the player. The heavy metal rock blasting from the speakers wasn't her preference, but she found herself sitting in the parking lot of their apartment complex, listening until the very end. Of course she was just delaying the inevitable.

Instead of loading in another disc, she chose to face the quiet dark of their apartment. Although she'd spent many nights here alone, it felt different this time. Knowing if there was an emergency, if she really needed him, he couldn't come rushing home to her rescue.

On the floor of their closet she found the shirt he'd run in the day before. She kicked off her shoes and stripped down to her panties then pulled the soft gray cotton over her head. Holes dotted the seams in the armpits and collar, and the hem was split and frayed from age. Holding the fabric up to her nose, she breathed in Danny's scent, a combination of sport deodorant and sweat.

After double-checking the locks and turning out the lights, she checked her phone one last time for any messages. Then she crawled into his side of the bed, buried herself deep within the covers and cried herself to sleep.

Chapter Twenty-Three

THE AFRICAN SUN blazed down as Danny hurried across the tarmac to C-Co's makeshift living quarters in an airport hangar. Since landing in Niamey ten days earlier, they had been running round-the-clock missions along with French Special Forces. Their targets, Al-Qaeda-linked militants in northern Mali, were responsible for everything from tourist kidnappings to embassy bombings across northern Africa.

Ben waited for him within the shade of the hangar, offering him a bottled water. "Hot enough for you? Only forty-four today."

Gratefully, Danny took the bottle of water, unscrewed the cap and drank it down all at once. While catching his breath, he did the temperature conversion in his head. "Fuck, man. That means it's actually 111 out there." Which wasn't hard to believe. It had felt as if the soles of his boots were melting beneath him as he crossed the asphalt. "Why do you insist on using Celsius anyway?"

"It sounds cooler." Ben chuckled. "Literally."

Danny shook his head and headed for his cot.

"Did you talk to Bree?"

It hadn't taken long for Ben to figure out Danny's head wasn't in the right place and like the good friend he was, kept pushing and pushing until Danny told him everything. How Bree had been offered a new job. How she had asked him if she should take it. How he wished her luck and instead of telling her how he felt, he took the pussy way out. Again.

"Went to voice mail." Never before had he requested to call home. Of course, he'd always deployed as a single guy. Never had to fear the love of his life leaving him while he was gone. Although this had been their plan from the very beginning, Danny now hated it was coming to pass.

"Did you leave her a message at least?"

Danny scrubbed a hand over his face and fell back onto his cot. "No. Probably pointless to call her anyway." Bree wasn't expecting his call and likely wouldn't answer without an identifying caller number. "I'd bet she's on the way to Greensboro if she's not already there."

Fuck. He was an idiot for letting her go.

"So that's it? You're just gonna let her go?"

Danny shrugged his shoulders. "What am I supposed to do?"

Ben shot to his feet and began pacing the same ten feet of concrete floor. Then just as quickly as he started, he stopped. "Get up," Ben said, throwing his hands in the air. "Come on. Get your ass up."

Danny moved to sit on his cot, but nothing more, wary of Ben's sudden change in demeanor. "What the hell for?"

Ben cracked his knuckles. "Because I'm going to single-handedly knock some fucking sense into that god-damn thick-headed, dumb-ass skull of yours."

Danny's jaw dropped. "The heat is making you fucking crazy."

"I'm crazy? I'm crazy?" Veins he didn't know existed popped out on Ben's forehead as his face went beet-red. "I'd rather be crazy than a fucking idiot!"

Danny made no move to get up. "This is what she wants."

"Are you sure about that? She's making a decision based on bad intel. If you'd had the balls to tell her how you really feel, I bet money she would have stayed."

"You don't know Bree like I do. She's so very smart. Bad luck combined with rotten timing is the only reason she hasn't been a huge success so far. This job is a huge opportunity. I couldn't ask her to give it up."

Having calmed down a bit, Ben dropped onto the cot next to Danny. "Then go with her. You've only got a few months left on your contract. You could leave the military and follow her."

"Really? And do what? This is all I know. It's all I'm good at."

"That's not true."

Danny pointed at him. "It absolutely is fucking true. If

leaving the military is such a damn good idea, why aren't you considering it? Why aren't you putting that good ol' GI Bill to use and living off your wife's business, huh?"

Ben remained silent.

"You and I, we're not cut out for boring office jobs. And we sure as hell aren't cut out to teach Crossfit to middle-aged soccer moms. This—" he said, waving a finger at the hangar full of men and equipment around them "—is what we do. We like the adrenaline. The camaraderie. But most of all we've got each other's backs. We equally support each other. If I were to leave the military, I'd have nothing."

"But you'd have Bree. If ever the day came that Marie said it was her or the army, I'd choose her. Every. Single. Time. I'd choose her. And I'd never spend a day regretting it. Because she is the single most important person in my life."

Exhausted, Danny rested his elbows on his knees, his head hanging from his shoulders. "It's my job as a man to take care of her and support her and keep her safe. If I can't do that, then what's the point?"

Ben rose to his feet, all the while shaking his head in disbelief. "I don't get your thinking, Danny. I don't get it at all. We're Rangers. We don't know the meaning of quit. And yet, that's exactly what you just did."

Before Danny could respond, Ben turned his back on him and walked away.

By the time Bree reached the second-floor landing she was an exhausted, sweaty mess. If she was having issues hauling the flattened cardboard boxes she purchased across the parking lot and up the stairs while they were empty, she sure as hell wouldn't be able to move them once they were full.

Thankfully, Marie knew a couple of college guys with a truck and nothing but free time who were willing to help her out with the move. It wasn't as if she had much, so all she had to do was pay for their food, gas, and a day's work.

Within a matter of days she'd be more than 300 miles away, starting her new job, her new life. Although she didn't really want to go, she also knew she couldn't stay. Ring or no ring. Vows or no vows.

For ten days she'd held out hope Danny would change his mind and ask her to stay. That time and distance would somehow bring them closer. Instead, there had only been silence. Which, of course, played right into her insecurities, letting her imagination run wild with reasons as to why he let her go so easily.

Like the thought that Danny had changed more in the past ten years than she'd realized and he had no desire to marry, ever. That their temporary arrangement was nothing more than a chance to play house, to try the idea on for size to see if marriage was or wasn't for him. In which case, so be it.

Or maybe he did like being married, but what she felt in her heart was completely one-sided and his love for her wasn't more than as a friend. With or without benefits. Which completely sucked.

Or even worse, he liked being married to her and

loved her, but now that he'd had a taste of family life he wanted to have it all, including children. Or at the very least he didn't want to rule out the possibility. In which case, she was completely shit out of luck. And that hurt like hell.

Her phone chimed, alerting her to a new voice mail. A phone call she'd obviously missed while getting more boxes from the car. The call came from a number she didn't recognize, but instantly her stomach twisted in knots.

She followed the prompts and waited for someone to speak but there was only deafening silence and instantly she knew who had called.

She held her breath, hoping, wishing he would say something. Anything.

I love you.

I hate you.

She could make out the sound of his breathing in the receiver. Voices in the background, but nothing distinguishable.

All too soon, the message ended.

Instead of choosing to delete ten seconds of dead air, she saved it and listened all over again just to hear his breath. And maybe if she listened hard enough, the beat of his heart.

RISKY MISSIONS WEREN'T just part of the job. They were the job. But on the pushing-your-luck scale, some missions were far worse than others, and this one in particular didn't sit well in his gut. Danny returned to C-Co's makeshift quarters where he quickly briefed his squad. When he was done, instead of preparing his weapons and ruck, he went in search of pen and paper.

His mind had been with her for much of this deployment. When he was kicking in doors and leading his men, his focus was one hundred percent on the mission at hand. But those other times, before he drifted off to sleep after being awake for thirty-six hours straight, his thoughts were of her. Of what he wished he had said to her before he left.

There was so much he had to say to her and no fucking idea where to start.

He did what he could, scribbled down what came to mind, unsure if what made its way onto the paper made any sense at all. It was a far cry from poetry, wasn't a decent love letter, either. But he got the important stuff down. That he loved her, would always—underlined twice for emphasis—love her. And that he hoped someday they might figure out a way to be together forever.

He folded the page, sealed the envelope tight, and shoved it in his pocket.

From there he went to find Mike, who was helping Lucky and the other medics stockpile their kits for the upcoming mission. He waited patiently out of the way, not wanting to interrupt. But his face must have revealed the uncertainty he felt inside, because Mike took one look at him and came marching over.

"What's wrong?"

Danny pulled the once-white envelope, now smudged

with dirt, from his pocket. Using his fingers he attempted to lessen the stain, but only succeeded in making things worse. "I need to give you this."

"What the fuck is this?" Mike asked, refusing to take the letter addressed to Bree from his brother's outstretched hand. "I'm not taking a death letter."

"It's not—"

There was no point in arguing. Mike called it what it was. And for the very first time in ten years, Danny was scared to death. Not even as a snot-nosed kid fresh out of RIP, dropping into Iraq under the cover of darkness and into the middle of a war zone had he been this scared.

But it wasn't the mission at hand that frightened him as much as never having the chance to tell Bree face-to-face how much he loved her. Had always loved her. Even when he left her.

"—I just need her to know."

Reluctantly, Mike took the envelope from his hand. "What is it about this mission?"

"I don't know." That was the honest truth. The feeling hadn't been there two nights before or the mission before that. But he could no longer pretend that everything was as it should be. "Just got a bad feeling about it, Mikey. They're dropping us on a compound in broad daylight, which is bullshit for one and fucked up for another. We spend most of our lives training in the dark and then they go and do this. But whatcha gonna do?"

He turned to walk away, but then stopped himself, remembering one final thing.

"Just so you know, I bought her a ring. It's in the left pocket of my dress blues."

Anger crossed Michael's face. "Why the hell didn't you give it to her?"

"I had a whole thing planned because I wanted to do it right this time, not like in Myrtle Beach. And I sure as hell wasn't gonna hand her a velvet box before I boarded a plane. Then she told me about the job offer and . . ." He still couldn't believe it. How in a matter of hours every one of his plans had taken a deep dive into a steaming pile of shit. "Anyway, if something happens—"

"*Nothing* is going to happen to you."

"—I'm just saying, if it does, then you can give it to her or return it or maybe you can use it someday. So . . . I've got to go."

Before he reached the open hangar door, Michael chased him down and grabbed him up in a fierce embrace.

"Do me a favor. Remember that you have a lot to live for. Don't go out there putting yourself in harm's way unnecessarily." Still clutching his shoulders, Michael stepped back so he could stare Danny in the eyes. "You may not have kids at home like a lot of these guys, and at this point you may or may not have a wife, but that doesn't mean you aren't loved. That you wouldn't be missed. Do you hear me?" Michael shook him hard for good measure. "Dad loves you and it would kill him to lose you. Same goes for me."

"I hear ya."

Danny affectionately slapped his brother's shoulders with both hands then pulled himself from Michael's grasp. "Gotta go."

He was halfway across the tarmac when Michael called out to him. "I'll see you on the other side, Danny!"

Without turning around, Danny waved his hand in the air. There was no point in drawing out their goodbye.

In the past ten years he'd seen it happen more than once. A guy got a bad feeling in his gut, a sixth sense about something going wrong, and it always came to pass. Maybe they died because they were scared and lost their edge. Or maybe they died simply because it was their time to go.

No one would ever know for sure. He could only hope that in this case, he was fucking wrong.

Bree stretched the tape across the cardboard flaps, sealing the last box shut. Being filled with only candle holders and throw pillows and towels, it was far lighter than the others and she carried it into the living room.

Danny's space was his own again, having returned to the dull, monochromatic style it was before. The photos she'd found that first week and put into frames remained untouched. And beside them, a large framed print of the two of them, the same photo taken during the parade that appeared in the paper.

She wanted to take it. Even had it wrapped and packed in a box at one point. But it didn't feel right. That picture belonged here, in this place. If Danny wanted to take it down after she was gone and bury it in the bottom of a box along with the other photo he kept of the two of them, then so be it.

Bree looked around the apartment one last time to be certain nothing had been missed. Her clothes and shoes and everyday things she'd wait to pack, saving them until the morning she moved, just three days from now. That meant there was only one more thing.

She stared at the ring on her finger. It definitely wasn't right for her to keep it.

As much as she loved Danny, as much as she wanted to spend the rest of her life with him, being in a one-sided relationship could only last so long. Sooner or later it would only bring both of them misery. He didn't intend to marry, but he'd done so out of some sense of duty and misplaced guilt. She would forever be grateful for what he did, helping her get her life back. But she would always feel they threw away another chance at happiness.

"No time like the present."

She sat down on the end of their bed and attempted to remove the ring in a single pull. Despite her fingers being slender, the vintage wedding band was snug and required some effort to remove it. She'd twisted the ring halfway over her knuckle when someone knocked on the door.

"Just a second," she yelled as she pushed the ring back on for the moment.

Without looking through the peephole, she flung open the door.

"Mrs. MacGregor?"

The men standing in front of her were clearly military

although she didn't recognize either at first glance. The one closest to her had a patch between the buttons of his jacket with two bars, but she couldn't recall what rank it meant. She studied his name and didn't recognize it, either.

But the black stitching on his right chest was a symbol everyone knew.

Chapter Twenty-Four

MARIE ONCE TOLD her how to know if your husband was injured or killed based on how many men came to your door and what they were wearing. But she couldn't remember a bit of it now it was actually happening. Once the cross on his uniform caught her attention, she lost all focus and only vaguely heard him introducing himself along with the man standing beside him.

"How is he?" she heard herself ask.

"May I come in?"

If she said yes, she didn't hear it. Wasn't sure if she nodded or spoke or if they just came in anyway. The chaplain guided her to the loveseat while the other man closed the door behind himself and remained outside.

"Your husband is alive, but in critical condition," he began. "What I have been told is he suffered three wounds. One to the leg. Two to the torso. I do not know the severity of each. An initial surgery was performed in theater before he was transported to Landstuhl."

"Where's that?"

"Germany, ma'am."

She was trying to wrap her brain around what he was telling her. "Where was he that they transported him to Germany?"

"I'm afraid that's classified, ma'am."

Of course it was. That was the operational security stuff Danny had warned her about.

Meanwhile, her imagination ran wild with bloody scenes from every military movie she remembered. And the fear was slowly replaced with anger.

Why, after all, should fathers and mothers and wives and sons and daughters be told where their loved ones have been sent to fight? She'd watched the evening news every day since he left. Searched the internet for any clue to his whereabouts. So many places in the world they could have sent him. So many places for him to die far from his family. From her.

But she had no choice but to accept the fact she might never know what happened to Danny simply because the mission or whatever they called it was *classified*.

Her flash of anger quickly gave way to acceptance and numbness.

The chaplain took her hand in his. "Mrs. MacGregor?"

She turned to look him in the eyes for the first time. They were an interesting shade of gray. Not quite blue. Not quite green. It reminded her of the early-morning fog the day Danny left.

"Is there anyone you'd like to call or someone I can call for you so that you're not alone?"

"I can do that?"

He nodded. "Yes, ma'am."

As the chaplain watched, she sent a text message to Marie, asking her to come over. Ten minutes passed without response, leaving her to assume Marie was busy with the kids.

She fought her way through another wave of tears and before she knew it and without any prompting, she began to tell the chaplain the story of her and Danny. How they grew up together, how they once meant everything to each other, how they eventually went separate ways. Then she told him of that early morning in a Myrtle Beach grocery store, of his backyard proposal and the courthouse wedding. She told him of the laughter and tears and everything in between.

Turning over her hand, he pressed a brass coin into her palm and folded her fingers over it. "In the hours and days ahead, I'm sure there will be times of darkness, times when you will feel very alone. When you do, look at this and remember that is certainly not the case. You have your family. You have your military family. You have your heavenly family. All will be there for you when needed."

As she clutched the coin tightly in her hand, letting the edge dig into her skin, there was a knock on her door for the second time that afternoon. Marie came rushing through the moment Bree opened it, immediately throwing her arms around Bree's neck. "I'm so sorry. I didn't hear the alert for your text message and only saw it after the call came in regarding unit injuries."

Assured she would be taken care of, the chaplain left and Bree began telling Marie everything she knew, which in the end amounted to very little. For now she was waiting on a call from the hospital in Germany. She had no idea if he was on the way to Landstuhl or already there, whether he'd be shipped back to Walter Reed within a matter of days or if his injuries were so significant the army would send her overseas.

"Have you talked to his father?"

She'd dialed Mac a dozen times in a fifteen-minute span before she forced herself to put down her phone. "Voice mail."

"They'll get ahold of him," Marie said, patting Bree's leg. "So what are you going to do in the meantime? Stay here, or go to Myrtle Beach and wait there with your family until Danny's stateside?"

Bree shrugged.

"You are going to wait for him, aren't you? Don't tell me after everything you two have been through, you're just going to take the easy way out?"

"I'm supposed to be in Greensboro—"

"Don't make me smack some sense into you," Marie said, pointing a finger at her. "You know you don't want that job. I know you don't want that job. In fact, I think the only person in the world who doesn't know this is Danny. So here's what you're going to do." Marie grabbed Bree by the arm and towed her into the bedroom where Bree's empty suitcase sat beside the bed. "You're going to pack your suitcase with only the essentials." She opened the top dresser drawer and pointed inside. "Get at it."

Then she calmly took a seat on the corner of the bed and kept a watchful eye on Bree while messing with her phone.

"Here's the thing," Marie said a few minutes later. "There's a flight that leaves for Myrtle Beach in ten minutes, which you wouldn't make even if there was a seat available. Do you think you're okay to drive there? It's how far?"

Having gathered her essentials from the bathroom, Bree stopped short in the doorway. "You're looking up flights for me?"

"Of course I am. That's what friends do."

Tears threatened once again. "How am I—"

"Listen to me. You can do this." Marie crossed the room and took hold of Bree once again, guiding her to the suitcase. "If there's one thing I've learned being an army wife all these years, it's that I have a pretty good idea which marriages are strong enough to survive military life. Which spouses can ride this wild lifestyle out. You've made it through your own battles and that's why Danny needs you. You're strong enough to handle this."

Bree took a deep breath and composed herself. Marie was absolutely right. So was the chaplain. As her dad would say, it was time to buck up. She owed it to Danny to be there for him. As to what would happen between them afterward . . . well, she'd worry about it later.

"Depending upon traffic, it takes about four hours from here to there. When is the next flight?"

Marie checked her phone. "Not until eight. So you might as well drive to Myrtle Beach. If you leave in the next hour, you can be there around nine."

They threw the last of her things in the suitcase and headed out the door.

"For the longest time I wondered why Danny didn't marry. Why he bounced from one woman to another, can't even call them relationships. Now it all makes sense. He was waiting for you."

"No, he wasn't," Bree said as she loaded her suitcase in the Tahoe. "Trust me. I was right where he left me."

"Okay, maybe waiting is the wrong word here." Marie followed her around to the driver-side door. "Maybe it's more like hope. He was hoping for a second chance with you."

A LITTLE BEFORE ten that night, she pulled Danny's Tahoe into the driveway of his childhood home. Only once she turned onto their street did Bree realize she'd completed most of the drive from Savannah on autopilot. She remembered stopping for gas and placing a quick phone call to Mac, but aside from that she recalled nothing of her trip. An accomplishment that was equally amazing and disturbing.

Even before she shut the engine off, the porch light flickered to life and the front door opened when both Mac and her dad appeared on the front porch. By the time she'd reached the top step, she was overcome with tears for what seemed like the millionth time that day.

"Don't you worry," Mac said, his voice a low grumble

in her ear as he clung tightly to her. "My son will make it home. After all, he's got a lot to live for."

She could only wonder what Mac would say if he knew they'd decided to go their separate ways just minutes before Danny boarded his plane.

When her father-in-law finally released her, she was immediately caught up in her father's arms.

"Just hang in there, pumpkin," her father said, alternating between rubbing her back with one beefy hand and kissing the top of her head.

As they followed Mac into the house, her dad held her steady with one strong arm wrapped around her shoulders. Then her mother met them just inside the door, took her by both hands and led her to the sofa, all the while asking if she'd eaten, if she was thirsty or needed to lie down. All that smothering care and concern she'd run away from months earlier, she gladly welcomed now, willing to take any and all support she could get.

And then from out of nowhere Father Bryant came in.

She wanted so badly to tell him to get out. To say things weren't so critical with Danny that it required all the prayers and consolation.

But she didn't know just how dire the situation was, nor was she the one suffering. So she held her tongue.

Everything they were saying, the prayers they recited, reminded her of last rites.

They had prayed over her in the same way when she was at her weakest. When she was most vulnerable. When she wanted nothing more than to sit up in her bed and tell them to get the hell out because she wasn't going anywhere.

But this time they couldn't force her to sit there and take it.

So she politely excused herself and headed down the darkened hallway to Danny's old room. She flipped the switch and the single overhead bulb snapped, shrouding the room in darkness. For a moment she wondered if she wasn't supposed to be here. If the universe was telling her she was violating Danny's personal space and the burned-out lightbulb was a sign to go.

But if she wasn't here, where was she supposed to go? Back across the street to her parents' house, to her old room? Going there felt like giving up.

From memory she crossed the room to where a small desk sat in the corner. Surprisingly, the gooseneck lamp still worked, casting odd light and shadows across the room. Exhausted from the emotional roller coaster she'd been riding most of the day, Bree sank down onto the edge of his bed to start, then slowly lowered herself onto the mattress, placing her head on the pillow. Her eyes scanned the room. Dusty books high upon a shelf. Ribbons and medals and trophies. A Major League movie poster. Several framed pictures.

Atop the dresser was one of Danny and his mother. In it he wore a Braves T-shirt while sitting in his mother's lap, her arms wrapped around his middle, squeezing him as she kissed his ear. A big smile as he tried to wriggle from her embrace.

He couldn't have been older than five at the time. He would have lost her soon after. She wondered if that was the last picture of them together.

Bree pulled her phone from her pocket, swiped the unlock screen with her thumb. No voice mails. No emails. No text messages. She quickly sent a message to Marie, letting her know she'd arrived in Myrtle Beach. A few seconds later she received one in return.

Get some rest. Keep me posted.

Then, refusing to put it off any longer, she fired off an email to her friend in Greensboro, explaining Danny's injury, that she was awaiting news on his condition, and would likely be delayed a week at minimum. Whether or not she held the job for Bree was a different story.

From there she opened the photo gallery on her phone, swiping through the many pictures she'd taken since arriving in Savannah. She stopped on a selfie of the two of them, last photo taken of them together the night before her birthday. In it, with Talmadge Bridge in the background and the sun setting behind them, Danny pressed a kiss to her cheek.

At this point she didn't care if they stayed married or divorced. All she wanted was for him to live. Nothing else mattered.

BRIGHT SUNLIGHT STREAMED through the open blinds, waking her. At some point in the evening she'd fallen asleep in Danny's room and the problem of whether to stay here or across the street was easily solved. Her suitcase had been brought in from the car and sat near the closet door and her phone was—

"Shit!"

Just seconds later she heard the distant ringing of a telephone. Instead of digging the charger from her handbag, she raced through the living room and into the kitchen where Mac was talking on the phone. She'd barely rounded the corner when he told someone on the other end, "She's right here. Hang on."

He covered the mouthpiece with his palm. "It's someone in Germany calling with an update on Danny," he said, handing her the corded phone. "Give me a second and I'll get on the other end."

"Hello?"

"Mrs. MacGregor, my name is Anne and I have news about your husband."

This stranger had the voice of an angel, kind and soothing. She said Danny had recently come out of a long surgery, that he suffered significant internal damage as a result of multiple wounds. Although he survived, his list of injuries was extensive.

Ruptured spleen. Damaged kidney. Perforated bowel.

There were other words like significant blood loss, transfusions, low blood pressure, and high risk of infection.

"Barring any post-surgical complications and if his vitals remain stable, he will be transported to Walter Reed within a day or two."

The woman promised to keep an eye on Danny and to call if there were any changes.

Bree hung up the phone and took a seat at the kitchen table. Once again, all she had to do was sit and wait.

Chapter Twenty-Five

DANNY'S EYES SHOT open and he quickly scanned his surroundings. He was in the cool, sterile confines of a hospital room, no longer in the extreme heat and dusty surroundings of Africa. No longer with his men.

"You're okay, Daniel." His father stood at his bedside, one strong hand resting on Danny's shoulder. "Just relax."

Through the haze of pain meds, his father's voice sounded muffled and distant. It would be so easy to slip back to sleep, but at some point he'd have to fully wake up, have to face the reality of why it was his father at his bedside and not Bree. So he focused on his breathing and tried to get his heart rate under control.

"Do you know where you are?"

"Yeah," Danny huffed. "I remember being loaded on a medical transport and vaguely recall someone telling me I'd arrived at Walter Reed. How long have I been here?"

"Couple of days. Your temperature spiked en route.

You had a pretty good infection going, but they've got it under control now." His dad patted his leg and Danny shifted slightly so his old man could take a seat on the edge of the bed.

"Is that all?"

"You mean aside from the fact you're minus a kidney and a spleen and a section of your small intestine?" Mac laughed without humor. "Sure, that's all."

So he'd lost a few organs. But as far as he knew, they were all things he could live without. Which hopefully meant that as soon as he could get the hell outta here, he'd be back with his unit and doing the one thing he was good at.

"Have you heard anything about Jenkins?"

"I received an email from Michael once the communication blackout was lifted. He said you'd ask about him. Jenkins has some facial wounds, a ruptured eardrum, and a concussion. But otherwise he's okay."

Danny breathed a sigh of relief and closed his eyes. "That's good to hear."

"Your brother also said that's how you were injured, that you went back for him. Do you remember that?"

"Yes."

Of course he did. He remembered all of it. Jenkins set the charge and blew the compound gate, stepping aside as the squad team rushed inside through clouds of dust and smoke. Then there was a second blast, likely from an RPG. And although the enemy missed their target, Jenkins was close enough to impact that he was hit with debris and shrapnel in the face. By the time

Danny had turned around, Jenkins had fallen to his knees, blinded by his own blood and completely out of it. A sitting duck.

So Danny did what he was trained to do, what any other guy in his place would have done. He charged into the open space, grabbed Jenkins by his vest, and dragged him to safety.

"What else do you remember?"

Danny remembered the feel of hot metal slashing through his leg and back. Of pushing forward, but only managing several more yards before he fell to the ground, unable to get back up despite his best effort to ignore the pain. Then hearing someone call "MacGregor's down" in his tactical headphones and knowing he was well and truly fucked. He remembered Ben pulling a tourniquet from a front pocket, wrapping it around his thigh, and cinching it tight, all the while screaming, "Fuck, Danny. I can't fix this!" Then Lucky appeared out of nowhere and used both hands to roll him like a rag doll onto his side, before pulling at his vest and body armor. He remembered the look of devastation on Ben's face as he helped carry Danny to the medevac and how he placed a kiss upon Danny's forehead before the doors slammed shut.

But he wouldn't dare tell his father any of that.

"I remember Mike saying, 'Dad is so gonna kick your ass for this.' " Danny began laughing, only to have it quickly transition into excruciating pain. "Do me a favor. Let me get out of here before you do that," he said through gritted teeth.

Only then did he look at his father, who wore an

expression saying he found Danny's attempt at levity far from funny.

His father rose from the bed. "I need to go tell Bree you're awake. Let me see if she's back from the cafeteria yet."

Danny could hardly believe what he was hearing. "She's here?"

"Of course. She is, after all, your wife." Mac folded his arms across his chest. "Thing is, she's stayed in the waiting room the entire time. Why is she out there when she should be in here?" he asked, shaking his head in disbelief. "Wanna tell me what's going on?"

"YOU CAN'T STAY out here in the hallway the rest of your life." Mac plopped down in the plastic chair beside Bree, the metal legs creaking beneath his weight. "I'm not sure what happened between you two, but at some point in time you're gonna have to go in there."

"I don't think he'd want me in there." She pulled off the plastic cover from her sub-par coffee and blew on it, helping it to cool.

He sucked in half the air in the waiting room then huffed it all out again in one big exhale. "God damn you two are difficult. Proof you're made for each other."

"Because no one else would have us?"

"Because you two don't want anyone else is more like it." Mac ran a hand across his face, the stress and exhaustion of the past several days catching up with him. "Listen to me. He's confined to bed for now. Couldn't come to you if he wanted to, and believe me he wants to."

Her heart leaped in her chest. "He's awake? Has he said so?"

"Not in so many words. But he knows you're here. And he kept one eye zeroed in on the door." Mac pointed to Danny's hospital room door. "I need you to go in there. Danny needs you to go in there."

Silently, she nodded in agreement and Mac softly patted her knee. "Good girl."

Bree rose to her feet and dropped her mostly full coffee cup in a nearby trash can. It wasn't as if she'd wanted it anyway. But from the moment she arrived here, she'd been suffering from a constant chill in her spine, unable to chase it away.

With Danny now awake, the time had come for her to tell him how she felt. She only hoped that Marie was right that Danny's feelings for her ran far deeper than friendship. In one hand she clutched the coin the army chaplain had given her with Psalm 23 engraved upon the back, the verse now committed to memory, she'd spent so much time reading it. Although the verse didn't apply in this circumstance, she did fear his breaking her heart for a third time.

She passed by two beds, the first with the curtain completely drawn and hushed whispers coming from the other side. The second she assumed was temporarily vacated, with disheveled sheets on the bed and a water pitcher damp with condensation on the nearby tray. And then there was Danny at the end of the room, facing away from her as he stared out the window. Heavy stubble shadowed his face and the blankets settled around his waist, revealing the even rise and fall of his chest. From a distance, it looked like he was just lounging in bed, like nothing terrible had happened to him at all. Only as she came closer did she notice the many tubes and monitors attached to him and the orange stain of betadine on his skin.

Without warning his head turned toward her, his eyes meeting hers.

But there weren't any answers in those dark blue depths. Her stomach twisted and her heart ached. Tears welled in her eyes and her chin trembled as she struggled not to cry. She didn't know how this would end, only that she wouldn't survive saying goodbye to him again.

GOOD GOD, SHE was a beautiful sight, even wearing a worn-out T-shirt, ratty jeans and that god-awful hat she loved. Dark circles shadowed her eyes and her expression was completely unreadable. He couldn't tell if she was happy he was alive or resented the fact she was here in the first place. But now that she stood only mere feet from him, he would say or do damn near anything to get her to stay.

A squeak of rubber on tile followed by voices alerted them to the return of his neighboring roommate. Immediately, Bree grabbed hold of the striped privacy curtain and guided it around the track, isolating them from the rest of the world. But still she remained out of reach when he desperately wanted to touch her.

Danny pressed both fists into the mattress, trying to push himself into a more upright position when a stab of pain traveled through his body.

Immediately, Bree rushed to his side, her hands suspended midair as if she was afraid to touch him. "What the hell are you trying to do?"

Ignoring the pain, he quickly grasped one slender wrist before she could move away. "This," he whispered, tugging her even closer as he eased back against the inclined bed. With her face just inches from his now, he cupped the back of her head with his free hand and guided her mouth to his. Although their kiss was little more than a gentle press of his lips against hers, neither were in a hurry for it to end. But when it did, he wasted no time in telling her everything he'd written in that letter.

"I love you, Bree," he said in a rush. "I know you really want that job in Greensboro—" She silenced him with two fingers against his lips.

"I don't want that job," she whispered. "I never wanted that job. I love you, and I want to stay with you in Savannah."

For the first time in weeks, the heavy weight pressing on his chest lifted and he could breathe again. By some miracle, despite making one idiotic decision after another, he hadn't lost her a second time. "Thank God."

Bree must have felt a similar relief, resting her forehead against his as tears slid down her cheeks and dripped off her chin onto his chest. He tried to hold her as best he could, rubbed her spine with the flat of his palm until she pulled away.

"I'm getting you all wet."

"It's okay. I'm in need of a good shower."

There was something else going on in that head of hers; he could see the uncertainty in her eyes.

"What about kids? Are you sure you won't want them someday?"

He slid sideways, giving her room to sit on the mattress next to him. Taking her hand in his, Danny waited until she looked him in the eyes.

"I'm sure. If things were different and you could have children, I'd probably let you convince me otherwise for the simple reason I would move heaven and earth to make you happy. But at the end of the day, having kids doesn't matter to me. All I want is you. Just you."

Mindful of his IV, Bree climbed into bed, pressed a kiss to his cheek, and carefully stretched out alongside him. Her head rested on his shoulder and her hand cupped his jaw, her fingertips gently stroking his beard. Danny wrapped his right arm around her and pulled her tighter to his side. For now this was as close as they could be. But he wouldn't trade it for anything in the world since she was, without a doubt, the best medicine he could ever ask for.

Her familiar scent surrounded him and his entire body relaxed. The pain dulled. His mind quieted. Her soft exhales warmed his skin, and he knew he was home.

Sometime later they both woke when the curtain was whipped open by the new shift nurse.

Bree sat up quickly, like she'd been caught doing something wrong. "Do you need me to leave?"

"You're fine right where you are, hon," the woman said with a smile before turning to Danny. "It's nice to see you awake today. How are you feeling?"

"Couldn't be better," he said, unable to hold back a smile.

"Well, I doubt that's completely true, but it's nice you feel that way," the nurse said with a wink. "Anything I can get you this evening?"

"I'd kill for a shower." How Bree tolerated lying next to him, he didn't know, because his own stench was getting to him. After all, it'd been a solid week, maybe longer, since he'd had a quick rinse, much less a shower with real soap.

"Now, now. No need to go to the extreme." She gently patted his arm. "You can't get up to take a shower yet, but you can have a sponge bath. And since your wife's here, I think she's just the person to help you with that."

Bree, however, wasn't convinced. "I'm not so sure—"

"You'll do just fine." The nurse placed a reassuring hand on Bree's shoulder. "Just mind the sutures and his IV and don't get them too wet. I'll be right back with everything you need."

With a flick of her wrist, the curtain closed just as quickly and they were alone once more.

Danny cradled her face in his palm, his thumb stroking the soft skin of her cheek. "There's an extra twenty in it for you if you can finish me off with a happy ending," he whispered. "What do you say?"

It took a second for her to catch his meaning, her eyes widening the moment she caught on, followed by her soft laughter. He joined in with a chuckle or two before the pain got the best of him.

"Are you okay?" Her smile replaced with concern.

"I'm fine."

Although Bree fought it, the corner of her mouth lifted. "You're terrible, you know?"

Of course he knew. And even better, he knew she liked him that way.

Danny pulled her close for another kiss. "I know, sweetheart," he whispered against her lips. "And I'm all yours."

Chapter Twenty-Six

August

BREE WOULD BE late for her own wedding if she didn't hurry up. Of course, in all fairness, she didn't know the real reason he was rushing her out the door.

Danny took another look at his watch. "About ready?" he called from the living room.

"Just another minute," she yelled back.

The plan, as far as she knew, was for a weekend getaway to Tybee Island. It included a night at a bed-and-breakfast and candlelight dinner for two on the beach. And to make up for not having a single picture from their courthouse wedding, a professional photography session at sunset.

What she didn't know was that a hundred of their closest friends and family were waiting for them at the beach.

The idea of a second wedding came about while he was still recovering at Walter Reed as they sat upon his hospital bed and whispered words of love and renewed commitment to each other. Despite it being just the two of them, no witnesses, no officiant, their vows held greater meaning than the first time they were spoken. But something was missing and Danny soon realized renewing their vows in front of their family and friends would mean even more.

But paying for a wedding would mean financially they would have to sacrifice something else.

When given the option of buying a house once his apartment lease expired or renewing their vows in front of family and friends, Bree chose a home for them to start their new life together. For the next few weeks they searched the real estate listings online, made wish lists and budgets, and looked forward to the next step in their lives.

More than once Danny suggested they wait another year to buy a house. Each time, Bree refused. "A wedding is nothing more than one big party," she had said. "A waste of money in the grand scheme of things." Although she said it more than once and quite convincingly, the disappointment was there in her eyes.

And so he decided a surprise for his wife was in order.

He heard her coming down the hall, flip-flops smacking the bottoms of her feet as she walked. She wore denim cutoffs and a Gamecocks T-shirt, carrying her dress in a garment bag instead of wearing it.

Maybe pulling off a surprise wedding wasn't going to be as easy as he previously thought.

Danny took a deep breath, his nerves stretched to the limit.

"What are you doing?"

"I decided to change after we checked in at the bed-and-breakfast." She sauntered up to him and pressed a kiss to his lips. "You look nice," she whispered, her breath fanning across his jaw. "Smell good, too." Her empty hand smoothed over his chest as she nipped his earlobe.

Damn, she was making this difficult.

And late. Very late.

Danny put his hands on her shoulders and stepped back, forcing space between them.

"No time."

"What's the rush?" She attempted to close the distance but he kept her arm's length.

"We're running late as it is and won't be able to check in until after the pictures. So you need to get dressed now."

He took hold of her shoulders and turned her toward the bedroom.

"But Danny," she said over her shoulder to him, "my dress will get wrinkled in the car."

"This is Georgia, sweetheart. Everyone wrinkles the minute they step outside. Trust me when I say no one will notice."

"But the pictures—"

"Will be beautiful anyway." He placed a kiss upon the curve of her neck and followed it with a little swat across her behind, starting her down the hallway.

After being discharged from Walter Reed, they returned to Savannah where Danny continued with his physical rehabilitation, working hard to rebuild his strength and endurance to return to active duty. Not far from where Ben and Marie lived, they found a single-story bungalow in desperate need of renovation. Marie went with them the first time they looked at the house and she and Bree chatted excitedly about all the possibilities. He could practically hear the cash register ringing up in his head as they spoke of how to balance historic charm with modern amenities, especially in the kitchen and bath.

In the end, he couldn't deny her. Once they closed on it in a matter of weeks, they'd be living in the middle of a construction zone with all of his weekends and vacation time dedicated to honey-do's for the foreseeable future.

He could hardly wait.

Using the spare minute or two made available to him, Danny pulled his phone from his pocket and dialed his brother. This was one time when his brother's penchant for secrets and weakness for sweets worked in Danny's favor, Michael's silence only costing him a dozen snickerdoodles and a freshly baked peach pie from his favorite bakery.

"Everything good on your end?"

"All good," Michael answered. "We're on the way now. ETA fifteen minutes. Everything going as planned?"

Danny groaned, scrubbing his palm over his face. "She's still getting dressed."

Michael laughed. "Should've told her."

"Too late now. I'm committed to it being a surprise. See you in a bit."

After ending the call with Michael, his phone buzzed with a text message from Marie.

All ready to go. Just waiting on you.

Thank you for all your help, he replied. **On our way.**

His phone buzzed a second time. **Gibby wants to know if they can tap the keg.**

Jesus Christ. Yes, it was hot as hell. Yes, the guys were likely wearing more than board shorts and flip-flops. At least they'd better be. But knowing these guys and the amount they could drink, they'd float the damn thing before he and Bree even got there. He glanced at his watch again and yelled down the hall. "Bree, we've got to go."

Then he texted back. **Not just no, but hell no.**

With the message sent, he tucked his phone into his pocket and looked up just in time to see Bree step into the hall. His heart stopped.

The dress was long and flowing, transforming her into a Greek goddess, her short, trendy hair accentuating her neck and shoulders and collarbones. Simply stunning. And then she turned around and he forgot how to breathe. The dress dipped low, low, low in the back, overwhelming him with an urgent need to trace the length of her spine with his tongue.

God Almighty.

"Is this okay?" She searched his eyes for an answer because he didn't respond quickly enough as far as she was concerned. Actually, he couldn't respond because she'd successfully short-circuited his brain.

"It's too dressy, isn't it?" she questioned. "And white? I really wasn't sure about this but Marie insisted. She said light colors look best in beach photos and the photographer agreed. But I don't know. It screams wedding dress to me."

She started for the bedroom again. "Give me one more minute. I bought a backup. Something less—"

He grabbed hold of her hand, pulling her back to him, her palms splaying across his chest. "It's perfect," he whispered. When she tried to protest again, he silenced her with a gentle kiss before emphasizing his point. "Perfect."

Of course, one kiss led to another, and another, leaving them both breathless in the end.

Bree caressed his face, her thumb dipping into the dimple of his chin. "Maybe we should reschedule the photo shoot?" Her lips were wet and rosy and swollen from his kisses. A pretty blush stained the hollow of her throat and spread upward to her cheeks. There was no doubt what she had in mind.

Danny groaned, wanting nothing more than to oblige. "I promise you'll be glad we didn't cancel."

Bree pouted her lip. "Promise?"

"Absolutely."

It took every ounce of self-restraint to not spill the beans and tell her they had a hundred people waiting for them. But he'd made it this far. No way would he ruin the surprise now. He grabbed her things and ushered her out the door.

So THEY WERE running a little bit late. Not a big deal. Traffic going to the island was fairly light considering it was tourist season. No accidents. No backups. And yet, Danny was super impatient, cursing under his breath at each and every slowdown. Not to mention fidgety, tapping his thumb atop the steering wheel whenever the traffic began to crawl. He caught her watching him more than once; in each case he'd taken another deep breath and smiled at her.

Something was definitely up.

And so she started mentally preparing herself for what was to come. Were they not getting the house? Were they being transferred? Was he being sent overseas far sooner than they expected?

When he found an open parking spot on the north beach of Tybee Island, Danny threw the Tahoe into park and hopped out, quickly placing a call on his cell phone before he'd even closed the car door. "We've made it. Finally," he said. "Give us a few minutes."

"Are we meeting the photographer at the lighthouse?" Bree asked when Danny offered his hand to help her out of the car.

"No. He's waiting for us just down the beach."

Danny closed the door behind her and hit the lock button on his remote. Twice. After patting down his pockets, he took a deep breath and quickly swiped at his brow. Taking Bree's hand in his, he was raring to hit the beach. Except when he took a step, Bree remained firmly in place.

"Are you okay?" she asked. "You seem really nervous."

"It's only pictures. Why would I be nervous?"

Bree shrugged her shoulders. "Got me."

"Just come with me. I promise I'll explain everything in a minute."

This time she allowed him to take her by the hand and lead her down the beach to where a large group of people gathered.

"Oh, look. Someone's getting . . ." Bree stopped in her tracks. "What are my parents doing here?"

Danny stepped in front of her then, taking both of her hands in his, momentarily blocking out the rest of the world. She looked up into his deep blue eyes to see his earlier nervousness replaced with confidence and strength.

"When we married six months ago, a courthouse wedding was good enough for the short term. But you deserve better than that. Actually, we both deserve better. We're kind of like cats with nine lives, you and me," he said, smiling wide, that rare dimple creasing his cheek. "We've both been through the wringer and survived the worst. Seems to me the odds are on our side now and things will only be getting better for us here on out. Starting now." From his jacket pocket he pulled out a diamond solitaire ring and knelt on the sand before her. "Aubrey Grace Dunbar MacGregor, will you marry me? Again? This time, once and for all."

She stared down at him, stunned speechless.

Danny squeezed her left hand and whispered so only she could hear, "This is where you're supposed to say something. Preferably a *yes* seeing as we're already married."

"Yes." She smiled. "The answer will always be yes."

Danny wrapped his arms around her middle and twirled her in a circle, finally setting her on her feet and kissing her lips.

Their friends and family cheered and clapped and whistled, while one lone voice shouted out from the group.

"You're not to that part yet!"

IN THE SHADOW of the Tybee Island lighthouse, Bree watched as Danny spun her mother across the dance floor. Laughing and breathless, it was clear her mother was having the time of her life. Mac followed suit, albeit at a much slower pace while dancing with Marie. And seated at a table at the edge of the dance floor sat her father, holding court of sorts, telling who knows what kind of stories to a dozen men from C-Company. They all listened intently as he spoke, then when he must have reached the punch line, laughed boisterously in unison.

And just as he'd promised all those months ago, Danny's marriage proposal not only helped her out of her rut and start anew, that newfound happiness also extended to their family members. All except one.

She raised her chin to meet her dance partner's eyes. "I never thanked you for saving Danny's life."

Michael blushed slightly as he maneuvered them across the dance floor. "All part of the job, ma'am," he said with a faux twang. The only thing missing was a cowboy hat so he could flick the brim.

"It makes it easier knowing you're there with him. Wherever the army sends you."

"For Dad, too."

"But who takes care of you, Michael?"

He looked directly at her, the surprise evident in his eyes. It was there only a moment before the walls went up and he looked away. "I'm rarely placed in the same kind of danger as him."

"That's not what I mean and you know it," she said, poking him in the chest. "Your whole life you've looked after your father and Danny. After me. And now all of these men. You deserve someone who will put you in their safekeeping."

He chuckled at that. "Don't go getting any ideas, Bree."

"I'm not."

"Sure you aren't." He smiled and shook his head. "The minute you started working for Marie, Ben, Danny, and I just knew it was only a matter of time before you'd be sucked into Marie's matchmaking ways." He leaned closer so only she could hear. "Too much time together and too little supervision."

"Hardly." Bree slapped his chest. "We just want you to be happy, Michael."

"I am. But I'm even happier for you and Danny."

She studied him closer, trying to decide if he was just paying her lip service on her wedding day. "You mean that? Not too long ago you were against this marriage."

"I was never against you two marrying," he said, shaking his head. "I was against the imminent divorce. I hated that you two would be so stubborn as to willingly walk away from each other. Again. Because you both hadn't been miserable enough for the past ten years. So yes, I'm very happy." He leaned over to press a noisy kiss to her cheek. "I'm especially happy you're officially my sister-in-law. It's been a long time coming."

"Yes, it has."

The song ended and Danny made his way across the floor to retrieve his wife.

"It's about time," she said as Michael handed her off to his brother. "I was wondering if I'd get to dance with my husband again."

"Of course. But before that happens there's one thing we need to do before Lucky heads out. This includes you, Mikey."

In a far corner, the men of the 75th gathered around a lone table beautifully decorated like all the others. Except this table was set for one and went unused. As they made their way across the dance floor, Danny told her of the regiment tradition, how a table is always set in memory of those who did not return from combat.

Her eyes misted at the memory of how close he came to being one of those men, of her losing him forever. As if reading her mind, he wrapped his arm around her shoulder and pulled her close, pressing a kiss to her temple.

Bull handed out whiskey-filled shot glasses to each of the men and offered one to Bree, as well.

"Are you certain? Shouldn't this just be for the men?"

"On other occasions, maybe. But today you're drinking, too, Mrs. MacGregor," Bull said with a wink.

Once everyone had a drink, Gibby raised his glass

high, offering a toast. "To those who fought alongside us and now watch over us from above. Fair winds."

"Fair winds," they replied in unison before quickly tossing back the tiny glasses of amber liquid. Bree followed suit, the whiskey burning a path from her throat to her belly. She'd barely caught her breath before Bull was attempting to refill her shot glass for a second round.

"Oh, no." Bree placed her hand over the glass. "No. No. No."

"But we're not done yet," said the giant blond warrior standing in front of her. "And it's practically un-American to refuse a toast to those who protect your freedoms."

Bree gave Danny the side-eye as he chuckled at Bull's manipulation, but she reluctantly lowered her hand, allowing him to fill her glass. "How many more?" she whispered for Danny's ears only.

"Not sure."

"Are you wanting them to get me drunk?"

"Do you think I'd complain?" Danny suggestively waggled his eyebrows.

Bree narrowed her eyes at him. "You're so bad. So very bad."

Gibby turned to face Lucky and raised his glass. "To goodbyes—may they never be spoken. To friendships—may they never be broken."

"To Lucky," they all said in unison before downing the second shot.

Afterward, Danny slapped his hand upon Lucky's shoulder. "Seriously, man, good luck in Oklahoma. Put that GI Bill to good use and show those snot-nosed college kids how Rangers do things."

"Will do," Lucky said. "Just as long as you promise not to take any more bullets. The organs you have left are essential items."

They finished off their conversation with a bro-hug as Bull made his way around the circle, filling their glasses for a third time.

"Gibby's really good with these toasts." Bree leaned heavily against Danny's chest as she hoisted her glass. "I have to admit I'm impressed."

Danny lowered his head to whisper in her ear. "He Googles them all."

Oh.

"To Danny and Bree."

This time the group turned to face her and Danny, and she couldn't help but smile at these brave, strong men raising their glasses in toast to them. And then, much to their delight, she threw back her shot. Which surprisingly went down far easier than the first two.

Bree took a deep breath and steadied herself. "Please tell me we're done?"

"Even if Gibby's not, you are."

DANNY PRIED THE shot glass from Bree's hand and placed it on the table before leading his wife to the center of the floor for one last dance.

He liked thinking of Bree that way—*his wife*. More

than he ever could have imagined. And he couldn't believe there would ever come a day when he would tire of hearing those two beautiful words.

His beautiful bride, who was more than a little tipsy, limply tossed her arms around his neck and leaned into him. Which of course gave him a good excuse to hold her a little closer than appropriate in his arms.

Bree tipped her head back and looked up at him with those big brown eyes. "You certainly know how to carry out a covert operation, Daniel MacGregor."

Her eyes were a little glassy, her speech a little slurred. Damn, she was cute.

"Anything you would have done differently?" he asked

"Not. One. Single. Thing," she said with half-mast eyes and a giant smile on her face. "It was absolutely perfect."

Bree pulled her arms from around his neck, choosing instead to wrap them about his waist as she rested her head upon his chest and burrowed beneath his chin.

He should call it a night, say their farewells and take her to their room for the weekend at the bed-and-breakfast across the street. But he wanted to finish this one last wedding dance with his new bride. His wife.

"You should know I used part of the decorating money to pay for this shindig. That means we're stuck with my old furniture for a while."

"That's okay."

"You won't mind having a new house and no real furniture to put in it?"

"Doesn't matter one bit," she said, snuggling closer. "After all, we'll always have the bed."

Acknowledgments

WHEN WRITERS BEGIN the querying process, the mantra chanted most is "It takes only one." Luckily, it wasn't long before "the one" found me and I couldn't have wished for anyone better. Thank you Stephany Evans for pulling me from the slush pile and setting this whirlwind in motion. Many thanks to Rebecca Lucash, Amanda Bergeron, and everyone at Avon Impulse. You have made my dreams come true and I look forward to working on many more books together.

Although writing is a solitary pursuit, I have many friends who were always there to cheer me on. Special thanks to my dear friend, Liz, who read eleven billion versions of this story. Thank you for all the times you listened when I called to bounce off the latest ideas, but especially for dragging me along to the RWA 2011 convention. If it weren't for you, I'd probably be writing some depressing book that no one would want to read—including me.

Many thanks to Gloria and Gena, two strong and beautiful women who inspired me to write a cancer survivor that had spunk and a sense of humor. Thank you to all "mah gurls" from the place that shall remain nameless. Your friendship and support means so much to me. Next time we all get together, drinks are on me.

Many thanks to George Kohrman, MD, who taught me I can do just about anything I want to a character as long as I follow the third rule of surgery—stay away from the pancreas. Any medical mistakes in this book are the fault of the student, not the teacher.

Thanks to Mom and Dad who let an eight-year-old spend hours pounding away on a gray IBM Selectric typewriter and not once complaining about the amount of paper I wasted on my stories.

I need to give a shout out to my girls for eating large quantities of pizza, tolerating mommy's excessive computer use, and having to hide my extensive collection of shirtless-man books when your friends come over.

Lastly, many thanks to my husband, who was always ready with a well-timed pep talk or kick in the track pants whenever I began to doubt myself. It seems only appropriate that this book will be released on our 19th anniversary. So here's your gift. I've spent a lot of time on this sucker. I hope you like it. And, no, you can't retire just yet.

About the Author

CHERYL ETCHISON graduated from the University of Oklahoma's School of Journalism and began her career as an oil and gas reporter. Bored to tears and broke as hell, it wasn't long before she headed for the promised land of public relations. But that was nearly a lifetime ago and she's since traded in reporting the facts for making it all up. Currently, she lives in Austin, Texas, with her husband and three daughters.

www.cheryletchison.com

Give in to your Impulses . . .
Continue reading for excerpts from
our newest Avon Impulse books.
Available now wherever ebooks are sold.

YOU'RE STILL THE ONE

Ribbon Ridge Book Six

by Darcy Burke

THE DEBUTANTE IS MINE

A Season's Original Novel

by Vivienne Lorret

ONE DANGEROUS DESIRE

An Accidental Heirs Novel

by Christy Carlyle

Give in to your Impulses . . .

Continue reading for excerpts from our newest Avon Impulse books.

Available now wherever e-books are sold.

YOU'RE STILL THE ONE

A Ribbon Ridge Book Six

by Darcy Burke

THE DEBUTANTE IS MINE

A Season of Scandal Novel

by Vivienne Lorret

ONE DANGEROUS DESIRE

An Accidental Heirs Novel

by Christy Carlyle

An Excerpt from

YOU'RE STILL THE ONE

Ribbon Ridge Book Six

By Darcy Burke

College sweethearts Bex and Hayden were once the perfect couple but is five years enough time to heal broken hearts . . . and give them a second chance at first love?

Ribbon Ridge, July

Hayden Archer drove into the parking lot at The Alex. The *paved* parking lot. He hadn't been home since Christmas, and things looked vastly different, including the paved lot instead of the dirt he'd been used to. The project to renovate the old monastery into a hotel and restaurant was nearly complete, and his siblings had done an amazing job in his absence.

He stepped out of his car, which he'd rented at the airport when his flight had arrived that afternoon. Someone would've picked him up, of course. If they'd known he was coming.

He smiled to himself in the summer twilight, looking forward to seeing his brothers' surprise when he burst in on Dylan Westcott's bachelor party. Hayden glanced around but didn't see anyone. They'd all be at the underground pub that Dylan had conceived and designed. It was fitting that its inaugural use would be to celebrate his upcoming wedding to their sister Sara.

Hayden could hardly wait to see the place, along with the rest of the property. But he figured that tour would have to wait until tomorrow. Tonight was for celebrating. And shocking the hell out of his family.

He made his way to the pub and immediately fell in love with what they'd done. He'd seen pictures, but being here in person gave everything a scale that was impossible to feel from half a world away.

They'd dug out the earth around the entrance to the pub and installed a round door, making it look distinctly hobbit-like. He wondered how much of that design had come from his brother Evan, and was certain Kyle's fiancée, Maggie, the groundskeeper of the entire place, had tufted the grass just so and ensured the wildflowers surrounding the entry looked as if they'd been there forever. A weathered, wooden sign hung over the door, reading: Archetype.

As he moved closer, he heard the sounds of revelry and smiled again. Then he put his hand on the wrought-iron door handle and pushed.

The noise was even louder inside, and it was nearly as dim as it had been outside. There were recessed lights in the wooden beams across the ceiling and sconces set at intervals around the space, all set to a mellow, cozy mood.

Hayden recognized most of the twenty or so people here. A few tables had been pushed together, and a handful of guys were playing some obnoxiously terrible card game while others were gathered at the bar. Kyle, one of his three brothers—the chef with the surfer good looks—stood behind it pouring drinks.

Hayden made his way to the bar, amused that no one had noticed him enter. "Beer me."

Kyle grabbed a pint glass. "Sure. What were you drinking?" He looked up and blinked. "Shit. Hayden. Am I drunk?" He glanced around before settling back on Hayden.

"Probably. Longbow if you've got it."

Kyle came sprinting around the bar and clasped him in a tight hug. He pulled back, grinning. "Look what the cat dragged in," he bellowed.

The noise faded then stopped completely. Liam, his eldest brother, or at least the first of the sextuplets born, stood up from the table, his blue-gray gaze intense. "Hayden, what the hell?" Like Kyle, his expression was one of confusion followed by joy.

"Hayden?" Evan, his remaining brother—the quiet one—leaned back on his stool at the other end of the bar. Like the others, he registered surprise, though in a far more subdued way.

"Hayden!" This exclamation came from the table near Liam and was from Hayden's best friend, Cameron Westcott. He was also the groom's half-brother.

The groom himself stood up from where he sat next to Evan. "What an awesome surprise." Dylan grinned as he hugged Hayden, and for the next several minutes he was overwhelmed with hugs and claps on the back and so much smiling that his cheeks ached.

"Why didn't you tell us you were coming?" Liam asked, once things had settled down.

Kyle had gone back behind the bar and was now pulling Hayden's beer from the tap. "Do Mom and Dad know you're here?"

Hayden looked at Liam. "Because I wanted to surprise

everyone." Then he looked at Kyle. "And no, Mom and Dad don't know." Hayden took his glass from Kyle and immediately sipped the beer, closing his eyes as the distinct wheat flavor his father had crafted brought him fully and completely home.

Kyle leaned on the bar. "Mom is going to be beside herself." He slapped the bar top. "Now this is a party!"

An Excerpt from

THE DEBUTANTE IS MINE

A Season's Original Novel

By Vivienne Lorret

USA Today bestselling author Vivienne Lorret launches a new historical romance series featuring the Season's Original—a coveted title awarded by the ton's elite to one lucky debutante . . .

The Season Standard—the Daily Chronicle of Consequence.

Lilah read no farther than the heading of the newspaper in her hand before she lost her nerve.

"I cannot look," she said, thrusting the *Standard* to her cousin. "After last night's ball, I shouldn't be surprised if the first headline read, 'Miss Lilah Appleton: Most Unmarriageable Maiden in England.' And beneath it, 'Last Bachelor in Known World Weds Septuagenarian Spinster as Better Alternative.'"

Lilah's exhale crystallized in the cold air, forming a cloud of disappointment. It drifted off the park path, dissipating much like the hopes and dreams she'd had for her first two Seasons.

Walking beside her, Juliet, Lady Granworth, laughed, her blue eyes shining with amusement. Even on this dull, gray morning, she emitted a certain brightness and luster from within. Beneath a lavender bonnet, her features and complexion were flawless, her hair a mass of golden silk. And if she weren't so incredibly kind, Lilah might be forced to hate her as a matter of principle, on behalf of plain women throughout London.

"You possess a rather peculiar talent for worry, Cousin," Juliet said, skimming the five-column page.

The notion pleased Lilah. "Do you think so?"

After twenty-three years of instruction, Mother often told her that she wasn't a very good worrier. Or perhaps it was more that her anxieties were misdirected. This, Lilah supposed, was where her *talent* emerged. She was able to imagine the most absurd disasters, the more unlikely the better. There was something of a relief in the ludicrous. After all, if she could imagine a truly terrible event, then she could deal with anything less dramatic. Or so she hoped.

Yet all the worrying in the world would not alter one irrefutable fact—Lilah needed to find a husband this Season or else her life would be over.

"Indeed, I do," Juliet said with a nod, folding the page before tucking it away. "However, there was nothing here worth your worry or even noteworthy at all."

Unfortunately, Lilah knew what that meant.

"Not a single mention?" At the shake of her cousin's head, Lilah felt a sense of déjà vu and disappointment wash over her. This third and final Season was beginning on the same foot as the first two had. She would almost prefer to have been named most unmarriageable. At least she would have known that someone had noticed her.

Abruptly, Juliet's expression softened, and she placed a gentle hand on Lilah's shoulder. "You needn't worry. Zinnia and I will come up with the perfect plan."

As of yet, none of their plans had yielded a result.

Over Christmas, they had attended a party at the Duke of Vale's castle. Most of those in attendance had been unmarried young women, which had given nearly everyone the hope of marrying the duke. Even Lilah had hoped as much—at first. Yet when the duke had been unable to remember her name, she'd abruptly abandoned that foolishness. And a good thing too, because he'd married her dearest friend, Ivy, instead.

The duke had developed a *Marriage Formula*—a mathematical equation that would pair one person with another according to the resulting answer. Then, using his own formula, the duke had found his match—Ivy. As luck would have it, both Ivy and Vale had fallen deeply in love as well. Now, if only Lilah could find her own match.

"I have been considering Vale's *Marriage Formula*. All I would need to do is fill out a card." At least, that was how Lilah thought it worked. "Yet with Vale and Ivy still on their honeymoon, I do not know if they will return in time."

Then again, there was always the possibility that the equation would produce no match for her either.

Juliet's steps slowed. "Even though I couldn't be more pleased for Ivy, I'm not certain that I want to put your future happiness in the hands of an equation."

Lilah didn't need *happiness*. In fact, her requirements for marriage and a husband had greatly diminished in the past two years. She'd gone from wanting a handsome husband in the prime of his life, to settling for a gentleman of any age who wasn't terribly disfigured. She would like him to be kind to her as well, but she would accept any man who didn't bellow and rant about perfection, as her father had done.

"A pleasant conversation with someone who shares my interests would be nice, not necessarily happiness, or even love, for that matter," Lilah said, thinking of the alternative. "All I truly need is not to be forced into marriage with Cousin Winthrop."

An Excerpt from

ONE DANGEROUS DESIRE

An Accidental Heirs Novel

By Christy Carlyle

Rex Leighton dominates the boardroom by day and prowls the ballroom at night. Searching for the perfect bride to usher him into the aristocracy, he abandoned the idea of love the last time he saw the delicious May Sedgwick. But when he's roped into a marriage bet, Rex is willing to go all in. There's just one problem—he's competing against the only woman he's ever loved.

The duke strode into the sitting room first, stopping and gesturing toward the American.

"My dear, you must help me convince Mr. Leighton to join us next week. And see here, sir, we can even supply a fellow countrywoman to encourage you. Miss Sedgwick, may I present Mr. Rex Leighton."

The duke was speaking, making introductions. The minuscule part of May's mind still capable of processing words and considering polite etiquette told her to curtsy or extend her hand, but she couldn't manage any of it.

A man she'd relegated to her dreams had crashed in and collided with her Thursday afternoon. Impossibly, *he* stood before her. The man she kept confined in her heart and mind. The same man, and yet so changed. He looked nothing like the poor shop clerk she'd pined for, impossibly yearned for year after year until she'd almost forgotten how to yearn for anything else. The eyes were the same mercurial brew of gold and azure, and all the angles of his face still aligned with irritating perfection, set off by a divot in the center of his chin.

That gleaming dark hair she'd once sifted through her fingers shone like rich mahogany in the afternoon light.

But his gaze was remote, impassive, as if a pane of murky glass separated them. She was the one stuck on a curio cabinet shelf, and he was coolly examining her from the other side. His clothes were those of a prosperous gentleman, not the outdated and oft-mended single suit owned by Reginald Cross. Worst was the arrogant tilt of his chin. The Reg of her memories had only ever looked at her with admiration and pleasure, what she imagined in her silly youthful way was love. No one had ever made her feel as important with a single glance.

He wasn't the same man. Couldn't be. The duke called him Leighton, not Cross. A striking resemblance. Nothing more.

May reminded herself to breathe and stepped forward to be introduced to the polished gentleman who could not be the shop boy who'd broken her heart in New York City.

Mr. Leighton took two steps forward, and her momentary grasp on composure faltered. *Reg.* His scent, the firm line of his mouth, the large, elegant hand extended toward her—they belonged to Reginald Cross. Smarter, wealthier, older, and with an abundance of confidence his younger self lacked, but still a man she'd once known. The only man she'd ever loved.

Emily touched her arm, urging May to accept his offered hand. She obeyed and moved toward him, sliding her fingers against his until their palms met. Warm. How could a memory be so warm? But he wasn't a memory. He was real. Alive. He was in London, had been for goodness knew how long, and she was meeting him in her dearest friend's sitting room. By complete and utter chance.

"A pleasure to meet you, Miss Sedgwick."

Same deep-toned voice. Same ability to raise shivers across her skin. Even when there was something silvery and practiced in his timbre, even while he still wore that placid mask.

"How do you . . ." The rest wouldn't come. May knew the words she was expected to say. Felt the gazes of Emily and her father. Sensed their discomfort at her odd behavior.

His hand tightened around hers and the glass between them shattered. He blinked, a quick fan of sable lashes, and then those unique eyes of his saw her. Not as a stranger to whom he was being introduced, but as the woman he'd held and kissed. The woman to whom he'd broken every promise he'd ever made. She detected his recognition in the tremor of his lush lower lip, felt it through the heat of his skin, read it in his blue-gold gaze that flitted from her mouth to her eyes and over each aspect of her face.

"May." He breathed the word quietly, intimately, just for her to hear, as if a duke and his daughter weren't standing nearby.

Grief, too long repressed, welled up like floodwaters, fierce and fast and just as unstoppable.

May wrenched her hand from his with a burning friction of skin against skin. When she spun around, Emily's face whirled past, a blur of confusion and concern. Moving, walking away from him, felt good. Like victory. Like strength. Like she would finally get to choose the conclusion to their tale. She needed it to end and had never gotten the satisfaction of a proper parting. She would explain her rudeness to Emily later, but for now she needed to find the mettle to keep going, to leave him as he'd left her.

"A pleasure to meet you, Miss Hedgewick."

Same deep-toned voice. Same ability to raise shivers across her skin. Even when he'd been [illegible] always [illegible] in his timbre, even while he still wore that pirate's mask.

"How do you . . ." The rest wouldn't come. Maybe now the words she was expected to say. [illegible] the gazes of Emily and her father. Sensed their discomfort at her odd behavior.

His hand tightened around hers and the space between them shortened. He blinked, a quick flutter of pale lashes, and then those unique eyes of his saw her. Not as a stranger to whom he was being introduced, but as the woman he'd held and kissed, the woman to whom he'd broken every promise he'd ever made. She detected his recognition in the tremor in his hand, felt it through the heat of his skin, read it in his gaze that flitted from her mouth to her eyes and over each aspect of her face.

"Ada." He breathed the word quietly, intimately, just for her to hear, as if Emily and his daughter weren't standing nearby.

Grief, one long repressed, welled up like flood waters, fierce and fast, and just as unstoppable.

Ada wrenched her hand from his with a burning friction of skin against skin. When she spun around, Emily's face whirled past in a blur of confusion and concern. Walking away from him felt good. Like victory. Like strength. Like she would finally get to choose the conclusion to their tale. She needed it to end and had never gotten the satisfaction of a proper parting. She would explain her rudeness to Emily later, but for now she needed to find the means to keep going, to leave him as he'd left her.